Also by Dora Levy Mossanen

Harem

Courtesan

Dora Levy Mossanen

A Touchstone Book
Published by Simon & Schuster
New York London Toronto Sydney

TOUCHSTONE
Rockefeller Center
1230 Avenue of the Americas
New York, NY 10020

This book is a work of fiction. Names, characters, places, and incidents either are products of the author's imagination or are used fictitiously. Any resemblance to actual events or locales or persons, living or dead, is entirely coincidental.

Copyright © 2005 by Dora Levy Mossanen
All rights reserved,
including the right of reproduction
in whole or in part in any form.

TOUCHSTONE and colophon are registered trademarks
of Simon & Schuster, Inc.

For information about special discounts for bulk purchases,
please contact Simon & Schuster Special Sales at
1-800-456-6798 or business@simonandschuster.com

Designed by Melissa Isriprashad

Manufactured in the United States of America

10   9   8   7   6   5   4   3   2   1

Library of Congress Cataloging-in-Publication Data
Levy Mossanen, Dora.
    Courtesan : a novel / Dora Levy Mossanen.
        p.   cm.
    "A Touchstone book."
    1. Jews—Iran—Fiction. 2. Jewish women—Fiction. 3. Iran—Fiction.
    I. Title.
  PS3612.E94C68 2005
  813'.6—dc22   2004059880

ISBN-13: 978-0-7432-4678-1
ISBN-10: 0-7432-4678-0

For

Leila Michaela

And For

Adam,

My Angels

And For

David A.

For the Bible

Acknowledgments

I have been blessed with the inspiration and support of many.

My literary agent, Loretta Barrett, guided and encouraged me with patience and unparalleled wisdom.

My outstanding editors, Marcela Landres and Doris Cooper, led me through the labyrinth. Their insightful suggestions were critical.

I am indebted to my marvelous publishing team: Mark Gompertz, Trish Todd, Chris Lloreda, and Marcia Burch, whose continued support I cherish. A million thanks to Jonathon Brodman for managing all the intricate details, and to Cherlynne Li for the gift of beauty. Praise goes to Brad Foltz, who did the beautiful cover for this novel, just as he did for my previous title, *Harem*. My gratitude to Sara Schapiro, without whom I would have been lost in the maze.

My colleagues Maureen Connel, Alex Kivowitz, Joan Goldsmith Gurfield, and Paula Shtrum read and reread draft after draft. Without their perceptive comments, *Courtesan* would not have been.

Words cannot describe my gratitude to Nader, whose encouragements afforded me a haven to write, and kept me sane and ever hopeful.

Carolyn's invaluable networking made the creative process much more enjoyable. I am grateful for that.

Thank you, Negin and David Ascher. You are more than a source of inspiration. Your astute contributions, endless research, and technical knowledge cast light upon paths that, at times, seemed impenetrable.

My heartfelt gratitude to my most cherished fan club, my family, Parvin, Sion, Laura, Ora, Sol, and David, whose constant support kept the pages turning.

Courtesan

1

❧

Persia

March 1901

I pinch my nose shut and gulp down two raw rooster gonads.

"Do not make that face, *khanom* Simone," Pearl, the midwife, commands. "Do what I say, or your womb will continue to cough up blood each month."

The woman pounds a brown concoction in a cast-iron mortar, her expression so serious she must imagine herself creating life. She rambles about mixing the pulp of a rare fish found in the Caspian Sea, five pulverized pearls harvested in fertile oysters, two grams of gold, and another secret elixir.

I dig my hands in the pockets of my riding breeches as the one-eyed witch raises a thimble of rosewater to my nose to hold back my vomit.

Why would I, the daughter of Françoise and granddaughter of Mme Gabrielle, idols of seduction, banish myself to a stone house on top of the Persian mountains? Why would I ingest gonads? Why would I follow the advice of a mad midwife?

The catalyst was Yaghout, my mother-in-law.

 ∽

Tired from months of travel from France to Persia, upon arriving
at the port of Anzali on the Caspian Sea, Cyrus and I joined a
caravan that made its way over tortuous passes toward Tehran.
My first glimpse of Persia on approaching Anzali from Baku was
the red-tiled roofs of a small town. And, in the distance, a mountain range hidden by clouds. From here, we crossed a vast desert
on *kajavehs*, two-passenger vehicles resembling chicken coops
balanced on donkeys. Our faces caked with dust and fatigue, we
arrived at Mahaleh, the Jewish quarter. Sabbath candles flickered
on windowsills. We negotiated a web of narrow alleys and crum-
bling walls to Sar-e-chal—the pit's edge.

A sobering odor assaulted me.

A large heap of decomposing refuse sat in a pit at the center
of the quarter. Traders, shopkeepers, and residents, a populace
covered in a cloak of sadness, toss their daily garbage into this
gorge. Men wear strange hats—the conical or lambskin of the
middle and upper class, the woolly muff of the Cossack, half
bowl felt of the working class. The cleric's turban is reminiscent
of my mother's fluffy swan pillow. Strange little shops with
fronts open to the street line the bazaar. Shopkeepers sit where
they can reach everything without rising. Public cooks broil
mutton en brochette over hot beds of charcoal. A water carrier,
his sheepskin jug on his shoulders, handed me a tin cup. Cyrus
waved him away, pulling my foulard over my red curls. I must
drink nothing but hot tea, he said, until I become accustomed
to Persian germs. Concealed under chadors, weary eyes peeping
through horse-hair blinders, women shuffle around like black
tents. Even Mme Gabrielle's ghosts would have rejected this
gloomy place, where Jews have to comply with the custom of
wearing a chador.

To think I fought to leave Château Gabrielle for this.

The camel carrying our belongings had difficulty squeezing

through the narrow cul-de-sac. We hired a mule to finish the task of transporting our valises.

"Houses at the end of alleys offer a degree of protection from periodic raids by Muslims," Cyrus explained, causing me further alarm. I clung to his arm and asked the significance of the patch worn on certain jackets. "Jews must display identifying signs so Muslims won't come in contact with us and defile themselves."

"You don't," I said.

"I refuse to comply," he replied.

"But *you*, a Jew, are the shah's private jeweler?"

"Being the only Persian gemologist with a degree from France, I am needed in court. And I have invaluable connections to the European diamond markets."

Before I had occasion to show more concern, he took me by the hand and led me to my future mother-in-law, Yaghout. Informed of our arrival by the quarter news bearer, she greeted us at the door. She wore the type of pants, vest, and ballet skirt the present shah's father had admired at the Paris ballet and that the women of his harem later made fashionable. If only Cyrus's mother knew that my grandmother had pleasured the present shah on his last visit to Paris.

"*Madar*, meet my fiancée," Cyrus said, kissing her forehead.

"*Pesaram*, my son!" she cried out, ignoring my outstretched hand.

I cringed under her scalding stare that traveled the length of my body to rest on my red hair. Bursting into fits of violent sneezing, she feigned an allergic reaction, which I did not realize then was to me. She held a Bible above Cyrus's head as we stepped into her home. In her other hand, she swayed a fire turner, a coal-filled, crackling wire basket. I had an urge to unstopper the tiny pores of my skin and unleash my perfume to mask the pungent odor of the smoking wild rue seeds she used to ward off the evil eye.

Cyrus pulled me into his arms. "Welcome to Persia, *jounam*."

Yaghout turned on her heels and stormed out into the garden. I glanced back to see her toss the fire turner into a small pool. The dying embers hissed in the water.

I suddenly missed Paris. I missed Françoise and Mme Gabrielle. I even missed my grandmother's repertoire of spirits wandering Château Gabrielle and the surrounding Valley of Civet Cats.

During the two weeks I lived with Yaghout, I tried to ingratiate myself to her. I flaunted the Farsi I had learned from Alphonse, our Persian butler back home. I brewed tea and chopped herbs for rice. I prepared *ghormeh sabzi,* an herbal lamb stew of red beans and dried lemons. But despite her endless insistence, I refused to wear the chador.

The volley of sneezes my presence triggered, the gurgling of her *ghalian* hookah, the shuddering rose petals in the foaming water, and the smoke shooting out of her nostrils were rude and frightening. How long was I expected to live with this woman? When she began to pop pills under her tongue to thwart a looming heart attack, I was ready to flee. Nothing Cyrus had said, and certainly none of my fantasies, had prepared me for the dark-eyed, mustachioed Yaghout.

"Is she a virgin?" she hissed to Cyrus one morning. "Do not give me that look, *pesaram,* but reconsider your decision to wed her. Because if she fails to produce a bloody sheet with Rabbi Shlomo the Penitent's signature on four corners, you will be dead to me."

"Consider me dead right here and now!" Cyrus snapped back.

I had been late for breakfast, still patting my forest of curls into place, when he grabbed my arm and swept me out the door, across the dusty garden with its ancient walnut and mulberry trees, emaciated chickens and loud roosters, and past the outhouse, an open-mouthed grave.

᠃᠁

"Stop daydreaming, *khanom* Simone," Pearl, the midwife, scolds, startling me back to the mountains, the lingering taste of gonads bitter in my mouth. "If you do not become pregnant, your husband will flee to *yengeh donyah*."

Beard, the owner of the teahouse around the corner, considers *yengeh donyah* the edge of the world—somewhere very far from Persia. Somewhere like the Valley of Civet Cats, I suppose.

Out of her chemise, Pearl retrieves a stretch of flesh that resembles puckered leather, rather than the breast she directs under her armpit into the mouth of the child bundled up in the chador around her shoulders. "You see *man hameh kareh hastam*."

Oui, oui, I suppose, she might be proficient in all manners of child rearing. But I would rather return to Tehran and face Yaghout than allow this woman to nurse my baby when I have one.

Her good eye stares at me, the other milky dull and forlorn like a dead goat's. She lost the eye to the trachoma epidemic in Rasht, a town in the north of Persia, she explains, adding that her one good eye is sharper than my two. She pinches some of the concoction out of the mortar and rolls a smidgen into a lewd colored blob between her callused fingers.

I shake my head, assuring her that I will not consume chicken droppings, which is what the mixture looks like.

"Well, then," she threatens, tying her bundle, "if you do not care to become pregnant, so be it. I came here to make you a proper wife. What else would a devout Muslim do, *khanom,* than come to the aid of a foreigner in the mountains?"

Pearl had first appeared at my doorsteps a week before. She had a message from Yaghout: *Although Cyrus married a French goy, he is still a Persian Jew. And like every one of us he deserves a son to recite the kaddish over his grave.*

That day, facing Pearl at the door, right there and then, a

palpable fear bled into my veins. What if I never conceive? What if I fail to become pregnant with Cyrus's child?

I opened the door wide, stepped back, and invited the midwife into the stone *maisonette* that was becoming home.

Wedged between two cliffs with an awesome view of the Damavand Volcano, a source of Persian mythology, the house stands thousands of meters above the capital city of Tehran. The surrounding mountains gush with streams, waterfalls, and wells that join the Karaj and Jajrud rivers to irrigate the thirsty city below. At daybreak, when clouds lounge low on our slate roof, hikers knock on our door. They seek a cup of hot tea, a glass of pomegranate juice, or a date-and-onion omelet before continuing their climb to the summit, before the summer sun bakes the boulders into stony ovens, or winter winds whip the carpet of snow into crystalline shards. The ever-changing shades of stone and earth, rain and snow, give the impression of four seasons encapsulated in one day. The silence, punctuated by the occasional clattering of hooves, cawing of crows, and braying of mules, is profoundly different from the sensual chaos of Château Gabrielle.

The décor of our boudoir with its ancient mirror reflecting images in mottled hues is primitive. The divan is covered with my stitched-together petticoats. Gradually, tentatively, the house reveals its charm, and I come to realize that what would have been impossible in Château Gabrielle—to love one man— is probable here. Here it is possible to love a man who, in the high altitude of the mountains, dethorns wildflowers that might prick my fingers, who calls me *jounam*—my life—who gathers back his shoulder-length, silver-peppered hair, and who wears a red diamond earring. In a backward society where bare skin is not tolerated, his white shirt is left carelessly open to reveal a muscular chest the color of almond husks. This is his way of showing his disapproval of a rigid culture that continues to challenge his choice of a wife.

Nevertheless, Château Gabrielle and its women are ever present in the trunk I salvaged from Mama. I pull out her costumes, capes, and masks to coil threads of memory around the mountains and keep my family alive.

And on the mantelpiece above the wood burner, eternally visible as a reminder of what he lost and what he gained, is Cyrus's tallit bag. The taffeta bag is square and flat, and when sunlight pours through the window onto an embroidered Star of David, the threads cast silver webs on the ceiling. Tucked inside is Cyrus's Old Testament, skullcap, and tallit with tzitzit fringes on both edges. Although secularly inclined, he has started attending the synagogue in Mahaleh. His Bible and prayer shawl, his only inheritance, have reconnected him to his faith. In full view on the mantelpiece, the bag must remind him of more than I could guess.

"This prayer shawl and Torah," his mother said, "Are all you will have to turn to if you marry that goy."

"She is Jewish," Cyrus said.

"She is the daughter of prostitutes," his mother replied.

2

It is the spring equinox, *Noruz,* the Persian New Year. Our ceremonial table is laid with *haft-seen,* or seven S's—symbols of rebirth, fertility, and wealth. We are in the company of *Grand-mère's* friendly ghosts—you have to have special ears and eyes to hear and see spirits, Mme Gabrielle said, and you, my beloved Simone, possess that blessing. Having invited themselves to the celebration, they hover above and around the table, their translucent images reflected in a silver-framed mirror signifying life. They swirl about candle flames that represent light and perch on gold coins symbolizing wealth. They lick wheat pudding for sweetness; settle on sprouts of wheat for fertility, hyacinth for beauty, and garlic for health. Avoiding a bowl of vinegar for patience, they circle rosewater apples representing health, plant kisses on painted eggs, rice cookies, and my cheeks.

We are neither alone nor lonely, Cyrus and I, cuddled in the ottoman, flush from the fire in the potbellied stove and from a dinner of smoked white fish and herb rice. The evening calls of muezzin from mosques around the city echo across the mountains. The aroma of jasmine tea is soothing.

"Come closer, *jounam*," Cyrus whispers, thrusting his hand into my copper curls, his tongue sliding along my neck. "I want you to know me the way no one ever has. Last night, what a treat to be soaked in your ambergris perfume."

"Recite a poem for me," I say.

He narrates the love tale of *Layla and Majnun* by the twelfth-century poet Nizami, then the legend of *Khosrow and Shirin* from Ferdowsi's tenth-century epic, the *Shahnameh*. I lose myself in the ebb and flow of his voice. He embarks on a mystical journey into the hearts of ancient lovers and the fatalistic poems of the Sufi Saadi. Why is Persian myth and romance always unrequited? I am finding peace in the solitude of the mountains, a sharing that culminates in a perfect togetherness that makes words superfluous.

He shuts the book and rests it on his lap. He hands me a box, his wide-set eyes seek mine. "The ivory frame is South African. But the photograph is by Antoin Sevruguin, a Russian raised in Persia."

I am riveted to the grace and mystery of the image of the *Veiled Woman with Pearls*, her profile seductive under layers of gossamer. She wears a crown of gold coins; her neck is adorned with pearls. Despite being covered, she exudes a muted yet powerful sensuality.

He runs his thumb down my cheek. "A chador can disguise a woman's strengths and skills and make her more agreeable to our culture. It could be liberating to observe everyone knowing that no one recognizes you or knows whom you are appraising."

"I'll never wear a chador—not even for you."

"It is a way to comply with public restriction without succumbing to its limitations. It's not always a choice here."

"If the mountains become home, I might."

"In that case, let us invent a past and a history for our home." He assembles his writing supplies, the litmus paper and indigo ink. I am fond of Cyrus's eccentric ways of revealing his defiance—his open shirt, the color of his ink, and the broad tip of his pen, as bold as a shout. "It makes a statement about me, *jounam*. It warns my enemies to keep away from my loved ones."

I marvel at his baritone and the power of his imagination as he summons a time when the Damavand Volcano had not fallen into smoky lethargy, and the boulders at the floor of the Rostam Ravine had not been burnished by time, when stars were still colliding and oceans had not matured into their present symphony. Even then, so long ago, a man dreamed of and built a stone house for his Parisian bride on the summit of the snow-capped mountains. I elaborate on this long-ago universe with my own embroidery, embellish it with my personal flavors to further validate and anchor us in this solitary confinement. I evoke a faraway land where evil thrives despite the abundance of ash berries and bitter grass, where spirits lurk in autumn leaves and teardrops.

And intense pleasures, I think.

"Come, my lovely wife, walk with me through my past."

Lost in his scent of cardamom, smoke, and leather, I ask, "Why do you wear the red diamond earring?"

"I received this in the rough from the father of my roommate at the Sorbonne—the man who would introduce me to red diamonds.

"A giant with a bone-breaking handshake, he sported bright-colored cravats, silk vests, and a Medusa-handled umbrella. His endless energy and charisma earned him acquaintances and connections all around the globe. But it was his strange eyes that were memorable. They did not seem normal. The dilated pupils and ax-heavy stare kept you in his grip.

"In time, I became indispensable to his trade. So much so that when I traveled on business, a bedroom was assigned to me in his mansion. BEDROOM OF PERSIAN NUNS was engraved on a plaque. I found that odd, never knew what that meant.

"One night, without his father's knowledge, my roommate invited a number of guests. Simone, you might not believe this, but in front of my stunned eyes, Monsieur Jean Paul Dubois greeted his son's guests. He then disappeared into a room and returned with a clay bowl. As if handing out pebbles, he plucked out and gave each guest a red diamond. Then, without the slightest show of displeasure, he bid them farewell. In a strange way, by not sending me away like the rest that night, he made me feel special."

I nibble on a rice cake, fascinated by Cyrus's account of this monstrous yet impressive man with whom Cyrus toured the Congo, Russia, and India, where he discovered the importance of discretion in a risky trade.

"I was introduced to influential men and exclusive clubs. I found out what strawberries, avocados, and pearl-sized beluga tasted like. My honesty earned the trust of merchants. The diamond business is rife with corruption. It can be brutal and dangerous. Money from the trade finances wars and other atrocities. Destitute men are shipped to South African mines to slave for unscrupulous miners. It is a heart-wrenching sight.

"I'll never forget my first big sale. June 1, 1898. The night of the inauguration of the Ritz Hotel at the Place Vendôme. The elegant hotel was the first to have electric lighting throughout and rooms equipped with private bath and telephone. I, a jeweler from Mahaleh, introduced myself to counts, princes, and kings. I was ambushed by mistresses who flaunted pearls, emeralds, and sapphires comparable to your mother's and grandmother's.

"But most astonishing was the unprecedented number of red diamonds. I am not certain, but it must have been then that I questioned the stream of red diamonds trickling into the circle of the elite.

"Red diamonds, Simone, are a mistake of nature. A rare abnormality—a deviation in their chemical structure—changes the way they absorb and react to light and thereby gives the impression of color. To me, as much as in the color itself, the beauty lies in the fact that the chemical difference that transforms such a hard stone is minute and even fragile. It occurs so rarely, yet when it does, the diamond becomes infinitely more valuable."

That night, at the Ritz Hotel, Cyrus met M. Rouge and his French mistress with a sleek sheet of red hair. M. Rouge was an eccentric *diamantaire*. His true surname and nationality were unknown. But his penchant for diamonds was legendary. He was having difficulty locating a red diamond for his mistress. Before the end of the next day, Cyrus, the newcomer, produced a five-carat red diamond.

He touches his earring. "This is my commission from that sale. I received it in the rough form from my roommate's father. I polished the gem myself instead of trusting it to a master cutter. Such magic, *jounam,* goes into this complicated and precise craft. I perfected each facet to coax and lengthen the path of light that passes through, allowing rays to travel farther and, in the process, deepening and enhancing the color. I set the diamond in a four-pronged platinum frame and haven't removed it since. It's part of me now."

I, too, have learned to appreciate the grace and power diamonds hold in their recesses. They inspire a certain awe not unlike what I experienced when my mother, drenched in diamonds, swathed in silk and velvet, sailed down the steps of the Théâtre des Variétés. Or when I happened to come across my grandmother's marble bust in châteaux around Paris. Diamonds are similar to Françoise and Mme Gabrielle—to have them, kings disregard their state and familial responsibilities, and ordinary men pay with their lives.

But more than anything, I fell in love with diamonds because a bracelet of red diamonds introduced me to Cyrus and because they became synonymous with freedom.

Focused on the red woven flowers framed by a border of blue arabesques on the carpet, Cyrus murmurs, "I need to go to South Africa to arrange for a shipment of diamonds. I hate to leave you alone, but this will be the last trip. I would never go if it were not necessary."

A rush of panic assaults me. I am rendered speechless with shock. I do not fear the mountains; they shelter me from the city. "I am scared, Cyrus, scared for you, conducting business with Muslims, and in court, no less."

"There's nothing to worry about, I assure you. I generate a lot of profit for the Qajar dynasty. In fact, I am not only respected, but liked."

"You are still a Jew."

"A good Jew!" He smiles, leaning forward and caressing my forehead with a hand that feels hot. "Please, *jounam,* trust me. Please don't make it more difficult. Beard is down the path and will get you anything you need. I have asked Pearl to drop in on you. Yes, you don't like her, but in case of emergency she would know whom to seek." He presses one hand to his eye, pleading for understanding, saying he loves me more than the pupil of his eye.

I sip hot jasmine tea that burns my tongue and chokes back further questions.

"Thank you for your understanding, Simone. In the meantime, if you need help in Tehran, go to Mehrdad. He is a trusted colleague. Beard will know where to find him."

Cyrus takes me by the hand and leads me into the bedroom. With the broad tip of his pen, he inscribes Mehrdad and another Persian name. "Here, this is another person to seek if you need assistances. You see, you are not alone." He lifts the taffeta tallit bag and tucks the note between pages of his Bible.

3

"Did you miss your menstrual period?" Pearl the mid-wife asks.

"Non, not yet." In Cyrus's absence, I find myself welcoming Pearl, who rides the lift to Beard's Café and climbs to my house to check on me. The infant she nurses rocks on her back in the black chador wrapped around her. She presses her ear to my belly, murmurs incantations, peeks into my womb with her primitive tools, and consoles me that in no time I will swell with a son.

"My sons enter the world with wide smiles," she says, as if they are hers, and as if her potions fashion boys.

"Do all Persian mothers want boys?"

"Albateh," she replies. Of course. "And I am always the one to nurse them." She taps the sleeping child behind her. "You, of course, will need me more than other mothers. Once you go into labor no one will come to your aid in this godforsaken place. And if my breasts, *astakhfol'Allah,* God forbid, dry up." She bites her thumb and forefinger and spits to her left and right to

ward off evil thoughts, her incriminating stare crawling up and down my petite figure. "I sacrificed three roosters so their souls would enter your womb and make you fertile. Now I shall ward off the evil eye, so your womb will stop coughing up blood."

My alarmed gaze follows her hand as it disappears inside the deep pocket of her wide trousers to reappear with an egg. No, I decide, I will not eat raw eggs.

She continues to spread herself out on the carpet and knots herself into a cross-legged position. From her bundle of potions, she retrieves a lump of coal and begins to draw circles on the egg. She murmurs incantations under her breath, and I make out the names of Beard, Cyrus, and Yaghout. She presses a coin to each end of the egg and wraps it in a handkerchief, squeezing the egg in her palm. A splitting sound that could not be caused by the mere cracking of an eggshell bursts out of her clenched fist. The baby in her pouch screams. The handkerchief turns the color of sour *vin*.

I am ready to toss Mama's mantle across my shoulders and run out, flee this suspicious affair.

"Did you hear that? The evil eye exploded! You were certainly struck." A gold tooth gleams in her mouth. I hope Cyrus is not paying her more than she deserves. She sways faster on her buttocks to calm the startled baby. She holds up a stained calico bundle for my inspection. Her good eye winks fitfully, and I am unable to tell if she is pleased or distressed. I look away from the assortment of concoctions, mortified at other horrors she might have in store. Last month, I ingested the *merde* she brewed in her mortar. Now, with Cyrus away, I cannot risk becoming sick; so whatever she is unfolding from its wrapping as she swears under her breath on all the great imams that it cost her more than a shah's coffer, she might as well shove down her own throat.

She balances the open bundle on her palm as if it were a treasured jewel offered to Françoise by a wealthy admirer. A pinkish pile of what resembles some vile part of an animal emits the acrid odor of rotting meat. "Have one for fourteen evenings with castor oil, preferably warm."

I wave to chase off the offensive odor, then step closer and sniff. Could this be true? I grab her by the collar. Shake her fat shoulders. Jostle her back and forth, unable to stop myself. "Foreskins?" I shout over and over again.

She loosens my grip with the sudden slap of her hands. "Women kill for foreskins!"

I snatch her bundle and run to the window. "Go away! We'll make beautiful babies without your magic." I hurl the bundle out, horrified as its contents—mortar, pestle, potions, coal, rags—scatter about the garden.

"*Ahmagh,* stupid foreigner!" she hisses, stomping out the door and aiming a spurt of spittle at the threshold.

"*Adieu,*" I call behind her, relieved to be rid of the witch.

"Whatever that means, may it come to pass on your own head," she shouts behind the door.

I smile at the silliness of her counsel—sudden movements tangle the umbilical cord around the baby and choke him, a pinch of saffron strengthens the heart, salt-soaked lingerie under the pillow chases nightmares away. Still, I did try that last remedy, I am ashamed to confess. But it did not dispel nightmares of my mother-in-law dragging me down to the foreign city at the foot of the mountains. *À Dieu ne plaise,* God forbid my coming face-to-face with Yaghout, having to suffer her again. But if I become pregnant, if Pearl refuses to deliver the baby, I would have to give birth in Yaghout's house. That horrible prospect sends me to my feet and flying to the door. Pearl is at the gates. "I apologize, Pearl. Come back. We foreigners can't control ourselves. I'll fire the samovar, brew cardamom tea, jasmine if you prefer."

She stops in her tracks, not coming forward, nor turning away, expecting me to grovel, I assume. "Please, Madame Pearl, if it were not for you I would die here alone. You are like a Persian mother to me."

That last lie seems to touch her. She wiggles her backside to adjust the baby in its pouch and, grumbling that she has no desire to replace my mother, storms past me into the house. I pile her plate with last night's dinner of roasted lamb and crunchy saffron rice. Spreading a tablecloth on the carpet, I set peeled cucumbers, roasted hazelnuts and pistachios on it, then serve glass after glass of steaming tea. When she has had her fill of every edible item in the kitchen, she belches and imparts another nugget of wisdom. "If you happen to smell food, have a bite, or the fetus will not form. And if you get scared, drop a pinch of salt under your tongue, or the baby's heart will shrink. Excitement is deadly." Her lips flap like hummingbirds. "The placenta will swell into such a putrid growth even Allah . . ." She throws her hands up in surrender, one good eye squeezed shut, the other staring at me like dull glass. Then, she utters her pièce de résistance: "No sex from the first month you miss your menstrual period until you give birth."

My mother's image on the bed "Seraglio" as she fans her breasts after an exhausting ménage pops across the screen of my mind. I purse my lips to trap my laughter in my chest.

Pearl's gnarled finger points toward my smile. "I am not surprised at your shameful appetites, khanom, not at all, offspring of prostitutes."

"Exceptional women," I correct. "Nothing short of royalty."

4

⚮

Paris
August 2, 1900

Enfolded in layers of red gauze, orange tulle, and violet chiffon, her blue curls cascading about her straw bonnet, Mme Gabrielle d'Honoré fixed her indigo gaze on the horizon. The faraway rumble of a carriage and the synchronized *clop-clop* of advancing horses echoed across the Valley of Civet Cats.

She was not expecting visitors today.

From her vantage on top of the clover hill, she had a panoramic view of the Valley of Civet Cats and the surrounding lavender hills. A carriage whirled at the last bend of the dirt-packed road that snaked around the neighboring villages and turned into a cobblestone drive to end at her château. Twelve postilions jogged alongside twelve golden stallions. Coachmen yelled and whipped up a dust storm.

She slapped shut her journal and locked away her past. Raising herself on one elbow, she reached for a tumbler at her side, tossed back her head, and drank the absinthe normally reserved to mark the culmination of her afternoon séances. The fiery liquid raced down to pool into soothing warmth in her belly.

With the advancing clatter of hooves, the scent of roses became dizzying. A whinny of restive horses rose from the stables
to join the honks of edgy geese from the lake below and the
shrieks of courting peacocks from her hilltop perch. Farther
around the hills, civet cats scurried out of burrows, trampled
the lavender underfoot, and clambered up chestnut trees,
marking their territory with their musky scent.

The carriage came to an abrupt stop by the two red-veined
marble lions that flanked the grand gates above which shone
Mme Gabrielle's bronze family crest. The wrought iron panels
were flung open to accommodate the entrance of the gold-
fitted carriage. The postilions slowed down along the panting
stallions with elaborate cheek pieces, crimson-plumed headgear, and leather harnesses inlaid with jewels. Coachmen
yanked upon reins to keep the beasts in line and prevent the
trampling of the bordering roses. Six uniformed men sprinted
out of the carriage. They marched briskly into the park and toward the clover hill.

Mme Gabrielle replaced the tumbler of absinthe on its
cobalt saucer, picked up a chocolate-covered almond from the
gilded rim, and popped it in her mouth.

M. Günter, the malevolent ghost of a once demonic lover,
whose pleasure stemmed from the misfortune of others, coiled
his absinthe-steeped nebula around her ear and whispered—
impending doom, chère madame. *Your fate is about to take a turn,
and not for the better, I am afraid.*

A petit mal of melancholia scurried across her legendary
hands. Had Jew haters finally caught up with the valley? Was
France going mad? It would behoove everyone to learn a lesson
or two from her dear friend Émile Zola. Every citizen had a
right to assert her individuality against society's demands for
conformity. She was who she was, Mme Gabrielle d'Honoré,
Jew or gentile, and proud of her accomplishments. Her gloved
hand shading her eyes, she squinted at the men who marched

toward the clover hill as if negotiating familiar terrain. With their advance, the details of their uniforms and medals came into sharper focus. What did high-level government officials want of her? Emissaries of the president of the Third Republic, no less!

This was not good. Not good at all.

Alphonse, Mme Gabrielle's butler, heard the commotion from inside the château and ran out. "No! No! Messieurs!" he bristled. "Madame may not be disturbed. This is unacceptable."

"We deliver the president's orders," one of the couriers shouted, waving a newspaper in the air. "A terrible thing has happened."

The indignant butler straightened his spine to its full impressive height. His intense eyes churning, his elegant features readjusted into their habitual high-brow manner. He seized the newspaper from the man and led the way with a great huff and a squaring of his shoulders.

The couriers' swords pressed against their muscular thighs, heralding their advance through the park, past canals and reflecting pools, streams that bore paths into limestone, curved and twisted to flow into a man-made lake the shape of an enormous peacock, which, to Mme Gabrielle's mortification, had attracted gaggles of geese she found insufferably crude.

The entourage stopped at the foot of the clover hill. They stared up at Mme Gabrielle's celebrated galleries, an exhibitionistic Mecca visible from kilometers away.

Breathless with the effort to warn his mistress, Alphonse ran ahead. Reaching the clearing at the top of the hill, he handed her the newspaper, clasped his hands behind his back, and positioned himself in front of her. He shook his head dolefully. The polished expression he had carried on his face for the thirty-two years he had served his mistress was peeling away like onionskin to reveal an older man underneath.

Mme Gabrielle shooed away a flock of peacocks and lifted

a veil from her face. Her gaze swept across the bold headline of *Le Monde.*

Assassination Attempt on Persian King
Foiled by Minister of Court

"How do you pronounce your shah's name?" she asked her Persian butler, the languorous roll of her smoky voice staggering the couriers.

"Mozaffar Ed-Din Shah, madame." Alphonse stressed every syllable, his nostrils quivering indignantly. The fuss had nothing to do with Gabrielle, after all, but with his country. He had left Persia in protest of the Qajar dynasty's pro-British policy, which had sold his country to the pitiless empire. He had settled in France for Gabrielle's sake, and she did not even attempt to pronounce his shah's name properly.

"Ah! *Oui!*" she murmured, returning to the newspaper.

Thursday 1st of August 1900, a French anarchist intercepted the Persian king's open carriage on the way to the Versailles. Mirza Mahmud Khan, the minister of the Persian Court, thwarted the attempt by redirecting the revolver aimed at the king. Lodging his finger under the hammer, the minister twisted the gun free of the anarchist and held him captive until the police arrived.

Mme Gabrielle studied an artist's rendition of the event—the shah's fearful face cowering behind the wide-shouldered minister of court. She stared curtly at the tips of her ink-stained gloves and wiped them against her cocoon of colorful gauzes, tulles, and chiffons. Although not impressed by the shah, she was fascinated by his minister. His loyalty was contrary to the senseless campaign of terror anarchists had mounted throughout Europe. An Italian had assassinated Sadi Carnot, president of the Republic. Another had murdered King Humbert of Italy. Rumor had it there were impending conspiracies to eliminate leaders of every Western country while Paris was hosting dignitaries for the 1900 exhibition. She was thoroughly and completely appalled by impotent, chicken-brained extremists who were envious of the aristocracy. Folding the newspaper into four neat squares, she set it down on the carpet of clover. Her startled gaze fell upon the journal she had overlooked in the preceding commotion.

Conscious of her every move, Alphonse stepped forward to retrieve the journal of vellum leaves bound in brocade from under the chaise longue. In the process, he scattered her spirits, who kept court at her side when she chronicled her history. Aware of the role time played in shaping the past, they fine-tuned her memory when she embellished reality or slipped into self-serving lapses of reverie. Alphonse, unaware of having startled the ghosts, clutched the journal until an opportunity to conceal it presented itself.

"Well, messieurs, and what do you want from me?" Mme Gabrielle asked, once her journal was secure.

His cheeks as red as watermelon hearts, one of the couriers clicked his heels, snapped his hand in a salute, and informed her that Émile François Loubet, the president of the Third Republic, demanded her presence at the palace.

"Pray, why," she sighed, "does the president demand my presence?"

Another courier stepped forward and handed her an envelope sealed with the presidential emblem. Her hands slightly trembling, she tore the envelope open and scanned the handwritten script.

A quickened pulse fluttered in her throat. She, Mme Gabrielle d'Honoré, daughter of Rabbi Abramowicz of Warsaw, was summoned to the palace by the president of the Third Republic to entertain the Persian king.

The congratulatory soprano of Luciano Barbutzzi, the ghost of the Italian castrato, confirmed her triumph. When still alive and at the height of his fame, the castrato had sought her celebrated hands, which were reputed to bring any creature to orgasm with their supple acrobatics and without help from the rest of her able self. And she had not failed him. When he died from a premature affliction of the bones, the inevitable consequence of castration, he returned to lodge in her armpit—where he found the acoustics ideal. Depending on her victories or failures, Handel's operas, Baroque music, or religious hymns resonated in the foamy-white tucks of her arms. If not for her insistence that he leave her in peace every now and then, her armpit would have turned into his permanent opera house. Now he celebrated with a joyous opus from Handel.

She was going back to court.

Her precious hands had, once again, proved a blessing. Their magic had helped her accumulate unparalleled wealth. And the same magic had impressed the president to choose her from among many other able—and much younger—Parisian courtesans. It was not for nothing that she slept with her cotton-gloved hands dripping in aromatic oils of sesame seed and musk and loosely tied to her four-poster bed so as not to inadvertently nick the tapered fingers, or the polished nail beds the shade and shape of peeled almonds.

She ran her gloved fingers through the curls Alphonse tinted with a blue dye from the glands of hermaphroditic snails. She had aged gracefully, elegantly, and without much fuss—as all women were meant to, but rarely do, she liked to say with a seductive wink. Nonetheless, being a sensible woman of depth and character, she had come to terms with the three lines in the center of her still-plump breasts, the appearance of which she softened with gossamer foulards. She did not mind the crescent-shaped wrinkles at the corners of her mouth, either. Or the two around her eyes, providing her with the expression of a woman who scorned the surrounding irrelevance. The seashell glow of her complexion was enhanced with veils. Her milky skin was pampered with an elixir created by the eminent Claudius Galenus, which the French had named Crème Ancienne. As a result, Mme Gabrielle had the appearance of a much younger woman nowhere remotely close to her marvelous forty-seven years.

The butler assisted her out of her gossamer cocoon and with a spectacular bow tossed a cape over her shoulders. She assessed the president's men. They were riveted to her famous and infamous galleries, which provoked the surrounding populace into heated debates about her frivolity and exhibitionism. To those accusations, she would throw her shoulders up and indicate that the galleries were reflections of her triumphant life and that she was entitled to create her own reality however she desired. Consequently, she had achieved her objective to stir controversy during her lifetime rather than when she was gone. Her life was a stage, after all, and she the main performer and at the height of her theatrical aplomb. "Gentlemen," she purred, the sweep of her arm taking in the galleries, "time permitting, I would have shown you around. But the president must not be kept waiting!"

And once again, with a few simple words, she transformed common men into potent emperors, and with as many words, caused her butler unbearable grief. It was in Gabrielle's nature to flaunt her sexuality, he reflected, and the main reason he failed to wash her out of his blood.

A flock of shrieking peacocks followed her down the clover hill, pecking at her heels, fanning resplendent plumage as if courting a peahen. Her fingers waltzed on top of their iridescent heads, tapped edges of their soft feathers, and tickled their oily underwings.

She cut through the courtyard of mermaids where sixty-nine statues spewed water out of mouths, nipples, and other orifices. She stepped back to admire *les grands jets d'eau*, the arabesque reminiscent of art nouveau coming into vogue. A time of change, she reflected, an invitation to rekindle her dreams.

The indigo-eyed woman approached her mansion, a gift from her first serious protector, a living edifice that shimmered in pomp, glowed in moonlight, and pulsed with possibilities.

The château stood on the remains of a long vanished sea rich with minerals, limestone, and nourishing algae that created healthy equine bones. Fragrant fields of lavandin, a lavender hybrid, cast purple blooms across the surrounding hills. In the evening, hundreds of civet cats clambered out of a network of underground tunnels, transforming the hills into a spread of mottled fur.

Pursued by the presidential envoy, she ascended the limestone stairs curving up to an expansive terrace that led to the first level of the intricate façade of the twenty-five-bedroom brick-and-stone Louis XIII château.

A rose tumbled out of the window above, gyrated, danced, and twisted in the breeze, pink petals fluttering against the backdrop of an azure sky. The stem shuddered and, with a muted snap, landed on the brim of her straw bonnet. She gazed up at the open window on the second floor, the principal boudoir of the château that had once witnessed her dealings and business acumen. Now the boudoir was the scene of her daughter Françoise's clandestine meetings with the best of men and the worst of the worst.

At this very moment, in that boudoir, her daughter was initiating her granddaughter, Simone, into the marvelous world of Honoré women.

5

The Persian king, Mozaffar Ed-Din Shah, leaned in his high-backed chair, a scepter encrusted with a red gem propped against his thigh. Medals covered his topcoat, a belt studded with emeralds, sapphires, and rubies girthed his waist. He drew deeply from a *ghalian* supplied for his addiction. The aigrette on his hat fluttered with every puff of exhaled smoke. The tip of his nose touched the handlebar mustache he twisted as he addressed Mirza Mahmud Khan, his minister of court.

Having recently saved the shah from death, the minister had become indispensable to a king who had reigned for fewer than four years. He was a prime target for manipulation by a shrewd man such as the minister, who had insight into the inner politics of the Qajar dynasty, inundated by rumors, innuendo, and propaganda. Taking advantage of the shah's trust and exploiting his superstitious nature, the minister advised and influenced the shah in selecting his viceroys, advisory council, and women for his harem. And those he enjoyed abroad.

The world Mme Gabrielle had entered was clearly controlled by the man whom she found even more charming in person than in his newspaper rendition. His ebony eyes, his strong chin, and the arrogance he flaunted without a trace of modesty demanded attention. To the king, she concluded, she must be an exotic novelty, a femme fatale who would introduce him to foreign sexual delights. The minister, on the other hand, observed her with the calculating expression of a politician. She did not mind engaging in his political game. In fact, she decided to engage *him*.

The minister's thoughts paralleled those of Mme Gabrielle, who had come highly recommended by the president of the Republic. Cordial relationships between France and Persia were reinforced by the shah's state visit and Persian involvement in the recent Paris Exhibition. But the French minister, Ernest Bourgarel, had yet to prove an ally. The overall Franco-Persian relationship remained guarded in deference to British and Russian wishes. And Persia was in dire need of agricultural and financial concessions. At any rate, the minister's mind was not preoccupied with his country; his personal interest was at stake. And this was where Mme Gabrielle could prove invaluable.

Within the last few years, red diamonds were replacing gold as the economic backbone of the affluent in certain countries, among them Persia. He was informed by the shah's private jeweler of a red diamond vein in South Africa. The mine was rumored to produce a rare breed of diamonds of an exquisite crimson shade.

Mme Gabrielle had entertained an army of influential Frenchmen. She might supply information about a certain French art collector who had purchased the mining license to this pipe.

Mme Gabrielle stepped behind the king as required by royal etiquette.

The shah gestured to her to come closer, permitting a degree of familiarity.

"*À votre disposition,*" she exhaled, and her *V* rolled in her mouth like sin.

Never once did the king acknowledge two other women who, quite nervous in his presence, stood across the room. The only woman whose exotic folds he longed to explore was Mme Gabrielle, concealed under vibrant layers. But being superstitious, he required divine guidance from his astrologer to discover if providence proposed he spend the night with the fairy. He tapped his scepter three times on the chair handle. An expectant silence levitated overhead.

The sudden appearance of a gnarled, white-bearded man, who seemed to materialize out of the shah's hookah, startled Mme Gabrielle.

Face wrinkled like aged quince, beard parted in the middle like two halves of an ax, the old man gathered his loose tunic under him and came down cross-legged to face the shah.

The minister positioned himself behind the king's high-backed chair.

Demanding the ancient rite of *Estekhareh,* the shah sought divine guidance regarding his choice of women. He dug his hand into the pocket of his coat and retrieved three pieces of paper, each inscribed with the name of one of the women. He unfolded the first note, glanced at the name, and handed it to his astrologer.

The old man's eyes aimed up at the minister, then turned to skim across one of the women. As if his worst nightmares were reflected on paper, his face turned into a mask of horror. He crushed the paper in his fist and shoved it into his pocket. The shah handed him the second slip. The astrologer studied the name. His skeletal legs shaking, he tore the paper into tiny shreds and sprinkled them over the embers on the king's hookah.

Mme Gabrielle crossed her arms across her breasts to calm Luciano Barbutzzi, who let loose his dynamic range, calling attention to the communication between the astrologer and the minister, who gesticulated behind the shah. The matter was quite suspicious, she concurred, especially since according to the castrato's libretto, the other women were summoned to pleasure the shah, too.

None of the medals pinned on his formal coat, nor the bejeweled egret on his hat, not even the giant red gem in his scepter made her fancy the evening ahead. The abacus of her mind began to click, adding and subtracting. She must take advantage of an encounter that was beginning to prove unpleasant. She thought of her granddaughter, Simone, who was never far from her mind. It was high time the rebellious girl made her debut. Her potential first lover would be critical in making or breaking her future as another Honoré *dame*. Mme Gabrielle found herself evaluating the shah. Was he a suitable candidate to introduce Simone to the taste of desire, facilitate her entry into the Honoré universe?

He had a presence that, if not regal, was impressive. But he was somewhat jaded, his heavyset limbs sluggish. The shadows his eyebrows cast gave the impression of chronic anger. He lacked Alphonse's elegant mannerism. He would not do for Simone.

Like a splash of sunshine, Mme Gabrielle directed her gaze toward the minister who, on the other hand, proved more charming than she had imagined. A wealth of experience had shaped a complex man in his fifties. Simone would appreciate his sophistication. But having lost his every innocent cell, he must have hardened into a rigid and possibly bitter man. That might not do for the idealistic Simone, either.

Having had the same romantic notions as a young girl, she empathized with her granddaughter. Still, Simone, too, would learn one day that impractical ideals never last in the face of universal evil.

At that instant, the minister of court, positioned as he was behind the king's chair, nodded his head as the shah handed his guru the last square of paper.

The shah seemed visibly annoyed when the old man wiped a tear from the corner of one eye and murmured Farsi words that sounded alternately harsh and poetic. The shah stood up, shaking himself like an elderly lion. He snapped his fingers and addressed Mme Gabrielle.

Certain she would not allow anyone, not even the king of Persia, to snap at her, no matter its cultural significance, she gazed around as if searching for another presence the king would dare address in such a rude manner. She, of course, was unaware that the guru had predicted that the union would result in chaos, that he had encouraged the shah to send her away. And that the minister had gestured emphatically, ordering the old man to give his blessing to her name inscribed on the last piece of paper.

His obsidian eyes twinkling, the minister cupped her elbow in his hand and, in perfect French and with an accent she found charming, directed her out the door. In the foyer, he assured her that before the night was over she would experience other customs she might find bizarre.

The shah's apartments in the president's palace lacked the elegance and grandeur of Mme Gabrielle's boudoir. She observed the olive green walls, the bed with its four oak posts and velvet canopy, the tapestry above the headboard with a hunting scene she found inappropriate for a bedroom. With the importance of the journey ahead of her taking precedence, she cleared her mind of all, save pleasing the shah, whose shallow breathing, drunken eyes, and impatient gestures revealed his eagerness. She tapped a space on the bed and invited him to settle next to her.

The shah, who had imagined she would belly dance out of her layered robes, and at a loss as to what to make of her, took his seat at the offered spot. He began to chatter about his outings in Paris. He attended the theater every night, leaving after the second curtain to address his prayers. He strolled in parks and engaged in target practice but was most interested in the zoo. He had ordered his *akkasbashi,* photographer, to purchase all necessary equipment for a "cinema" in Persia. He was awestruck by the Eiffel Tower, the tree-lined streets, the gas lamps, and cafés with windows open to the streets. He prattled on and on, riveted to Mme Gabrielle's cerulean eyes, a color he had not encountered in his harem or anywhere in his country.

Mme Gabrielle, who was getting bored with the shah's stream of consciousness, and who found it difficult to understand his French, began to tweak the tips of her glove and peel off the grenadine. With coquettish reluctance, she accepted a kiss from him on her fingers, then demanded that he blow on her fingertips to warm them. From her cape, she retrieved a tumbler of precious oils—a waxlike perfume from sap of styrax and benjoin trees mixed with spermaceti oil. A few drops of ambergris and the fixative civet, scraped from perineal glands of her cats, created the signature perfume French women tried to duplicate. She glided the balm on the tip of each finger, up and down each shaft, across each translucent vein, calling upon her entire repertoire of savoir faire, sensual aptitude, and deceptive skills.

One of a rare breed of women who were fortunate to boast a perfect balance of the preeminent male and female attributes, she utilized these assets to her advantage. Men had no difficulty confiding in her or being crass in her presence as they would in male company without fear of judgment. In a way, she was one of the boys. But she also possessed what men lacked—sensitivity, indulgence, and a healthy dose of intuition.

She had perfected the art of mentally challenging but never testing a man's fragile ego—so much so even Émile Zola sought her intellectual stimulation. She would engage him in heated discussions about Baudelaire's *Fleurs du Mal,* whether certain of his poems were intended for the great courtesan Appollonie Sabatier. She argued about the pros and cons of the Salon of Living Artists and the exoticism of mulatto women. She questioned whether talismans warded off evil, and if so, did *la peau de chagrin,* or skin of sorrow, shrink every time it carried out a wish? And she pondered why in the end, when shriveled to nothing, the skin of sorrow heralded death. She would hold Zola's gaze and ask if he believed that Balzac died of exhaustion, mirrors reflected reality, Courbet and Flaubert were the two pillars of realism, and Salammbô the symbol of perversity. She flaunted her knowledge of Impressionism, of *le Naturalisme,* and her familiarity with Zola's social history of the seedier side of the family, *Les Rougon-Macquart.* And she always sought his view of the Franco-Prussian War and whether love and hate were sister and brother.

At the crucial height of her verbal exhibitionism, when she was on the brink of conquest, and her lover, overwhelmed by her, felt a strong need to cuff her into submission, with one sensual glance and the most feathery touch she would convert his frustration into enormous sexual energy.

As she prepared to disarm the king, the door to the room opened. A yellow-skinned boy with billowing pants stepped in. A cage, in which a startled hen clacked, dangled from his hand.

The king reached into the cage and retrieved two recently laid eggs. He threw a meaningful gaze at Mme Gabrielle. "We never travel without our chickens," he explained. "We find it essential to consume fresh egg yolk after certain functions that deplete our strength."

She held the king's hand in hers and, from behind her veils, directed her indigo gaze at his lust-filled eyes. Her mouth a lush question mark, her smoky voice husky, she assured him that this occasion would be quite different. This time would be energizing rather than depleting. So much so that in the future he would find no need for his guru or his minister's guidance. And before he had occasion to react to her brazen remark, she settled back and encouraged him to share any intimacies he desired.

Mme Gabrielle was a master listener, a queen of moving under her men's skins and then, at the opportune moment, as-

34 *Dora Levy Mossanen*

sailing them like a lioness. As a younger woman, she had wrestled in bed with kings, counts, and princes, engaged in foreplay that had thrust her men into frenzy. But, alas, her bones had settled into the relaxed lifestyle of a retiring courtesan. She would have to replace wrestling with a different technique. "What bothers you, my king?" she asked when she noticed him shift about and wince.

How, he wondered, had she guessed his struggle with the embarrassing pain in his groin? He hesitated about sharing his dilemma, but just for an instant, since it would be impossible to lose face to an infidel and a courtesan besides. And he did not intend, at any cost, to spoil the long night of pleasure ahead of him. A drop of sweat rolled down his forehead and dangled at the tip of his nose. He squared his shoulders as if he were about to announce a verdict that would change the path of history. "We are having difficulty using Western toilets."

She struggled to contain her laughter. She had never heard of such a problem. However, this intimate information gave her tremendous leverage over him. "Oh! *Pauvre, pauvre petit roi,*" she murmured, her hand sashaying across his chest, skipping the length of his thigh, and lingering on his sex to measure the size. "I will intercede on your behalf, my shah. I will advise the authorities to disengage a toilet seat. Then your honor may squat down and take care of his royal needs. In the meantime," she purred, pointing to a pitcher of water at the bedside, "I will not take offense if your eminence relieves himself right here."

Luciano Barbutzzi's *Bravo! Bravo! Signora bella!* tickled her underarm, and she stifled a smile.

At that, the "Lion of Persia" took care of business with a copious stream of urine and without further ado stepped out of his attire, tossing each piece into a corner as if his attendants were at hand. He then ascended the steps to the high bed, sprawled out on his back, and presented his hairy self.

She observed his limp penis and realized she faced a man who, surrounded by a harem of fawning women and a court of flatterers, swayed on the brink of impotence. Luciano Barbutzzi's *potete farli* encouraging her on, she stroked and cajoled every receptive gland but failed to coax the shah into sustaining an erection for longer than a few sighs.

With a dramatic flair, she tossed her feathered fan, sweeping cape, and wide-rimmed hat on top of his pile of clothing. Removing her platform shoes, she revealed herself in all of her diminutive grandeur. At the apparent shock of the shah, who had imagined the cloaked woman with the powdered hands as much taller, she let out her throaty laughter. She freed her blue curls, undid her foulard, and embarked on disengaging the multitude of mother-of-pearl buttons that ran the length of her dress.

He watched her fingers slide each button out of the silk eyelet, reveal a glimpse of her creamy neck, ample cleavage, and blushing nipple. And with every revelation, a thimble of blood and a measure of oxygen pumped into his jaded veins.

She stepped out of her dress and stood before him with rouged nipples.

His women waxed, depilated, and threaded themselves clean, not a single hair on their bodies. He had never imagined body hair as such an aphrodisiac. The azure cloud of her pubis and armpits stunned him into full erection. He dug his hand into the pubic hair her beautician dyed, conditioned, and trimmed more diligently than the curls on her head. He lifted her off her feet, laid her down on her stomach, and mounted her, whipping her on the buttocks with his long, thin sex.

Her joints complaining under his weight, she worried that his acrobatic shenanigans might injure her. She folded her leg from the knee, raised her heel backward, and tapped him on the scrotum.

In fear of being hurt by a stronger kick, he jumped off her with agility rare for him. Unable to believe she had the audacity to kick the king of Persia, and at a loss as to what to make of her laughter that pealed like temptations, he lifted her up by her underarms and tossed her around.

And without further consideration, he thrust his royal face into her oceanic pubis and drowned himself in what he had craved forever.

∽∞∾

At dawn, he opened his eyes to encounter a lady-in-waiting rinse royal sweat off Mme Gabrielle's thighs, shampoo and brush her tangled curls. The blue cloud between her legs stirred him, causing a measure of consternation. Plans had been made. He was expected at the Paris Exhibition. It would be impossible to climb back into bed. He drew in a deep breath, feeling rejuvenated and stronger than he ever had. She was right, egg yolks were unnecessary. He pulled a bell cord and began to snap his fingers, a habit Mme Gabrielle found quite annoying.

As if he had been eavesdropping all night behind the door, the minister immediately entered and, in reply to the shah's question as to why his jeweler was late, called out into the corridor.

Mme Gabrielle wrapped her cape snuggly around her, deciding that if she were expected to perform a ménage à trois, she would forget the shah and the president. Walk straight out of the palace rather than, at her age, get involved in a Persian circus.

A single knock sounded and the door turned on its well-oiled hinges. A lean, tigerlike Persian appeared at the threshold. Jewelry boxes stacked high in his hands, he remained at the entrance. His informality made him appear superior in rank to the shah. His shoulder-length hair pulled back, a romantic sadness shadowed his hazel eyes, an indifferent smile tugging at the corners of his mouth.

Mme Gabrielle's earlier indignation took flight. A stream of energy filled her—a feeling she had not experienced since the day she walked out of the Marais and into the heart of Paris. She fumbled to remove her gloves, bare her hands, and toss her cape around her neck to conceal her age. In the process, she nearly tripped over her platform shoes, catching her balance with a dramatic sweep of the cape. Despite her rich repertoire of men, she had not encountered such aristocratic grace, such shapely shoulders, such a proud brow. She was too old, of course, to consider the Persian with the faraway look and the shy self-assurance for herself.

But Simone was not.

He would be the perfect candidate to initiate her virgin granddaughter into the magnificent universe of the most glamorous, emancipated, and sought-after women of Europe.

Before Mme Gabrielle had occasion to repeat the sensual theatrics of her hands, he stepped in. Placing the boxes on a table, he flipped them open to display an array of rubies, emeralds, and diamonds. She held the supplied loupe over the necklaces, bracelets, rings. She hardly heard the minister buzz in her ear, asking if she had by chance come across a certain owner of mines. She did not note that the minister, not the shah, instructed the jeweler what to display first. She owned a wealth of gems, gifts from kings, counts, and dukes, but she had never encountered diamonds of such clarity, emeralds of such purity, pigeon blood rubies of such depth and exceptional workmanship. She passed her hands over the suite of rubies.

The jeweler detached the necklace from its velvet cushion and held it up under the chandelier. He clasped the necklace around her neck, fastened earrings to her earlobes, and slid a ring on her love finger. She was stunned at the effect of his fleeting touch on her wrist. His breath on her neck as he locked the gold clasp burrowed a path into her heart. She would have considered trading her range of invaluable experiences for a renewed burst of youthful vigor if that were possible. No one, not even her *cochon*-headed granddaughter, would refuse such romanticism, charm, and a voice that had strummed Mme Gabrielle's often-used heart cords.

The shah tapped her wrist below the bracelet where her pulse pounded faster than the day she had experienced her first orgasm with Émile Zola. "I assume this is to Madame's liking," his royal highness said with newfound confidence.

Her eyes held his, but her fingertips sought the jeweler. She drew circles on his palm, stroked a vein, and slid up and down the grooves. "What is your name, young man?"

"Cyrus," he replied, a glimmer in his eyes, "like the great Persian shah."

She turned to the king and said that it would please her to no end if M. Cyrus came to Château Gabrielle with jewelry for her granddaughter. And before the Shah had occasion to consult the minister, she dipped into her purse and flipped out a calling card. "My granddaughter, Simone," she sighed, meeting the Persian's stunned expression.

Cyrus was riveted to the image of the girl on horseback, her profile avoiding the camera, impatient to dash into the forest behind. Without hesitation or shame, he held the loupe over her savage curls, her thighs gripping the stallion, and the curve of her white neck. It shocked and fascinated him that Parisian women would surrender sidesaddle and hand strangers calling cards complete with their granddaughter's address and photograph. He tucked the card in his wallet. "I will look for suitable jewelry for your granddaughter."

Finding his insipid response unacceptable, she scrambled to sweeten her invitation. What rare gem could even she, Mme Gabrielle d'Honoré, not conceive of owning? Her gaze slithered around the room, past the minister of court, and the jeweler, and came to settle on the shah's scepter. The answer looked her in the face.

"Cher Monsieur," she purred, embracing his hands, "for my very special granddaughter, nothing short of a red diamond will do."

7

Persia
August 1901

I close my eyes and listen with expectant pleasure to the echo of Cyrus's galloping stallion, the sporadic neigh as the animal negotiates its way up steep cliffs.

My husband is coming home from South Africa.

He is a strange sight astride his white stallion, a gift from M. Amir, the Persian chargé d'affaires. The dove-white animal has a mane the shade of Mme Gabrielle's hammered gold cuffs and black-speckled ears alert to the taps of its master's silver-tipped cane. Cyrus spurs the animal around the city where pedestrians, mules, and camels are customary, where men wear somber colors and veiled women shuffle around like wandering souls.

My heart slaps against my chest at the image of the horse twitching its speckled ears to shoo away fireflies overhead. Although fireflies seem harmless, the harlots lure each other's mates and gobble them up, Mme Gabrielle had warned, when a cloud of fireflies had greeted Cyrus on his first visit.

What a vision he was, stepping down from the president's carriage, his hair pulled back, his beard trimmed to perfection, his silver-tipped cane announcing his arrival, his pocket watch glinting in the sunlight.

Now, on his way back to me, he sways to the rhythm of the trotting stallion he directs around the city square, past stalls of shelled walnuts and almonds in water jars, pyramids of mulberries and currants piled high on tin trays, and sheets of dried sour cherries. From behind Mirza, the grocer, and his outdoor stove of steaming beets, Cyrus stirs the stallion around the alley of jewelers, where Turquoise, a merchant at the side of the dirt road, displays cheap jewelry. Raising his cane in salutation, Cyrus negotiates his way past the first sharp bend and up the narrow path smooth with the patina of time, behind Black-Eyed Jaffar's teahouse, where customers recline on carpet-covered pallets sipping tea and puffing on hookahs, their breath curlicues of steam, woolen-gloved hands stirring firewood in cans under mulberry trees. From here, he negotiates the route to our house, through an underpass, around a stony bend where whistling winds hurt his eardrum. He winces, shifting the reins to one hand, the other pressing against his ear. An infection left his ear sensitive to loud noise and lies.

The wind carries the echo of hooves, muffled and far apart, becoming more audible as he nears Beard's Café. A banner outside its lopsided brick wall announces today's menu: cream on top of sheep milk, goat cheese wrapped in lavash bread, onion-and-date omelets, hot lentil porridge, or—if you prefer—strong Turkish coffee.

An abandoned property looms on the horizon closer to our home. The grounds were once planted with trees transported with difficulty to this arid mountainous site. The man-made garden once belonged to a Jewish family that fled the wrath of a weak shah who found his voice with the aid of a Frenchwoman.

Cyrus tugs at the reins and circles the garden, where unattended trees resemble ancient, bearded men and gloomy, fossilized women. He will lodge, groom, and feed his horse here until chiefs of the mountains, whoever they might be at the time, evict him to claim another piece of land as their own. He pats his horse, then strides out and gazes at the imposing valley below and the majestic mountains above, bathed in savage hues of a rising sun. Emptying his lungs of the impurities of the long trip, he drinks in the crystalline air of the mountains.

I check myself in the mirror.

The grinding of boots on gravel sends me into the garden where Cyrus and I coaxed vegetation from between cracks, stones, and boulders.

He ambles toward the gate, unlocks and pushes it open, crosses the landing, leaps over one rock, then another, tapping his boot with his cane. "Simone! I will never leave you again," he says, the tips of his fingers touching one eye to reinforce his promise.

In his arms, I am lighter than miracles. Moonlight gleams off his silver strands, wet mouth, and the red diamond I lick. He carries me in, and we snuggle down into the ottoman. Nesting in its velvet embrace like hatchling birds, surrounded by a potbellied stove and throw cushions depicting mythological scenes.

"Let me feel your hair," he murmurs, "inhale your scent. Give me your perfume."

I hug my knees to the content fullness of my belly. I laugh. I am happy. I want time to linger, want our lust to simmer and overflow.

His tongue roams around my breasts, my nipples flowering to greet him.

"I am pregnant," I whisper.

8

The sun gathers force above the outline of the snow-capped Damavand Mountains, shining its way past Beard's Café, sliding across the narrow bend toward the small gate and beyond branches covered for protection against frost, across the garden where Simone and Cyrus had coaxed the earth to yield now dormant ash berries. It casts its rays upon the stone house where Cyrus settles at a table pushed to the window to catch the strong beams of the noon sun.

The pregnant Simone is asleep in the bedroom.

Cyrus, drunk with her fragrance of amber and myrrh, has a few short hours to test a suspicious element he discovered in South Africa. Not wanting to cause her unnecessary alarm, he works silently, unfolding his handkerchief on the table, passing a loupe over the nearly imperceptible metallic powder. He is preoccupied with the configuration of the room he came across in the miner's home, its high-temperature ovens and harsh lighting.

When he had arrived at the gates of the city last night, he had considered soliciting the help of Gholam Ali, the one-eyed metallurgist, who is skilled in identifying peculiar chemical compounds. But Gholam Ali is a chronic gossipmonger, and the last thing Cyrus needs is to broadcast his suspicions. Consequently, putting his own gemological knowledge to use, he folds a handkerchief and ties it around his lower face and mouth like a makeshift mask in case the trace element in front of him proves toxic. He twists open jars of light elements he obtained from Tehran on his way back home—chrysoberyl, magnesium, lithium, aluminum oxide. A stack of magnifying glasses and leather straps is neatly arranged in front of him. Pulling his chair forward, he rests his arms on the tabletop for support. Cautious not to scatter the powders, he carefully sprinkles them out of various jars and coats the residue from South Africa. The chemicals will need an hour to work.

He rubs his bloodshot eyes and leans back in his chair, remembering a couple of years ago when red diamonds of two, three, and four carats began to trickle onto the market. To investigate this aberration of nature, he traveled from Persia to Europe and eventually to Africa, where he monitored the process of mining from rivers and open pits, the trade of rough from one hand to another, from the polishing wheel to the sawyer, and eventually from one *diamantaire* to the next. With critical eyes and strong loupes, he scrutinized the depth, color, and facet of every such diamond he located.

Failing to find proof of enhancement by heat treatment, he compared his own red diamond with those in the market. The properties, or fingerprint, of his diamond were identical to the others. Practically all, he realized, including his diamond, originated from the same mine.

He gazes through the window at the bright sun on the snow-capped mountains. It is early afternoon. Simone is still asleep. He is going to be a father, he thinks, and his grave expression breaks into a broad smile.

He holds the loupe over the trace powder he salvaged from

South Africa and leans over the tabletop to take a better look. He jerks back, nearly toppling his chair. Under the influence of chemicals, the powder has turned a metallic gray. He is facing a trace remnant of beryllium, a highly toxic metal isolated some seventy years ago. Normally invisible to the naked eye, unless coalesced with a metal such as copper or nickel.

He remembers a freak accident that occurred at the Sorbonne when he was exploring topics for his thesis. The accidental inclusion of chrysoberyl in a parcel of heat-treated sapphires had changed their color, and he had his topic. Further research had revealed that microscopic particles of beryllium—as little as a few atoms—could turn the color of sapphires to a more vibrant shade when diffused into the gems' minute open spaces. But diamonds are much harder stones, he reflects. Their carbon atoms are too closely packed for beryllium to get into.

Highly suspicious now, he decides to conduct two experiments. He removes his earring and places it on the table. He will have to work fast in the few hours remaining before sunset. But his hands are unstable and his eyes tired. He drops himself onto the futon in the corner, slips his hand under the cushion, and retrieves his Old Testament, reading the first few pages of Genesis. He lays the book on his chest and shuts his eyes. If his suspicions were to prove true, the diamond market would be thrust into panic. And the financial backbone of certain nations would snap.

He struggles with his options, the folly of questioning influential men such as the shah and the minister of court, planting himself and Simone in the eye of danger.

Now that he has a family, caution is of utmost importance.

He would use his findings as a trump card that would have nothing to do with greed but everything to do with principle and his desire to protect his pregnant wife.

~∞~

His mind wanders back to four years ago when M. Jean Paul Dubois had taken a liking to him. Cyrus spoke French without an accent and negotiated with clients the miner preferred to avoid. He soon learned to study a buyer's reaction, adjust the price accordingly, and sell a wealth of low- and high-grade diamonds in sealed packets. If a merchant as much as questioned the quality of the presorted diamonds, a shadow would darken the miner's eyes. He would offer the responsible party a cup of pepper tea and bid him farewell with a warm handshake and an icy glare.

He did not like what he discovered in Namaqualand and decided to return home. The miner did not object. He might have been expecting, even coaching him for this move. He would be infinitely more valuable in Persia, a country with vast resources but little trust in foreigners.

He embarked on the journey to Persia with a pouch of red diamonds for the minister of court and a note recommending Cyrus as Dubois's ambassador.

He was offered more than he had bargained for, the coveted post of royal jeweler. Traveling back and forth from Persia to South Africa took months. Storms, typhoons, and fatal diseases were a constant threat. Still, the obligatory journeys to purchase raw diamonds afforded months of relief from court intrigue.

Then remarkable, and unbelievable, circumstances had put Simone in his path.

He would not leave her alone in the mountains. But deeply entrenched in the import of diamonds that enriched the royal treasury and Mirza Mahmud Khan, he had to come up with a viable alternative before he presented his resignation.

The day he requested attendance is seared in his mind.

Mirza Mahmud Khan leaned back in his high-backed chair and listened to Cyrus's proposal. Exhibiting no sign of exploding into one of his volcanic rages, the minister removed his felt hat and tossed it on the table with a muffled thud, sending the medals on his lapel into a quiver.

Cyrus was aware that the South African mines yielded white diamonds of fine quality and competitive prices. He also knew that the minister had access to all the whites he desired. What he wanted was a cut of the extraordinary wealth of reds from a fertile diamond pipe that had cornered the market. Cyrus was the only merchant who was offered the courtesy of sorting out and choosing red diamonds from the sealed parcels forced upon others. The minister's dream—the merging of Mirza Diamond Inc., his distribution company, with Dubois Enterprises to create a conglomerate with the resources to take over the great De Beers and create a red diamond cartel—would unquestionably die with Cyrus's departure.

"I understand your predicament," the minister replied, his eyes boring into Cyrus. "You may train whoever you find most competent to replace you. Once the first shipment of diamonds sails toward Khorramshahr, you may resign."

Cyrus had to make one last trip to Namaqualand. And not only for the purpose of arranging for the transport of red diamonds to Persia.

He arrived before noon. M. Jean Paul Dubois had long left for his mines. His servant served him pepper tea with a casserole of cubed bread, eggs, cream, and fried chunks of ham. Cyrus did not reveal that he did not eat ham but invited the servant to join him at the table. The man remained standing as Cyrus spread a slice of bread with spicy butter and passed it along, a gesture of equality between master and servant. But the man was unmoved. "Don't stand on ceremony with me," Cyrus said. "We are both servants. I slave for the court, you for Monsieur Dubois." As if that were a cue to release the dam of his grievances, the servant began complaining about slavery and the rape of his beloved land by the stripping away of kilometers of coastal sand for no other reason but to steal diamonds

"Something suspicious is happening here," Cyrus agreed, "right under your nose. The only way I will be able to help Africa is with your help."

Glancing back at him from the corners of his soft eyes, the servant was silent for a long time. Then, as if shaking himself out of a trance, he gestured for Cyrus to follow him. Familiar with the complicated geography of the mazelike house, he led the way, Cyrus following him as close as his conscience. They crossed stone corridors to descend a staircase into a basement. The drone of machines was constant behind a door. The servant put a finger to his lips, suggested Cyrus return after midnight.

∞

The sun aims its rays through the window, startling Cyrus awake. He scrambles to his feet, pulling out his pocket watch. The sun is beginning to lose its strength, and he has not yet begun his experiments.

He sets the Old Testament on the tabletop and gazes at his diamond. He is not certain he has a right to jeopardize Simone's financial security. But they would both lose more than their wealth if he does not take this risk. The thought of her makes his chest squeeze with delight. He is a lucky man, he tells himself, a lucky man to have such a marvelous woman.

∞

My baby's first kick rattles me out of a languorous postlove sleep. I stretch toward Cyrus's side of the pallet, my hand wandering across the empty sheets. My mouth goes dry. Was his embrace a dream, his promises never to leave again? Another impatient kick startles me out of bed. "You will see your papa in a few months," I whisper. "For now, it's best to stay where you are. It's a safer place than where you'll spend the rest of your life." Will growing up in Persia be different for my child than it has been for me, the foreigner? Will I ever become accustomed to this culture, or forever remain a stranger, despite the shared intimacy with my husband?

"Cyrus," I call out behind the closed bedroom door, "I am hungry. Let's go down to Beard for dinner." Hearing no reply, I twist the handle and open the door. I remain paralyzed at the threshold.

His muscles tense, his jaw clenched, Cyrus is focused on different paraphernalia scattered on the table. His diamond is clamped in a jeweler's tongs and on some kind of three-pronged device. A horizontal leather yarn runs from the wall above the window all the way to the opposite wall. Magnifying lenses of incremental size and a loupe hang from the yarn. "What are you doing?" I cry. "Our diamond!"

He jumps to his feet. Grabs my shoulders. "Don't worry. I am not doing anything foolish." He removes his earring from the gadget and clasps it to his ear. "See. It's fine. Calm down, *jounam,* it's not good for you."

"You never answer my questions. Keep leaving me in the dark. What kind of love is this?"

"Love of a man who is protecting his family."

"Unacceptable! Tell me. Right now! Why did you move the table, the chairs?"

"I moved away flammable objects. I was experimenting with heat. And this is all I'll say for now. Come, let's go to Beard's."

"I am not hungry anymore."

"Of course you are," he says, lifting me in his arms.

9

The cold stings my face and settles in my heart. My breath coils across Cyrus's cheeks as he carries me down the mountain's snow-hardened slope to Beard's Café.

The teahouse stands on a landing where, weather permitting, a single lift deposits hikers. In winter, professionals who seek the euphoria of the mountains visit the café, their nail-dotted hiking boots piercing the packed mud and kilims underfoot.

Steaming samovars, ember-filled braziers, gurgling hookahs, and the aroma of mint and jasmine tea, butter, and sheep lard greet us.

Beard glances down, his Islamic principles and decorum demanding he avert his gaze from my yellow-green eyes that must proclaim my femininity and the jungle of red curls the scarf fails to conceal. Does he glance away because the wicked image of Cyrus and me in bed—one unusually tall, the other hardly reaching her husband's chest—pops into his mind? The *diable* in me wants to set his mind at rest, assure him we have

not yet encountered any difficulty in that area. He is a friend of
Cyrus, and I feel welcome here where, in his own way, Beard has
come to terms with my eccentricities, and I with his.

He is a stocky man of medium height. His bush of hair the
shade of a hayfield stands at the crown of his head like an inverted brush, his beard twisted ropes the color of overcooked
porridge. Sitting in a cross-legged position on the kilim-
covered floor, he lifts his beard from his lap and coils it into a
series of elaborate knots under his chin. Groaning, he prepares
to untangle his legs, which are as thin as saplings despite a
torso grown massive with the consumption of lard and goat
cheese.

A miracle occurred in his youth, a tale hard to validate but
one that he recounts with such passion that we listen politely.
Hardly fifteen, he was bitten by a tarantula on this very spot on
this mountain where he later built this teahouse as homage to
Allah and his miracle. With nothing short of sadistic relish, he
draws the gruesome details of the 175-millimeter tarantula—
one of the largest and deadliest—that paralyzes before sucking
tissue fluid out of its prey. The creature's claws latched onto his
calf and would not let go, the sharp, hollow stinger between the
segmented tail squeezing and pumping poison into his leg.
Venom had coursed through his blood with such speed that by
the time he was discovered and carried down in a makeshift
stretcher and deposited at the cabin of the closest shaman, his
body had swelled up and turned purple, and, in his state of
delirium, he began to recite poetry in an unintelligible language. The shaman had cut his calf open and had drained such
large amounts of blood that, for months, Beard's veins stood
out like thirsting branches. Although he survived to build this
teahouse, his legs never regained their strength.

He negotiates his way toward us, his muscles rippling like
angry snakes against his stomach and around his arms, a red
tattooed tarantula belly dancing along one biceps. Like two

marionettes cut in half from the waist, the thin legs of one attached to the bulky torso of the other, his legs struggle to balance the swaying ship of his upper body. He carries hot tea in narrow-waisted glasses and brass bowls of sugar cubes, dates, and dried mulberries. He never deviates from the proper manner in which tea must be served—ceremoniously, piping hot, and in narrow-waisted glasses that reveal the integrity of his tea. *"Shab bekeir, khosh amadid."*

"Good evening. It has been too long," Cyrus replies. "And how have you been the last months?" He cuffs Beard on the back as he would a favorite brother.

Beard glances sideways at me before turning his gaze to Cyrus. After months of visiting his teahouse, I still seem to puzzle him. How would he react to Françoise's décolletage, to Mme Gabrielle's blue hair, to the airy nothings I wear at home, so contrary to the wool skirt and black sweater I sweat in now.

Cyrus pulls my scarf up, tightening the knot under my chin. "Don't be angry with me. Not tonight. What would you like to eat?"

We are hungry, my baby and I, but I do not reply. For the first time, I *am* angry with Cyrus. I turn away from him and listen to Beard.

Standing on the hide of a vicious tiger he once hunted in the jungles of Mazandaran, he recites tonight's plat du jour, a litany of appetizing and not-so-appetizing dishes: brain and extremities of sheep, liver and fried eggs, sizzling kebab of onion with crispy sheep fat.

Cyrus orders hot *barbary* bread and Tabriz cheese with large glasses of sweetened tea. I lean against cushions, saliva pooling under my tongue.

Before I wash down the last morsel of bread with sweet tea, Cyrus flips his pocket watch out of his vest to check the time. I take in his scent of tobacco and the cardamom he chews to keep away the odor of his clients—the smell of their deceit, he tells me. Purple crescents shadow his eyes and paleness frames his mouth.

"I am tired from the long trip back home," he says, pushing away his untouched plate.

He carries me up the mountain as if I am a load of precious diamonds. He crosses the rocky road, the slippery landing, a short stretch of graveled path to our house, unlocks the gate, strides through the garden blanketed with a layer of scintillating snow and up the three steps into our home. His mouth grazes my stomach. The glint in his eyes makes him look younger than his thirty-two years as he strokes my once-small waist and flat stomach that seem to swell by the hour. As of this morning, fresh arteries are germinating in his heart to grow and connect to our unborn child.

"He is a boy. Name him Elijah."

"A girl will be lovely, too," I reply. "Will you tell me what you were doing with your diamond if I promise to give you a son?"

He burrows his face into my curls, sucks on my earlobes, his tongue sliding along my neck to linger beneath the curve of my chin. "We will talk tomorrow. I promise. I must go to the city early morning. You will be asleep then. Good night, *jounam*."

"Who conducts business that early?"

"Royalty." He smiles bitterly. "Dawn. Dusk. Whenever guilt keeps them awake."

"What are they guilty of?"

"Of more than you could imagine." The set expression of his mouth and the willful seriousness of his eyes leave no room for further discussion.

I nurse my apprehension and reason that he is concerned about our financial situation. "Sell the horse. It will bring good money."

"No! Not the horse. One day, it will belong to Elijah. Our son will not be a real man until he learns to handle horses." He pulls at the band around his ponytail, and it snaps against his hand. He winces, running his fingers through his loosened hair. "Promise to raise our son to be an honest man, Simone. And teach him to wear his dagger in full view." He turns away, his profile framed by the soft light, the silver tip of his cane nudging the door to our bedroom.

10

Paris
1900

Françoise flung open the doors to her apartment.

Simone lingered at the threshold of her mother's dressing room—a universe of yearnings and excess, love and hate, envy and obsession. Her lashes cast wicked shadows across her cheeks, the freckles along her neck amber in the candlelight. She was clad in riding breeches, knee-high boots, and a holster buckled to her waist to accommodate a revolver.

Sixteen, she was summoned, at last, to meet "Seraglio," her mother's mythological bed. Despite her indifference to a profession she neither respected nor intended to pursue, her curiosity about the bed had tempted her to accept the invitation.

Postcards of the bed were sold across the country in concession stands. Newspapers reported on the bed's aphrodisiacal properties. How a most famous photographer, who customarily charged thousands of francs for his services, had shouldered the expense of capturing its likeness. He must have been curious, too, Simone thought, remembering the lengthy debates between her mother and grandmother, after which they had determined that a photograph by such a celebrated photographer would not detract but add to the bed's reputation as a symbol of carnal pleasures. And they were right. "Seraglio" became notorious among the Parisian male aristocracy who had had the fortune of sinking into its satin folds. During Mme Gabrielle's reign, the bed's reputation as an aphrodisiac had spread beyond Paris to other cities and provinces. With Françoise's ascendancy, whispered tales of "Seraglio's" mythical attributes assaulted salons and masked balls, clubs and casinos, and peppered the gossip of envious wives and mistresses.

Silk-padded walls appliquéd with designs of fantastical birds, and an opulent wardrobe of lush fabrics, luxurious shoes, and colorful parasols greeted Simone. Her image reflected in the polished sheen of a door at the far end that led to her mother's boudoir. The fine hair on Simone's arms stood up in anticipation.

Why did the bed lure her like a giant embrace? Her ideologies were different from Françoise's, who looked down upon the concept of love and marriage. She could, of course, still turn around and walk out the door. She had learned more than enough about her mother's and grandmother's lives from living with them. Unless she had sleepwalked with her eyes shut, she could not have escaped the constant dramatic foreplay that occurred around the château. They began with the clattering of an arriving carriage, the adulating whispers of a suitor behind Françoise's shoulders in the foyer, lusting kisses on Mme Gabrielle's hands at the foot of the grand staircase, and shameless flattery on the landing above. And if Simone happened to cross the terrace under Françoise's window, she would try to guess which lover sighed endlessly, had a hearty laugh, or was generous with his sobs.

Her sexual data was complemented by the only pamphlet

her mother suggested she read—further proof, according to Françoise, of how the male gender treated their women. To her amusement, Simone learned that the banana slug's giant penis got stuck in the female slug during copulation, forcing the female to gnaw off the organ. Male lions could copulate 157 times with two different mates in less than an hour. During climax, male honeybees exploded, leaving their genitals behind in the queen bee to discourage further mating. Elephants in musth—a bout of sexual fury that lasted four months—rumbled and dribbled uncontrollably, their penises turning green with acidic urine.

Françoise glided across her dressing room, her naked silhouette swaying under layers of gauze. She peered into chests, flipped open hatboxes, fished out silk camisoles and flung them aside. "Simone, unbuckle your pistol and step out of your breeches."

Complying reluctantly, Simone slipped into the gathered folds of a pistachio-green peignoir that dropped to her ankles and flared in back. Françoise set a wide-rimmed bonnet with orange piping at an angle upon her curls.

Effat, Françoise's Persian *femme de chambre,* entered as graciously as her weight and crooked legs would allow, a stiff apron groaning against her ample stomach. She stroked the tips of her smoky hair and rolled her eyes. Her pin-sized irises, hardly noticeable in a pair of white, protuberant orbs, projected the unsettling appearance of blindness. But her gaze appraised every detail.

Alphonse discovered Effat on his weekly visit to the Sunday market, where *marchands de quatre saisons* lined fruit, nut, and cheese carts. Wiggling her hand among a pile of cod, she had selected the largest, examined the eyes for freshness, the scales for odor, and the stomach for firmness. Right there and then, the butler had offered her a job in Château Gabrielle. At the time, she was employed by a Persian family vacationing in Paris, and the thought of missing her ethnic meals had been reason enough to refuse. Week after week, the butler facilitated her defection by sweetening the offer. In the meantime, he convinced Mme Gabrielle that Persian women could bake exotic tidbits, and that no food was more delicious. Soon, the lure of the Seine, the newly invented electrical lights, glamorous women, and the French delicacies, which by her strange logic she thought would melt the extra fat off her plump thighs, proved irresistible. Effat not only joined the household that supplied her with ample fodder for gossip but also married the keeper of the grounds and became indispensable. Her chilling gaze now roamed her mistress's mind and riffled through crevices Françoise herself did not access.

Maids, ladies-in-waiting, and liveries scrambled to execute Françoise's most mundane orders. The better part of the day was spent preparing for her evenings. Noon began with a soak in a cast-iron tub filled with Sarah Bernhardt's Nerf Sédatif, camphor, sea salt, and tincture of valerian. While Françoise relieved the last evening's fatigue, Effat nourished her straight hair with herbal oils and softened her complexion with creams. The rest of the day, she scattered roses in the dramatic fashion of silent-movie actresses. But her mind was far from idle. Every fully awake moment was spent evaluating her last lover's anatomy and exploring novel methods of pleasuring him.

"Effat, the peignoir is not right," Françoise said, dipping her fingers in a pot of lip balm. "Have her try this skirt and, *oui,* the bodice. Maybe the ermine-trimmed cape. What do you think, Simone?"

"They are ugly," Simone said, annoyed. An hour had been wasted dressing and undressing, and she had not even entered the main boudoir.

"Ah! You will definitely like this one. Effat, *dépêche-toi.*"

Effat nodded in neither an affirmative nor a negative ges-

COURTESAN   59

ture, waddled to the closet, and selected a *robe de bal* with a tight bodice and a flounced skirt.

Simone felt a need to do something wicked to the sixteen-hundred-franc gown her mother had worn to the Théâtre des Variétés. A dress had to be simple and functional—flounces hindered activity, gala corsets were like armors, and crinolines mummified. She was most comfortable in boots and slacks that did not obstruct movement and accommodated her holster and revolver. She would compromise with a *petit costume*. But the horrible skirt Effat held up would not do. Not at all. She wished she were on horseback, exploring the Valley of Civet Cats with Sabot Noir, her friend and stableboy par excellence, as free and as unpredictable as the stallions he trained.

"Pay attention, Simone," Françoise said, flipping open a peacock fan, a stunning creation of the famous M. Rimbaud. She fluttered the feathers, nodding as if the skirt were her choice rather than Effat's.

Simone stepped into the skirt, straight into the seam of a flounce, tripped, and dived headlong onto the settee.

Françoise shrieked.

Effat rushed to salvage what she could.

Horrified at the look on her mother's face, Simone struggled to disengage the heel. In the process, the tip of her boot sank into the hem and ripped it with a delicate hiss. She burst into laughter.

Françoise slapped her fan against her forehead, consoling herself that she was done with the skirt anyway, since she had worn it once already. Yes, every nobleman worth his franc had admired her in it. "Once I am finished with you, Sweetfire," she said with a sigh, her pursed mouth concealed behind peacock feathers, "you will break hearts, not your ankle."

The nickname her mother used in anger was not lost on Simone as she fought for air among the folds of a skirt pulled over her head. "These dresses belong in a museum. I look ridiculous in all this fabric."

It was true, Françoise mused. They were delicate women—she, Mme Gabrielle, and Simone. Consequently, they had to apply more effort in selecting their attire. Still, men preferred petite women. Women like them made men feel taller, powerful. Not that most men—creatures of impulse and instant gratification—were conscious of this fact. But Françoise was Mme Gabrielle's daughter, and like her, she could smell a rose before the seed was planted. *Certainement,* she was the descendant of the wily Mme Gabrielle. A woman who tamed kings. An idol of her time. And so was she, Françoise d'Honoré—as long as she preserved her youth.

At the inevitability of old age, she twirled her fan, tapped it against her cheek, and tossed it across the room. Age crept up on women like her in a harsh manner. At the ripe age of thirty, danger of sliding down the slope of glory loomed. She pulled out strings of pearls from her jewelry box, displaying them around her neck and in her hair. Squinting at a pair of earrings, she dangled them in front of Simone. "A cheap gift from a cheaper man. The dimwit thought I would mistake glass for mine-cut diamonds." She tossed the earrings into a box of hairpins.

Simone retrieved the earrings, holding them against her earlobes.

"Oh, *non, non,*" Françoise screamed. "Mediocre taste is a woman's downfall." She riffled through her armoire and found a ten-carat emerald cut diamond. "This is your father's gift to me." At the mention of Count Mirfenderesky, a Bavarian who had caused her infinite pain, her eyes glinted like iron. When he fled with a repulsive, lowly grisette, Françoise had sought refuge on "Seraglio" the entire nine months of her pregnancy. Although he pretended to be a count, he was a simple per-fumer who stole her heart by thrusting her into explosive orgasms every time he unstoppered one of his perfume bottles. She had not loved any other after she lost him, her only *amant en coeur*. She presented the emerald ring to her daughter. "This is infinitely better than those cheap earrings."

"No," Simone said, adjusting the earrings in her earlobes. "I don't want a ring from *him*. I would rather wear these."

"*Pauvre* Simone," Françoise moaned. "You have such choices, *ma chère*. Don't settle for less. You are far more beautiful than I or your grandmother. Men would die to bury their mouth in your curls. Give them what they want—pain and more pain." She flipped her head back as if to whip her thoughts into order. "Still, you are missing that je ne sais quoi. Let's get to work. You have much to learn, Sweetfire."

While Françoise continued her monologue, her captivated audience her narcissistic self, and while Simone fought to hide her growing impatience, Effat had dressed Simone in an outfit Françoise had last worn to the Bois de Boulogne. She had created such furor that the Comte Valois de Medici and Duke de Soissons had vied for her attention for months and showered her with gifts until, tired of their petty jealousies, she had dispatched them both to their frigid wives.

The satin breeches squeezed Simone's crotch and the laced bodice squashed her breasts like pomegranates. She was about to throw her hands up and forget "Seraglio" when, with a wave of her white arm, Françoise invited her into her universe of senses.

11

"Seraglio," the legendary *lit à baldaquin,* the four-poster bed, presented itself in all its gilded glory. Gauze hangings gathered at the ceiling to form an Arabian tent around the ebony frame engraved with plump cupids. Golden cords swung from supporting pilasters. Cheval mirrors with bronze figurines of cupids reflected the bed's voluptuous image in their repeating depths.

Curved alcoves and intricate molding accommodated the recently installed electrical wiring. The lively notes of Chabrier's "Souvenir de Munich" permeated the boudoir.

Françoise tossed layers of gossamer off her shoulders and lounged across "Seraglio" in all her resplendent nakedness. The cobra stretch of her thighs sent a quiver through the strings of pearls around her neck. The metal glint of her eyes sailed over objects, secure in the knowledge that she and not "Seraglio" injected her men's limbs with desire. A lavender rose peeped through her yellow hair. She threw her head back, showing off her powdered armpits.

Simone was stunned by the surrounding excess—gold and silver leaked out of Limoges boxes, precious stones scattered on bed stands, undergarments of silk, ivory hairpieces, whips to match riding habits, and a cast of her famous feet on a bronze pedestal. Her mother had such appetite for excess. And for perfumes. Scents swirled off incense, drapes, and wall panels.

Armed with an atomizer, Effat emerged to circle Françoise and spray her with Rose de Mai. "Be a darling, Simone," she murmured, "and hand me another rose."

"I am dizzy, too many competing scents in here."

"Complementing, not competing," her mother corrected. "Memory and fragrance are intertwined in our emotional brain. Men will miss you when you leave your perfume behind."

Simone plucked out a yellow rose from a vase bursting with flowers.

"*Non, ma chère!* Never, ever yellow; pink is best—it reminds men of our nipples. Give me the one with crinkled petals."

Having selected the appropriate one, Simone fixed the rose behind her mother's ear and returned to face "Seraglio." Despite a breeze from the windows, she found it difficult to breathe. She wanted to run out. She longed for fresh air.

From the center of her massive bed, from where she ruled her universe of men, Françoise aimed her gaze between her daughter's legs. "Desire keeps us alive, Simone. Use your sexuality as a man would his sword or pistol. Feed his desire—this most vital of all emotions." She plucked the rose out of her hair, and to celebrate her past, present, and future, flipped it out the window.

The rose waltzed against the backdrop of a cloudless sky, arced downward to pirouette toward the park with its jasmine hedges and parading peacocks, to land on the brim of Mme Gabrielle's straw bonnet as she crossed the terrace below the window.

Françoise picked up a banana.

Simone jumped up, her yellow eyes on fire. "Mama, *non! Assez!* Enough!" The giant embrace of the bed where her mother's desires and dreams ruled supreme was closing in on her. If she did not walk out, she would certainly surrender an essential piece of herself.

"Do not stand like that with open legs, Sweetfire," Françoise scolded. "Have you lost all sense of decorum? First, expect your private box at the opera, promise of a mansion, then *peut-être oui, peut-être non,* even then do not just open your legs without a lot of coaxing on his part. Please, do not keep glancing out the window. You are not going anywhere, *ma chère,* not for a long time. And raise your eyes. They are your most valuable assets." For a moment Françoise contemplated this last assessment. "Well, in reality your second best," she corrected herself.

She curled her neck back and dipped the banana into her mouth, leaving behind no trace but the expression of bliss on her face.

Simone thought she would die of shame.

"To live in this opulence," Françoise purred, "to launch yourself as a highbrow lady and not a street urchin, to cultivate beliefs so contrary to other women is reason for celebration."

"To have the fortune of coming across the man who would make every other man inconsequential, *that* is reason for cele-bration," Simone replied.

"*Pour l'amour de Dieu!* What nonsense. When you have the good luck to start the day with no concern but pleasing and manipulating a contingent of men, why would you encourage the possessive imprisonment of love that invariably leads to pregnancy?" Always conscious of that looming danger—after giving birth to Simone at fourteen, Françoise had had to termi-nate a few pregnancies. She continued to use vaginal sponges soaked in vinegar and alum, douches of mineral and vegetable solutions, and the bidet, and insisted on coitus interruptus whenever possible. "Love is like combustible matter, Simone, like quicklime or naphtha. Love eats its own."

"Love is integral to a woman's emotional growth," Simone insisted.

Disregarding decorum, Françoise shot out a stream of spittle into an ashtray on the side table, grinding a foulard in it as if crushing an insect. "Love leads to marriage that eventually robs our identity."

"I believe in love," Simone said simply.

12

At the far end of the grounds, opera lorgnette in hand, Sabot Noir followed the arc of the pink rose that stumbled out of Françoise's window and landed on the brim of Mme Gabrielle's hat as she made her way to the Grand House. His lorgnette directed at Françoise's bedroom, he grumbled under his breath. Now that he saw less of Simone, he would have exchanged a stable of Arabian horses to learn more about the constantly unfolding drama in the upstairs boudoir.

Sabot Noir was tall and lean, with glossy brown locks that tumbled down shoulder blades as narrow as bird wings. The string of chestnut beads he wore around his neck, his café au lait complexion and delicate frame—so contrary to his masculine lust—gave him an effeminate appearance. His parents had emigrated from Algiers to settle in France with the support of the colonial French government. In Mme Gabrielle's employment, his father had started as a stableboy, rising to the rank of stable master and overseer of the grounds.

His mother named him Sabot Noir, or Black Hoof, because

he was born with a hooflike mark on the sole of his left foot. She came to believe that he had close kinship to the black-hoofed buffalo, whose gait, like her son's, was a dance of confident precision. She taught him the breeding and migratory habits of animals and to treat them respectfully, even when hunting, so their spirits would aid him.

One summer, to assimilate the power of horses, the mother ingested tall fescue and white clover from the pastures. She died of poisoning. Mourning her loss, Sabot Noir wrapped himself in buffalo hide, climbed to one of Civet Cats' highest hills, and threw fatty buffalo meat toward the east as an offering to her spirit.

From that day on, he lost the art of smiling.

Before long, he became indispensable to Mme Gabrielle's thoroughbred stud farm. He kept caterpillars in check, sprayed worms, and muzzled horses to keep them from grazing on harmful plants in the frost. Although the Valley of Civet Cats was blessed with mineral-rich soil that created healthy equine bones, he further strengthened the horses through racing and training exercises. He was an invaluable vet, trainer, and breeder. And he taught Simone, his playmate and confidante, the art of palmistry and the secret of taming horses. She, in return, taught him to read and write, the steps of a perfect waltz, and how to use a pistol—to defend his honor but never to murder.

With her hair the shade of foxes and her understanding of horses keen, she was of his world. She, like his mother, had assimilated the power of horses but in a far less fatal manner. He came to believe that Simone was his soul mate, his mythological goddess. He channeled his infatuation into scrubbing, feeding, harnessing the horses, and preparing the carriages for outings. He was admired as the most conscientious stable hand by the ladies and despised by the boys for the feverish pace they found impossible to match. No one suspected the source of his

energy. His every brushstroke on a mare's crest, every inspection of a hoof, and every caress of a spur vein were in prepara-
tion for Simone's invitation to ride out into the Valley of Civet
Cats.

To him, Mme Gabrielle and Françoise were mere women,
riding Balzac, Flaubert, or Nabis into the *bois,* where he carried
their lunch, fastened a loose harness, or secured a horseshoe
when necessary. Françoise's sword-straight hair pierced the air
like knives when her mare bound into full gallop; Mme
Gabrielle's blue mane churned like an ocean. But Simone was
altogether different. A flaming illusion he longed to capture
when he groomed her stallion and pressed his nose to the pelt
where her scent lingered.

Then, not long after his mother died, his father wed Effat,
Françoise's Persian maid, and his life changed. His father spent
his free time in the company of Effat. Simone attended the lycée
and drowned herself in books. She no longer fetched him from
the stables to divine her future through the geography of her
palm or to introduce her to a just-born gelding. They no longer
hid under the bridge across the lake, his ears burning at her
gossip.

Once in a while Simone found time to ride with Sabot
Noir, to give him gifts—a pair of onyx cuff links, a book of
mythology, the ivory opera lorgnettes—but he never saw her
enough. He began to question the wisdom of living in a paradise that was becoming more elusive. In this house of women
he could not afford, the hellish fires of his flesh would soon
consume him.

He rarely left the compound for fear of missing Simone if
she sought him, except when he found out in the newspapers
that a poor woman would go under the guillotine. Then he
would go lean against the walls of La Roquette prison, between
Bastille and the Père Lachaise Cemetery, to say a silent farewell
to the soul that would join his mother's. Or he would ride to

the cour d'assises, the main criminal court where offenders went on trial. Staring intensely at the person standing before the judge of the cour d'assises, Sabot Noir's muscles taut from the pleasure of his danger, he would suffer the stimulation his body required.

Now, he gazed up at Françoise's bedroom to discover if Simone, despite her promise to him, would embrace her mother and grandmother's lifestyle. He aimed his lorgnette toward the façade of the château with its thirty-two windows. He had scrutinized them more than he was willing to confess, with or without his lorgnette; from the farthest end of the grounds to the closest he dared approach behind the courtyard of mermaids, where sixty-nine statues spewed water from between their thighs, electrifying his veins.

He imagined Simone in the frame of the window, arms spread out on the ledge, inviting him to bask in her nakedness, her *rondes de jambes*—her wickedness painfully sweet—the whore of all whores, he the lover who held sway in her bed.

Detecting commotion at the window, he craned his neck. The lorgnette magnified the halo of Simone's red curls above the ledge. She was in Françoise's boudoir. She had given in to temptations. She had broken her promise. His heart flipping like fish in sizzling oil, Sabot Noir stood paralyzed. Her vision stirred him into arousal. The realization that she was in that bedroom devastated him.

13

Grâce à Dieu, Mme Gabrielle thought as she shut her eyes; her blue lashes scintillating in the sunshine. Her gloved fingers stroked the suite of rubies she did not have the heart to part with. Rubies that were fast becoming Françoise's envy. Mme Gabrielle sighed, content to be back in the familiar embrace of her gardens. Still, the night spent in the palace had proved a triumph.

She had been invited by no less than the president himself to entertain the shah. She had captivated a king, whom she had transformed overnight into an infinitely less jaded and more decisive man. She raised her arm to the sunlight, twisting the bracelet and sketching delicate netting on her skirt. She had worn the gift in the president's carriage as it had rumbled through the streets of Paris toward her home, too tired to wave to bystanders but never so tired that she could not enjoy her rubies.

Before she had further occasion to gloat about the fortunate turn her life had taken, the ghost of Oscar Wilde plopped down onto her lap. She gasped at the appearance of the handsome author who was enamored of her breasts in life. "What happened to you, Oscar? You are only forty-six, too young to die."

He embraced her right nipple in his mouth like a loudspeaker. His voice resonated across the tightly woven tissues of her breast: *Do not believe rumors that an ear infection killed me, my dearest Gabrielle. A plague far worse than any killed me.*

A deep sadness bore its way into her marrow.

Oscar Wilde was one of the very few lovers she had actually enjoyed. Their affair had taken place before he had met Bosie and before his trial, and while he was still struggling with his conflicting desires. When he had left her to embrace his innate sexual inclinations, she had missed his romanticism and wit. And now he clambered into her cleavage, going to work on her breasts, flexing them as though he were still alive and training his biceps.

As if that did not suffice, she had to cope with his added prodding to pick up her journal and get to work. "Yes, Oscar, I, too, find it necessary to keep the past alive. Simone's life may take many unforeseeable turns and she must be prepared."

Oscar Wilde sighed through cotton-puff clouds—those born with a platinum pacifier in their mouths remain forever naïve.

"It pains and saddens me to shake Simone out of her innocence and idealism," Mme Gabrielle mused, "but it must be done."

They shared so many similarities, the young Ester Abramowicz and Simone d'Honoré. With her savage, almost ruthless beauty and sly, defiant mind, Simone was a revolutionary at heart. She cultivated idealistic aspirations no one could pluck out of her *cochon* head. The girl imagined herself a horsewoman, a reader of palms, and an academician who cared about the art of *la conversation,* and nothing else.

Mme Gabrielle slapped Oscar out of her cleavage and into the sanctuary of her curls. "Yes, *cher* Oscar, Simone *has* become my raison d'être. Now leave me in peace."

She opened her journal of vellum leaves bound in brocade with silver clasps inscribed with enamel lettering. The lullaby of her golden-tipped pen put Oscar Wilde to sleep.

The Rabbi's Daughter
1865

I am Ester Abramowicz, known to Paris as Mme Gabrielle d'Honoré.

Now that you are sixteen, chère Simone, I will embark on a journey to record my history, a past I delegated to oblivion for thirty-five years but find impossible to do so any longer.

As of now, you are ready to come into the Honoré fortune, carry the mantle, and keep your legacy alive.

I have a vision of Honoré women going down in history as the Three Graces, the three most sought-after grand dames of Europe. When that comes to pass, you will have to decide for yourself whether to reveal your Jewish heritage or let it remain dormant under the simmering façade of your gilded present. A wise decision requires the facts not only of your present but also of your past.

Follow me to 13 Rue des Rosiers, Avenue of Rosebushes, in the Marais, to a dilapidated seventeenth-century mansion that Papa, your great-grandfather, the self-taught and self-ordained Rabbi Abramowicz of Warsaw, converted to a synagogue.

Every Sabbath, a crowd of Orthodox and not-so-Orthodox Jews, rich and poor, sad and joyful, came to witness Papa's miracles in our unconventional synagogue where men and women conversed, mingled, and danced as if it were the natural order of things.

A few taps of Papa's hands made barrels of wine bubble, ferment, and overflow long after the season for grapes ended—wine the color of pomegranate juice that tasted sweeter than manna prompted women to seek their husbands and men to find their wives more enchanting than Michelangelo's angels. A gentle puff from Papa's lips lit candles at the exact hour of sunset on the Sabbath. His warming gaze rendered plain women beautiful the moment they set foot onto our threshold. A morsel of our challah energized the lame and impotent. And no matter what the weather outside, a bright sun shone down on our courtyard, drenched in the fragrance of roses Papa fed with compassion and I watered with lofty ambitions that spiraled up from the wells of my imagination to rain down from my lilac dreams.

"She is a beauty, our magical rabbi's daughter, with her red curls and subdued fire," congregants whispered, concealing their mouth with a hand, the other tucking at a sleeve or tapping a shoulder.

"And hardly twelve, is she? Yes, certainly a child, but in a few years she will unleash that sparkle of je ne sais quoi in her blue eyes and prove more irresistible than our own rabbi."

I drank in sweet songs of praise thirty-five years ago as boys my age accompanied their parents to prepare for their bar mitzvahs. And although it was not customary for girls to study the Torah, Papa saw no reason why I, or any other girl who desired, should not. And I did not, either. Uproar shook our Orthodox community. But Papa did not care. He had fled Poland to practice, immigrated to France with his wife and daughter seeking freedom. He would not allow his own people to shackle him with outdated beliefs.

Papa had no way of telling, of course, that twenty-nine years later the Dreyfus Affair would force him to acknowledge the Jew haters who had always infested France.

Because of my friendship with Émile Zola, I was one of the first to learn that papers in the wastebasket of a German military attaché put Dreyfus, a Jewish captain in the French army, under suspicion of providing classified information to the German government. Despite his protestations of innocence, Dreyfus was found guilty of treason, stripped of his rank, humiliated, and shipped to Devil's Island. The right-wing newspaper, La Libre Parole, portrayed the incident as further evidence

*of a Jewish conspiracy to destroy France. When Émile learned of Drey-
fus's innocence, he was furious. "J'accuse," his open letter, denounced
the army's cover-up. Found guilty of libel and sentenced to imprisonment, dear Émile fled to England until he was granted amnesty. It was a
difficult time for us all.*

*The affair shattered Papa's illusions. If he could not live as a free
Jew in France, he concluded, he could not anywhere else in the universe.*

*In the meantime, in the Marais, every female member of our congre-
gation was secretly, or openly, enamored of Papa's charm and the chiseled
features that gave him an air of gentility. He continued to maintain his
compassionate patience even when he should have lost his temper—a rock
aimed at our window, a flaming bottle of alcohol tossed against our door,
our garden vandalized. Papa was intent on enjoying life. He danced to
Yiddish songs. His diminutive, agile body skipped around, the red, curled
pe'ot at his temples whipping against his cheeks, the tzitzit fringes of the
tallit katan swaying at his hips. He would belt out biblical psalms, praise
his wife, and welcome Elijah into his home. Tossing his fur yarmulke
overhead, he released the orange blossom scent of his cologne. So many
yarmulkes lodged around the crystal arms of our chandelier that it came
to resemble a cluster of civet cats hanging upside down from the ceiling to
sprinkle Papa's perfume upon us all.*

*After a glass or two of wine, he pinched Mother's buttocks and ex-
claimed in the baritone I love, "An honest man likes to dig his teeth into
ample flesh such as my lovely wife's, not into the bone-breaking thighs of
a thin woman!"*

*Directing a wink my way, he would assure me that I was neither
thin nor fat, just plump in the right places. I inherited the cobalt shade of
Papa's eyes, his joie de vivre, and the cuddling voice that makes up for
our small stature. You, too, Simone, resemble him in many ways. You inherited the shade of his hair and his mule-headed stubbornness. He has
to stir matters his own way, be in charge, scheme if necessary to assure
our happiness.*

*Now, in hindsight, I have come to realize that his overprotective
tendencies might have encouraged my flight and robbed my mother of*

her sense of self and individuality. But I digress. Ignorant of what the future held, we were a happy family then.

The luscious éclairs and Napoleon tarts Mama baked on Sabbath were the envy of the two local bakers—one on Rue du Pont aux Choux, the Street of the Bridge of Cabbages, the other on Rue des Mauvais Garçons, named after its fourteenth-century criminal inhabitants. You must understand, Simone, the Marais, a 310-acre triangle on the Right Bank of the Seine, was once a marsh that became a chic seventeenth-century neighborhood, but declined to a slum of narrow winding streets and wooden-shuttered windows in my time. Here patisseries set up shop close to synagogues to serve the devout after services. Leftover crumbs were collected in paper cones for sale to the poor. But our miracle house on 13 Rue des Rosiers did not require a patisserie. No one was turned away, especially not the poor who lost sleep before Sabbath dreaming of mother's delicacies that made them salivate so hard they had to rise numerous times to spit the excess into the bedpan.

A mere child of twelve, I swore to do everything in my power never to find myself salivating into pails and pots for a bite of éclair, never to narrow my horizons to the claustrophobic monotony of a four-walled kitchen.

The Avant-Garde

In our basement, to the gurgling of fermenting wines and the rising scent of orange blossoms, butter, and burnt sugar, Papa explained that Jews did not celebrate a girl's coming-of-age—although boys marked that milestone with prayers and festivities. Girls, in the same manner, became responsible for their own actions, but there was no ceremony to mark the occasion.

Now you will come to understand why I encourage you to apply to university, Simone, why I support your study of art and music. In some ways, I came to view the world as Papa did.

"I am a meshuggener rabbi," Papa said, "so if I were to believe in celebrations to mark one's womanhood, you would have had one, Ester, a feast to duplicate some sort of a coming-of-age ceremony similar to a bar mitzvah. But what is a fête? Fun and necessary prayers, of course. But that does not amount to much if you do not stand on your own feet and shape yourself and your world."

His gaze warmed the basement, sending my mother into a flurry of complaints over wines that began to sour in his presence. He placed his palms over his closed eyes, and when the temperature cooled down, he continued, "Do study the Torah, Ester, but visit the Louvre, too. For more than four years now artists have been studying the great masters in the museum. One of our central mitzvoth is to quench our curiosity. Observe the masters, analyze and dissect, then experiment with breaking free from tradition. I shaped my own identity. Why should you not? I am an oddity in our community, with one foot in the Warsaw shtetl and another in the French Marais. Yet when the time comes for my soul to depart to olam ha-ba, I will have no regrets because I lived, loved, and changed. And this, in the end, is what matters. Now go make something of yourself."

I adored this most in Papa, my mentor, his appreciation of music and art and his belief that women could achieve the same level of enlightenment as men.

My wish for you, too, Simone, is never to find yourself dependent. And that, ma chère, goes hand in hand with higher education and financial independence.

I followed Papa's advice and visited the Louvre every day. I was mesmerized by the masters in all areas—Wagner, Verlaine, and Delacroix. Walking back and forth from Rue des Rosiers to the galleries, I took the winding cobblestone streets, where de guingois buildings leaned over, slightly askew and melancholy. I loved Place des Vosges and its perfectly symmetrical arcades. The Henry IV seventeenth-century square was steeped in the aroma of strudel and apples, cinnamon and poppy seed cake. And, yes, this is where the poor, who had nothing to their name but the gathering pools of saliva in their mouths, congregated.

But then, on the other side of the Seine, in the vibrant city, I came to discover the architectural genius of Eugène Haussmann. Modern Paris and I were born the same year, for it was in 1853 that Haussmann, the city planner, initiated his grand design. There were no broad boulevards, gaslights, or elaborate carvings on stone façades and archways before Haussmann. And certainly none of the châteaux with intricate frescoes and gold gilt. I admire Haussmann, the perfectionist with the fearless disposition who fashioned the Paris that never ceases to surprise.

You, Simone, have inherited my Haussmannian ambition and talent. This is why you are the candidate I chose to take over the empire I created.

During the following reflective years of change and youth, a certain melancholy solitude crowded me. I longed for a more sophisticated life than what the Marais offered. I began to consider myself an "intellectual." I refused to follow my mother into a bourgeois future I detested. To Papa's mortification, I developed an affinity for Wagner's operas, which Papa shunned due to his anti-German sentiments. I saw myself in the forefront of the avant-garde movement, with Wagner the torchbearer of a new era devoted to pleasure. Papa was a romantic and a nationalist. He encouraged my interest in Lully and Rameau. "Our own priceless treasures," he would say. "Their melodies enter our soul and imagination and reemerge in a more profoundly beautiful way."

I developed certain disrespect for conventional customs. A slow transformation—an evolution rather than a revolution—emerged in my manners.

Now, as I record my memories between these pages, I look back with puzzlement and wonder. How could Papa not foresee that his encouragement would authorize my break from my family? How could a man as farsighted and intuitive as he fail to know his daughter? I am afraid of committing the same mistake, Simone. I do not want to encourage you to cut loose from Château Gabrielle. But I am not quite certain where to draw the fine line between supporting your sovereignty and instilling the importance of remaining loyal to the Honoré heritage.

⁓

Mme Gabrielle shut her journal, clucking her tongue. She had effectively erased the history of her childhood in 13 Rue des Rosiers, yet expected Simone to keep alive the Honoré heritage and tradition. As if that was not enough, she who had caused her papa such great pain demanded that Simone honor *her* wish.

Well, *c'est la vie*. Rabbi Abramowicz's only daughter did not sully her hands with baking dough, marry a Jewish boy, and cover her hair with deplorable kerchiefs. She had walked out of the Marais into the heart of Paris to emerge as the unparalleled Mme Gabrielle d'Honoré, an artist who re-created her own reality but never, ever copied anyone else's.

Alors! In the process of shaping her own future, her granddaughter would learn that life was a series of triumphs men considered their right and women had to fight for.

Mme Gabrielle shooed Oscar Wilde's ghost out of her ear, where he strove to ingratiate himself by licking her eardrum. She aimed her cerulean gaze toward the horizon and the distant hills bathed in melon rays. Alphonse expected her for dinner, and she was late. She gathered her skirts about her and prepared to join him.

14

⌀

Alphonse interrupted his task of setting the dining table, dropped the polishing rag into his apron pocket, and approached the windows. Outside, the magnificent Gabrielle made her way up the stairs and sailed across the terrace to join him for dinner. He would have considered himself fortunate if the glow on her gauze-covered cheeks was due to their rendezvous rather than last night's encounter with the shah. She never ceased to astonish him with her shrewd sophistication, her prophetic spirits, and the horses she named after authors, artists, and philosophers—Balzac, Flaubert, Zola, Cézanne. His heart squeezed in his chest as if she were coming to him for the first time when he was still a devout Muslim and mortified she might prove *najes*, impure, and afflict him with an incurable disease. At the time, he had read and reread the Koran: *O you who believe, the idolaters are surely unclean; so they shall not approach the Sacred Mosque.* In the end, love had triumphed. He was not defiled.

The exaggerated flare of Alphonse's nostrils added to the aristocratic look of his patrician features. His determined walk and erect spine further flaunted his long, shapely legs and extraordinary height. At the age of fifty-six, that habit had left him with a permanent ache in his back, which he failed to cure with painful stretching contraptions. Consequently, he acquired a bicycle, a novel gadget that relieved his cramps while allowing him time to meditate on why he had left Persia and what other surprises providence had in store for him.

When he went about his household chores, inspecting areas the subordinates invariably missed, his elegant attire was protected with a leather apron the pocket of which held polishing paraphernalia. He was responsible for overseeing more than seventy-five household servants who took care of laundry, fetched water, logs, and coal, plucked poultry, and cleaned fireplaces.

He passed his hand over his aristocratic head, thinning hair meticulously brushed over a balding spot. He tinted his hair with leftovers from Mme Gabrielle's coloring creams from the glands of hermaphroditic snails, the shade of which he altered with a pinch of powdered lapis lazuli so as not to emulate her exact color and arouse scandalous gossip. An added beaker of pigment of fermented woad leaves had recently replaced the indigo plant. Finding the shocking cobalt color, which gave her hair and lashes the shade of oceans and clouds, to her liking, she refused to replace the formula with the just discovered synthetic indigo from coal-tar derivatives.

He checked the dining room again, the table set for two, the shining candelabra, silver cruet stands, dish warmers all engraved with the interlaced MGH, the Honoré seal. He folded and tucked his apron in the mahogany secretary. One last time, he inspected himself—his silk stockings, white cravat, and coattail. He adjusted his most treasured companion, a gold chain Gabrielle had given him at a moment of frivolous flirtation after he had performed a tune on his sitar, a Persian musical instrument she found charming.

She sailed into the dining room, handed him her bonnet as he pulled out a chair and adjusted her skirts. His hands trembling, he slipped her fingers out of her gloves as if handling crystal branches.

She smiled as he stroked her naked fingers. Raising his hand, she planted a kiss on his palm. He was an invaluable asset. His dignified demeanor and skill in implementing dialogues of all manner of nobility from all parts of the world had over and over again deceived dignitaries into assuming he was employed by a highbrow aristocrat. But, above all, he was the only individual who knew everything about her—her secrets, triumphs, and every flaw. With him, she could be Ester, even as she remained Mme Gabrielle d'Honoré. He fluttered her napkin open and dropped it on her lap. Her eyes softened when they met his, and his anger for her previous indifference regarding the attempted assassination of his shah took flight. He no longer cared that she had not expressed a single conciliatory word, nor attempted to properly pronounce the shah's name.

She signaled for him to occupy the chair next to her. "Alphonse, I invited a Persian jeweler here. Please supervise preparations for his arrival."

"A Persian?" Alphonse asked. How and where had she come across another Persian? Alphonse rose to check behind the door and make sure no one eavesdropped. He returned and poured wine into a tasting cup a blacksmith had fashioned and that he attached to the chain she gave him. He swiveled the wine in his mouth before filling her goblet. "Who is this man?" he asked, his lower lip slightly trembling. "Must I suffer a Persian rival now?"

"No," she replied, her fingers skipping across the table to join his in a repartee. "It is not what you think. You are the only Persian I would ever desire. This one is for Simone—the shah's jeweler. You will approve of him, too. I am hoping he will whet her interest in men. Then it will be easier to initiate her into the Honoré profession. She has all the qualifications to become a *maîtresse en titre*. Be presented to court one day. Entertained as a queen."

Waving away the waiter who had served them, Alphonse turned a plate of *asperge à la dente* to face Mme Gabrielle. He did not want Simone to pursue Gabrielle's and Françoise's vocation. He anticipated, even hoped, that Simone, the illegitimate offspring of that yellow-blooded scoundrel of a Bavarian comte, would end up fashioning her own future, one not to the liking of her grandmother. Françoise would not have carried this golden child to term were it not for the fact that she had fallen into an obsession with that coward. At the first sign of her pregnant belly, he had taken off with a consumptive grisette—not even one of the demimondaines who had a semblance of style.

Thankfully, Simone had not inherited her father's yellow blood, nor her mother's capricious nature, but her grandmother's defiant temperament, whose potential Alphonse had detected when her blue curls and azure lashes were a deeper color than wine.

Alphonse reassembled his thoughts. "This matter is important to me, too, Gabrielle. What do you know about this jeweler?"

"*Bien sûr, cher* Alphonse. He is different from the French men Simone has seen around here. He carries this tragic look, as if struggling with heartbreak. Simone will find him romantic. More important, he will have to leave Paris with the shah, and no long-term romances will develop. It will be a liaison, a one-night lust to give Simone her first taste. Then she will readily welcome other suitors." Mme Gabrielle's gaze fell on Alphonse like a shower of sapphires. "I want Simone to experience what we had. It was lovely, don't you think, *mon cher*?"

He watched her sip wine, suck on the tip of an *asperge,* and he marveled at his fascination, which had not diminished but intensified with every one of her tragedies and triumphs. True, he had suffered at her side as much as, if not more than, he had rejoiced. He had squandered his wealth on her, had snuffed his desire to become a successful merchant, and had become her butler so as to remain at her side. Every evening, when she stepped into her carriage, she tore out his heart to ravage it in another man's bed. The X's he carved with a razor into his wall to keep track of her lovers had left their scar on the tip of his right thumb and in his chest. Still, he, who full-heartedly believed in reincarnation, prayed every night that Allah would dispatch his soul to wherever Gabrielle's went.

Now she communicated with him not as her lover but as a trusted friend, a confidant whose advice she sought. "I warn you, Gabrielle, the Persian culture is very different from what Simone is used to."

"I am French, too," she replied. "I never regretted knowing you."

"We are not all the same. Persian men can be opinionated, especially when it comes to women. You do not understand my culture, Gabrielle. I took yours to heart and never imposed mine on you. I do not want Simone to suffer."

"This is exactly what will fascinate her. The mystery of the unknown. The exoticism of it all."

Alphonse did not say more. Maybe Simone would fall in love with the Persian. Maybe the jeweler would prove as accepting as he himself had proved. Maybe he would marry Simone and introduce her to an honest life. Finding an enthusiastic student in her, Alphonse had embarked on teaching her the Farsi language. In the process, he revisited the country he missed. Now that providence was sending a Persian her way, her knowledge would serve her well. "Then why not encourage Simone to come to know the Persian better? Maybe she will keep him at her side as you kept me."

"No, Alphonse, never!" Gabrielle interrupted. "I have high

hopes for her. Consider the Persian a catalyst to speed her entry into her intended world."

He sighed at Gabrielle's firm response. Her dream was already solidifying into reality. He, too, had anticipated a chance encounter with her as a fleeting diversion from months of abstinence. But their relationship had bloomed into thirty years of devotion. She had wound her chain of steel around him, renamed him Alphonse, a name that carried enough weight not to require a surname. But he wanted more for Simone, a man whom she would find neither inferior nor superior to herself. "What can I do for you, Gabrielle? What can I do for Simone?"

Mme Gabrielle went to him and sat in his lap. "Embroider the exotic aspects of Persia; paint an irresistible hero she will want to meet. Remember when we first met, Alphonse? You stole my heart when you put your hand on my shoulder and invited me to dinner. Remember how you brushed your hair back behind your ears? This is the type I want Simone to imagine."

15

Before the jeweler came to the château and before Simone suspected what had taken place behind her back, Mme Gabrielle embarked upon assuring the success of her plan with the same energy she put into every one of her campaigns.

Alphonse, too, wholeheartedly immersed himself in the task at hand, but for a different reason. Whereas Mme Gabrielle considered the new bed Alphonse acquired as an introductory station from which Simone would step up to her intended future, Alphonse hoped it would end up as her nuptial bed. Mme Gabrielle and Alphonse each contributed to the décor, combining their tastes to please both Simone and Cyrus. The rosewood bed was inlaid with ivory nightingales common in Persian poetry and mysticism, the sheets white, as Alphonse considered that a pure shade. The draperies were as sheer as the elusive love Gabrielle considered the cause of a myriad of tragedies. Despite mirrors being essential tools of the trade, she had settled for two on either side of the bed. Framed with bamboo, the mirrors projected restraint—uncommon in the château but suitable for Simone.

Although Alphonse's intention was for the couple to find themselves in a conjugal tent, Mme Gabrielle was influenced by Baudelaire's "Invitation to a Voyage." The wall panels depicted scenes from the opera *Carmen,* the gypsy dancing among cherry blossoms and cucumber bushels—Alphonse's touch—Baudelaire's poem inscribed on the center panel:

> *While other spirits sail on symphonies*
> *Mine, my beloved, swims along your scent.*

Alphonse had his own beloved mystic, Hafiz, whose divination he sought at every turn. He settled on the bed with his book. The leather-bound cover smelled of home. He ran his index finger across the frayed spine of the much-used pages. "Oh! Hafiz the Great, your wisdom eternal, your compassion endless, enlighten me with your divination. Will the jeweler's visit end as Gabrielle desires, or as I, born an Isfahani, wish?" He cleared his mind of daily debris, sank into a trance, and opened the book. He fought not to shut his eyes at the attack of ominous words he faced. Verse after verse spoke of solitude, alienation, and betrayal. He smacked the book shut. Even the great Hafiz could be wrong.

Suddenly, he felt assaulted by the surrounding lavender flowers, Françoise's dizzying obsession. He marched around, snatching roses out of vases and tossing them away, as if they, not Hafiz, were oracles of bad luck. Out of breath, he stopped, smoothed his hair over a scalp that had, after countless applications, absorbed the blue dye he applied. Simone's nuptial bedroom deserved the appropriate flowers; he would no longer bow down to Gabrielle's wishes. He would take matters into his own hands. Energized, he tried to think of a proper flower that would not mask Simone's wonderful scent. He evoked the pink roses he purchased for Françoise, the blood-red of the Barbados lily he offered Gabrielle, which must have been fashioned after her heart. Then he remembered the flower he bought for himself when it was in season. It was called ice flower in Persia. Some Frenchmen called it witch hazel, others found it too exotic to name. The flower was shipped to France from another continent, bloomed once a year on the 21st of March, the spring equinox, and the first day of the Persian New Year. The leafless auburn stalk and the glassy, yellow-veined petals evoked the crisp mountain air of his youth.

He had found Simone's flower and one the Persian would appreciate as well.

16

Gas lamps shone in the gardens and chandeliers glowed dimly inside. The neighing of restless horses reverberated in the upstairs bedrooms as silk-padded walls failed to stifle the bray of donkeys. The shrieks of courting peacocks forced geese into early migration, their wings whipping a whirlwind around the valley.

Seamstresses stitched, embroidered, and hemmed gowns for Françoise and Mme Gabrielle. Muslin hangings replaced velvet drapes to make way for sunlight. Standing mirrors and railings with Françoise's colorful capes were readied as a backdrop for trying jewelry. *Le pâtissier* procured saffron, anise, cardamom, coriander, and nutmeg—whisking, baking, and tasting Persian delicacies from Effat's recipes.

A Persian from an exotic world would soon be visiting.

A streak of vanity ran through the servants, and the masters of ceremonies neglected their chores to linger in front of mirrors. Steeped in the scent of roses and intoxicated by a contagion of anticipation, the maids danced up the left flank of the grand staircase, where black-and-white photographs of Mme Gabrielle's dead lovers whispered flirtatiously. Ancestors, who did not want to be absent from family portraits, peered from behind a shoulder and above a head, or posed full figure next to the image of Rabbi Abramowicz of Warsaw.

Servants chose to go up and down the opposite staircase to steal a glance at Simone's life-size photograph, at the inaccessible girl on horseback whose eyes lassoed them wherever they went.

Unable to contain their curiosity, the household hands pestered Effat and Alphonse with questions about the shah's jeweler.

Sabot Noir, forgotten in the ensuing pandemonium, directed his lorgnette at Françoise's window. The thought of Simone on "Seraglio" with another man had pushed him to the brink of madness.

During her daily beauty soak, Françoise read terrifying crime stories in serialized *romans feuilletons* to scare her skin into an even paler hue. When a particularly chilling story made her heart skip in her throat, she tossed the book out the window. Wet and naked, she rushed to the mirror to observe her alabaster complexion and the delicate veins underneath.

Mme Gabrielle passed her hand over furniture, paintings, books, and sculptures, searching for traces of nonexistent dust. Her satin slippers sashayed across Venetian floors installed in the French château. She glided in and out of salons with motifs of marble in concentric circles, cubes, diamonds, Greek marble from the Mediterranean, and Verona marble the color of liver and spleen. The glitter of her indigo eyes and the smile of mocking disdain concealed the expression of a scheming woman. She, who noticed every detail, who allowed nothing to escape her scrutiny, now tolerated her daughter's mania for an imaginary bracelet of red diamonds. The Persian jeweler would not deliver the bracelet, of course. Red diamonds were the

scarcest of gems, and only a handful were known to exist—
never enough for a bracelet.

She even tolerated the pianist Franz Liszt. A halo of feral
curls surrounding his expression of cynical diabolism, he ended
his bouncing on her fingernails, as if on his private piano keys,
to clamber into her ear with his baton and conduct a symphony.

"Enough!" she ordered, the dramatic vibrations bouncing
in her cranium and causing a grand headache. "My eardrum
isn't any old drum! And, if I may be so bold as to ask, Monsieur,
for whom are you composing such a large-scale symphony?"

For Cyrus, his answer echoed in her head, *for your lovely Simone's husband.*

17

∞

Persia
1901

I prepare for my husband's arrival from the city. I shall do exactly what Pearl, the midwife, warns against. I will re-create myself in an intriguing image. Prove to Cyrus that his pregnant wife is even more desirable and willing.

Tonight, I will be his personal courtesan.

I rummage through Mama's chest, each costume with fascinating *histoire* that cast its brilliant hues upon her life. I step into a shantung skirt, high-heeled kid slippers, and lacy corset. Content to please one man, I appreciate Françoise and Mme Gabrielle's universe from afar.

Françoise loves the drama of stepping down from her shiny landau to enter Maxim's restaurant. Bells peal in church towers and the Seine ripples and gleams under a golden sun. Horses are groomed and carriages polished, gowns steamed and faces powdered. Her hair piled high like a cluster of golden rosebuds, her eyes capture a crowd gathered around her carriage. She is accompanied by Comte Jacques Saris of Bordeaux, who nibbled so savagely on her earlobes that throughout their affair they required soothing with snake oil. She lifts her shantung skirts slightly above a delicate ankle. Familiar with the exact distance between the carriage step and the sidewalk, she plants one diamond-buckled pump on the cobblestone. And before her admirers have a chance to steal a glance at her bare ankle, another foot comes into view below the raised petticoats she flips up to expose her sex framed by lace garters.

I wrap costume pearls around my rouged earlobes and swathe a silk stole over bare shoulders. My yellow-green eyes shining, my freckles stand out in anticipation. I undo the tiny mother-of-pearl buttons along the front of the corset to expose my glorious belly.

Cyrus's courtesan is ripe with his baby.

I refused Mama's parting gifts: the ten-carat emerald-cut diamond my father gave her when he left with a crude cocotte, the tortoiseshell combs and feathered masks she wore to yearly soirées at Carnival, the enamel bracelets the shade of her gray eyes that heralded her grand entrance into Café de la Paix. They suit her best. What good would jewels do up here but tempt thieves?

We will not live in the mountains forever, of course. A day will come when Cyrus and I will own a mansion high up on the Shemiran Hills. I will tack the entrance with golden nails, girt the door with silver bands, and install a loud bell to announce arrivals. We will hold lavish soirées and invite Mama and *Grand-mère* from Paris. Sommeliers will serve wine in crystal goblets, and maître d's in starched shirts will hand out bite-sized delicacies of stuffed mushrooms and puff shells with caviar. My son by my side, I will carry myself as befits a descendant of glorious women and will look down upon Yaghout, who scorned me.

I go to the kitchen and check on the casserole of marinated leg of mutton on the wood burner. Cyrus has never been so late. Thoughts collide in my head. For the first time in our married life, Cyrus went to bed before me last night. Is he still angry with me? I am the one who should be upset. Is he involved in something illegal, something that has to do with whatever he was doing yesterday? Grabbing my skirts, I pace the house, controlling the urge to open drawers, leaf through books, inspect the mantelpiece—anywhere, everywhere—for anything that would put my mind at ease.

Dressed in Françoise's gown, lips and earlobes rouged, I curl up on the pallet in the corner and wait for Cyrus.

18

Paris
August 1900

"A Persian jeweler is bringing a bracelet of red diamonds," Alphonse whispered in a conspiratorial voice, his gaze seeking Simone's. "Are you aware that red diamonds are linked to legends and myths? You do not believe me, do you? Then look around the château and our valley. Their mere mention causes a change of weather, affects the behavior of our animals and the mood of everyone—except you." He then suggested that, for once, she follow his advice and ask the seamstress to sew a gown. "The most feminine style you can bring yourself to wear, my dear." And summoning his most convincing expression, he added, "There is much I cannot divulge about Monsieur—such as his coming here for reasons beyond the sale of jewelry."

Since last week, when a splendid carriage with drawn drapes and gold fixtures had transported her grandmother from the president's palace, and she had emerged in an elegant suite of rubies to disappear into her bedroom, Simone had followed the ensuing drama with detached interest. She learned that in a single night, Mme Gabrielle had transformed the shah from a

rather indecisive man into a self-assured king who had garnered the courage to confront his minister of court. Now
Alphonse bristled with incomprehensible excitement about the
visit of yet another jeweler. Her mother's fascination with the
bracelet was in character. But with her grandmother's ever-
present fear of looming poverty, why would she consider the
purchase of such an expensive item? These days, more than
ever, nothing made sense. Something had propelled every creature into heat; even the butler's uncharacteristic behavior. He
was the voice of reason in Simone's off-balance universe. Now
his enthusiasm was complemented by the shimmying of lusting
horses, shrieks of aroused peacocks, and rustle of succulent
roses.

"Since when is the purchase of jewelry so important
around here?" she asked.

"It is not the merchandise, Mademoiselle, but the gentleman who has thrust the women into a state," he replied, his
forehead crinkling. "If I were you, I would pay attention, too.
The aforementioned gentleman is a native of my country,
where men are known for their charm and their devotion to
their women." In reality, Alphonse was not at all confident of
Persian men's loyalty. In his own time, he had come across
brutish men he could have strangled with his bare hands. But
there were exceptions. The jeweler might prove worthy of Simone.

"Why are you trying to impress me?" she teased, brushing
a leaf off his lapel. "Mama is the one to impress. She will be
more than happy to welcome this monsieur. And since you
choked the château with flowers, stick a few into the gas lamps,
and while you are at it, the mermaid statues can hold some too.
Really, Alphonse, I'm not interested at all." She tossed her magnificent hair back and said, "Nothing, and certainly no one, is
worth this fuss. It will not be the first time Mama and *Grand-
mère* purchase jewelry, or the last a merchant would visit."

At that, she gave Alphonse a stern look, turned on her heels, and wandered into the park. Farther away, she detected Mme Gabrielle and Françoise engaged in heated conversation. Her mother had applied every gram of her sexual talent to convince M. Gerard Fontanel, her present supporter, to purchase the red diamond bracelet. He was wealthy and rather obsessed with her, but far from generous. Unable to bear Françoise's tears, he had promised to obtain the bracelet even if he had to borrow. Eager to hear her mother and grandmother's discussion, Simone stole behind the jasmine bushes.

"*Ma chère,*" Mme Gabrielle said, "*s'il te plaît,* consider this one a supplier of jewels and nothing more. I want him to initiate Simone. She is sixteen and showing no interest in following in our footsteps. Remember how she chased away the poor Englishman who invited her to le Grand Seize? She riddled his retreating footsteps with bullets. You and I know, *chérie,* that the first time is critical. A good lover is bliss. A bad lover . . . Oh! *Non!* Such a horror."

Françoise slapped a rose against her breast, the petals tumbling into her cleavage. "Simone is not ready. She has not progressed one bit; on the contrary, she is fighting back to the extent of stoppering her perfume. And she has no interest in meeting the Persian."

Simone crouched lower as the two women walked past the hedges.

Mme Gabrielle pinched off the remaining petals that clung to Françoise's rose and scattered them across the fountain. "I will make sure she comes around. As for you, *chérie,* give up your thorny flowers and take better care of your precious hands. In the meantime, you are free to choose from a universe of men. Imagine the ennui of getting trapped with one man.

"Leave the Persian for Simone."

19

Françoise's head throbbed and her mouth was dry from last night's Bordeaux. She scooped a palmful of Venus Skin Food Balm of spermaceti oil from a pot at her bedside and massaged it on her face. Unable to go back to sleep, she sat by the window with a cup of *chocolat chaud*. The grounds shimmered in the sepia glow of dawn. Horses grazed and peacocks huddled along the slopes of the clover hill. She did not like to miss her morning sleep when her brain surrendered to delicious fantasies. Dreams were essential to her. They were her reality. The thought brought a wry smile to her lips. What was her reality, after all? The lessons she offered Simone suggesting she confine her identity to what she wore, how she consumed fruit, and the hours she pleasured men? Despite her talents and the Honoré title, high society remained closed to her. The aristocracy populated her boudoir as if it were their private bedroom, but she was not welcomed into the salons of the upper crust.

She heard footsteps on the terrace below and leaned on the window ledge. Alphonse, journal in hand, sneaked down the steps. Presented with the opportunity to discover why her mother, who lived her life freely and openly, made such an effort to conceal her journal, Françoise ran to her dressing room and tossed a peignoir over her shoulders. Dashing out into the park, she followed Alphonse at a respectable distance. He walked straight to the clover hill and climbed up to disappear into the Gallery of Bougainvillea. Concealed behind the flower-drenched trellises, Françoise waited. She felt deliciously naughty when Alphonse emerged without the journal to retrace his way back down the hill.

Inside the Gallery of Bougainvillea, as always, she experienced a wave of admiration for the boldness confronting her. Paintings of Mme Gabrielle in the embrace of British princes from the House of Hanover to the House of Saxe-Coburg, Russian Alexanders who became czars, and rich sultans with unparalleled stud farms were displayed here. French ministers who rose to the presidency were put on view among bougainvillea branches trained into frames. Lovers were portrayed lying down or kneeling to worship her mother in poses that conveyed her grandeur and infinite appetite.

The one man missing from the gallery was the one who intrigued Françoise most—her father. Perhaps Gabrielle's journal would finally reveal his identity.

Françoise coaxed her trembling legs across the gallery to a portrait that sent chills up her spine. She passed her hand along the canvas as if to make sure the image was other than flesh and blood.

In her lifetime, Mme Gabrielle had had any man she had desired. Except the man whose portrait Françoise faced. Gregory Efimovich Rasputin, the charismatic peasant and self-styled holy man, legendary for his bouts of drinking and endless womanizing, had fascinated Mme Gabrielle. But his mad spiritualism and presumed power of hypnosis had alarmed her. Consequently, she had decided against adding him to her roster of lovers. Settling on the next best alternative, she had engaged an artist to paint the likeness of a naked Rasputin in the throes of ecstasy, his chest beaded with perspiration, his legs coiled about her like a sinewy vise.

Beneath Rasputin's intimidating shadow, Françoise identified a freshly trampled spot of moss. She carefully prodded the moss-covered earth and dug under the ground to find the journal buried in a leather-lined hole. She settled down under the portrait and opened the chronicle of her mother's jealously guarded past.

She was unaware of Oscar Wilde's ghost supine on a bougainvillea branch, a chuckle in his throat, eager to inform his mistress that her secrets had been exhumed right under Rasputin's mean stare.

The War
1870

My precious Simone, wars and plagues are part of life. A lot of optimism and a bit of money can save us and our loved ones during such trying times.

I was hardly seventeen when the Franco-Prussian War assailed home and family, a ruthless whirlwind that destroyed everything in its path.

Paris was besieged by Prussians.

Parisians were starving, given the meager supply of oxen and sheep that grazed as food supply in the once lush Bois de Boulogne where races for the Grand Prix de Paris used to be held.

One chilling dusk, the three of us—Mama, me, and Papa—went out to the Champs-Élysées. With our hearts heavy and our arms weak, we stood in line with hundreds of others. With our tears, we watered the majestic trees that lined the Champs-Élysées, and then, raising our axes, we chopped them. We had to have firewood or we would have died from the brutal cold.

But 13 Rue des Rosiers remained as cold and silent as an ice cave.

Wine froze in barrels, the wood planks drying and cracking open with sudden claps. My father's eyes lost their warmth and his touch its magic. Congregants missed Sabbaths, huddling for warmth in their own corners. Spittle dried in the mouths of a contingent who had once missed sleep dreaming of Mama's éclairs. Mama did not knead bread with her cold fingers, much less bake when ingredients were scarce.

Her raging hands became opiates of her mind. She unraveled her sweaters, shawls, and socks and reknitted them into gloves for her husband and daughter. The more difficult our predicament, the faster she unraveled, stitched, and withdrew into herself. The speed of her fingers became the measure by which I gauged our growing misery.

My father complained to his God, as if He were an intimate friend breaking bread with us. "Hashem, please do not let our city turn into a place of misery and ash. Not again, not again!" And as if the Omniscient were not already privy to the dark, muddy Paris that sank under the stench of boiling fish and rotting cheese, Papa continued to reiterate our dismal condition. "How do You expect Your chosen to survive?" he called out to his Lord.

But the Lord was nowhere to be found.

I have experienced the ups and downs of life, chère *Simone, but you have not. You were fortunate to be born into the lap of luxury, raised and loved by two adoring women. You might find it unnecessary to look beyond your present and begin to shape the foundation of your future while still young and optimistic.*

I have been warned by my collective spirits that a pestilence of Jew haters is on the rise. But the Valley of Civet Cats, with its perfumed cats and fragrant lavender, will be the last to be infected. Consequently, I have embarked on constructing a new wing for my papa at the western corner of my château. I believe, and more than anything hope, that when you, Simone, with your integrity and diligence, occupy the helm of the Honoré estate, Papa will embrace the Valley of Civet Cats.

*Providence has a way of selecting a specific family member to over-
see the well-being of the rest of the clan. I was that chosen daughter. You
are, too. As you know, I took fate into my own hands and steered myself
toward our present reality. In due course, you will come to appreciate the
importance of securing your future and that of your entire family.*

Françoise slapped the journal shut, buried it in its grave, trampling the moss with satin slippers. Her cheeks were on fire. Her
mother's memoirs were addressed to Simone rather than to
her own daughter. How had she disappointed her mother?
Had she not embraced the life she had been raised to accept,
the same life Simone continued to reject? It was certainly true
that Simone was better educated, had enormous reserves of
willpower and level-headedness, but she had applied these
qualities to fight her intended future. Yanking herself back to
the crowding portraits, Françoise glared at Rasputin and
whacked his thigh with her fan.

Her mother was on her way to retire at the age of forty-
seven, quite late for a courtesan. Far from squandering the
wealth of property and precious gifts of art and jewelry she had
amassed throughout her professional life of close to thirty years,
she had invested wisely. She remained one of the wealthiest
women in Paris. Her business acumen had afforded her family
an extravagant lifestyle. Françoise pulled her peignoir tight
against her naked breasts. A puff of envy blew out of her mouth.
It was best not to agitate her present peace. She had no desire to
shoulder the onerous responsibility of managing the Honoré
empire. In truth, Simone might not be a bad candidate to follow
in the matriarch's footsteps, or the wealth one generation had
accumulated would vanish with the next.

Françoise attempted to riffle through her mother's past.
She was eager to locate anything that would illuminate the

identity of her father—a balm to soothe the chronic ache lodged in a neglected part of her heart that ruled her emotional life. That was fine by her, she concluded, since it discouraged intimacy. But having embarked on a rampage to exploit men, she was not certain who had ended up exploiting whom.

Mme Gabrielle's magical childhood and her Jewish roots were fascinating, since she seemed more of an atheist now than a Jew. But why did she will gaps in her narrative? Why did the wiring of her memory go awry when the matter of Françoise's father came up? The extent of information she had of her father was that Mme Gabrielle was inebriated with absinthe the night Françoise was conceived. He was a one-night lover. And dropped from the Honoré collective memory without further mention.

She might as well have been conceived by the full moon and absinthe.

20

Persia

1901

Awakened by the odor of burning meat, I run to the kitchen. The leg of mutton is charred and inedible. I toss dirt on the cooking logs in the wood burner, wait for the last embers to die, and then turn back to the bedroom. Something must have gone terribly wrong. It is past midnight and Cyrus is not home.

I step out of Françoise's gown, wash my face, lips, and earlobes of smeared rouge, and throw Cyrus's coat over my shoulders. Outside, a pale moon sinks behind the ghostly outline of the mountains. Northern lights blaze across the vast canvas of the sky. Cyclones of greens, reds, and violets rise and ebb. The firmament sounds like a Bach concerto, the wail of a hundred violins, the chorus of a thousand harps. Aurora borealis.

Bare branches of potted jasmine and Persian roses are covered in bags for protection against an early frost. Cyrus has unsuccessfully tried to grow *khiar,* cucumbers, in pots and ledges around the perimeter of our land. Winter is not here, but an early snow has settled on the mountains. Insects scurry into frozen potholes. A snake gleams fluorescent, slithering under a boulder. The cawing of crows reverberates above the indigo-shadowed mountains that catch momentary fire with the flashing lights. I aim a pebble up at the canopy of crows—such clamor these birds make after dusk. I miss *Grand-mère* and her spirits. She would have made sense of this early winter, the gone-astray aurora borealis. I brush snow off a boulder and settle down to observe the magic overhead. Drastic changes in temperature do not usually affect me, but a chill runs through me now.

The sound of boots crunching on snow.

"Cyrus!" I jump to my feet and negotiate my way to the gate, careful not to slide on the hardened snow. Nothing but the shadow of stone and mountain and the luminous streamers that twist and turn in the skies.

I settle back, shut my eyes and, for the sake of my baby, try to calm down.

The metallic sound of the latch at the gate startles my eyes open. I did not hear the clatter of Cyrus's stallion, the clink of dismantling saddle, or his approaching boots. "Cyrus?" The crackling orchestra of the aurora borealis stifles my voice. The light momentarily outlines his silhouette behind the gate. And beyond, the stark ruins of a world profoundly sad in its solitude.

I rise to my feet and go to greet him.

A faceless form, tall and heavyset beneath a black cape and hood, hovers over me. I fight to push the gate shut, keep my balance, stop myself from slipping on the snow. The figure steps forward. Blocks my way. Prevents the gate from closing. I open my mouth. A silent scream forms in my throat. I must summon the strength to dash to the teahouse to solicit Beard's help.

Violent bolts flash overhead. The northern lights seem momentarily to strike the stranger's cape with fire. He sets down a box at my feet. Grabs me by the waist, jams me against his chest, his breath steaming.

My screams reverberate around the mountains. Boomerang back over and over again, echoing my fear.

The outline of one arm rises from under his cape.

The silver glint of a blade against the canvas of the furious sky.

"Here!" I address the dagger aimed down at me. "In my heart! Not in my belly." I am no longer afraid. I will shield the curled fist in my womb. The northern lights swallow my words. I push my stomach against him to protect my belly.

A block of ice, his arm remains paralyzed overhead. His grip slackens from around my waist. He flails back. Stumbles like a drunkard, dragging me down. A lifeless doll, I fall on top of him. I free myself. Roll away and scramble to my feet on frozen bones.

Someone hurtles himself on top of my attacker. Drives him into the snow. "Cyrus!" I scream.

The blade gleams close to one, then the other. Let it not be Cyrus! Please! Not him. The dagger swivels in the air to swoop down and lodge handle up in the snow. One man shoves the head of the other down. Crams his mouth with snow that darkens with blood.

"Cyrus?" I call out to the demons above, and my voice echoes and gathers force, stirring phantoms out of the shadows, emerging from around cracks and boulders. My baby flips in my belly, my heart in my chest. An army? Enemies? Why? Ribbons of fire light the skies and, for an instant, night turns into day, illuminating the shape of numerous retreating figures in the horizon. "Cyrus!"

"It is me, Beard."

I scoop up snow and rub my face in razor-cold ice. "Where is Cyrus?"

"I do not know," Beard replies, breathless. "A stranger passed by the café, others followed—many more. This is unusual. I became suspicious." He kicks the box at my feet. "What is this?"

I wave toward the body farther down. "My attacker left it. Is he dead?"

"Yes, do not look. Wait, do not touch anything." He bends to check the box, turns it around, and passes his hands over the cardboard. He searches for the dagger lost in the struggle, yanks it out of the snow, and cuts a rope tied around the box. He lifts up the lid. Dropping the box, he leaps back.

I stand paralyzed as he bends down and retrieves an item.

Under the chaotic orchestra of light overhead, my gaze falls on the object Beard holds up. The acrid stench of putrefaction sends me reeling. I grab the gate to keep myself from fainting. The aurora borealis illuminates the dappled ear of Cyrus's stallion. The lead-colored dots. The severed blood-stiff border exudes a sickening odor.

The stink of blood in my nostrils, I fall to my knees. "Beard! Beard . . . Where is he?"

Beard grumbles something about evil djinns in the heavens—a premonition of further misfortunes. He tries to lift me up. "He must be dead, *khanom,* dead."

I slap him across the face. Push him off. Kick him away. I claw at his shirt, tear it off his back. "How dare you say he is dead! Leave me alone! He is *not* dead."

The truth stabs me in the belly.

I squeeze my thighs together to hold on to my son.

To the wet pain between my legs.

21

Yaghout throws herself on her son's imaginary grave, the starving arms of rosebush and jasmine.

A collective wail rises to echo against the mountains.

Two men lift her up and support her between them.

I walk into her arms. "Are they reciting the kaddish for Cyrus? Is he really dead?"

She pushes me away with one hand.

In the red jersey dress he liked, I stand in his garden, surrounded by his family, a haze of black. The mourning rituals are a blurry drone with temporary breaks of unbearable awareness. My only wish is to locate and shelter my husband's body from the ravages of time, to preserve him with precious oils and the pearls of my dying fragrance.

Men tear their shirts in mourning. I dig a finger into a flounce on my dress and rip it off. I will tear whatever I want. The vulgarity of wearing red on such an occasion, someone whispers. He wore white in his defiance. I will wear red.

My stomach is nearly flat, the pad between my legs blood

soaked. Do souls hover overhead like moths, like Grandmother's ghosts intoxicated with absinthe? Does Cyrus know that he lost the son he would have taught to handle horses and carry a dagger in full view?

With unblinking eyes, Rabbi Shlomo the Penitent recites the mourner's kaddish in the garden where Cyrus cajoled vegetation out of the earth. The rabbi prays to the Almighty to breathe peace into the soul of Cyrus and Elijah and to grant their family patience and a long life. Inspecting the pitiless white sky, the rabbi implores the Lord to reveal one of his miracles. "So I can resume blinking again, Lord, have mercy on your servant."

Something snaps in my womb, a dry, stubborn twig that clung to the twilight of hope. I grab the rabbi's bony arm and assure him that no miracle would occur in this house. "So blink if you have to, Rabbi. Don't torture yourself."

Book in hand, men murmur prayers that will not bring my son back. Would their prayers bring Cyrus back?

Buzzards circle overhead, preparing to swoop down as if invited to a fête.

What is left to prey on?

∞

In our home, where I am told sweets must not be served and flowers not be displayed, a clan that had ostracized us climbed up the tortuous pass to deliver tear-drenched food. They leave their shoes at the door and assemble on throw pillows, on the carpet, on the stone floor, everywhere. Trays of tea without sugar are passed around. Bunches of mint, peeled cucumbers, and bottles of rosewater are sniffed and blessings murmured. Copper trays of steaming lentil-rice, potato-and-onion omelets, mint, and spring onions permeate the house with the odor of death. Faceless women wail and blow raw noses with corners of chadors. Men sway back and forth in prayer. Children tuck themselves into corners, improvising with pots, cups, and ladles for toys. No one occupies Cyrus's futon. I imagine him enter, tap his cane against his boot, and wrap me in his arms to resume where we left, continue to create our own history and chronicle our love.

Overnight, a smoky ribbon appeared in the middle of my hair—the Red Sea parted—for grief to cross, I suppose. Another mystery added to his disappearance.

A brand of French harlots, a woman whispers, hand concealing her mouth, as if that would temper the bite. "Do not cry," Pearl says as she sips black tea. "You are strong; you will get through this. No, no, bite your tongue back, never curse. God is great. Time will heal." Why is Pearl here? I do not need her now. My mind a swamp of disbelief, my gaze swivels around the room seeking Yaghout—I need Cyrus's mother. Her voice comes from the kitchen. How could she care about dinner now? I nod like a marionette, acknowledge an emaciated woman with hair piled up on a cone-shaped head, two women nursing and dabbing wet cheeks. Children lie around the room or doze in their parents' laps. Beard sits cross-legged on the carpet in a corner, wearing the white, grease-stained shirt, a showcase for his bulging biceps, the tarantula tattoo gloomy across his arm. He lowers his head as if embarrassed, handles a pouch on his lap. I want to go to him, but such a move would be inappropriate. He clutches the pouch in one hand, the other pointing toward it.

I stand up to the clucks of disapproval and settle next to him. As if he had been expecting this moment, he places the pouch in my lap. From behind the leather, pebbly objects roll against my palm.

"This is yours," he whispers, averting his gaze. "You must leave Persia. Right away!"

I rise to my feet and move toward the bedroom. I am in

mourning. I know I should not walk around, others should serve me if I need anything—a bite to eat, a glass of water—but this I will have to do myself. My heel catches in a flounce, pulling my neckline low.

I come face-to-face with Yaghout.

Her once red lips are pale and lifeless against sallow skin. Her thick, arched brows knot into a frown, and her date-colored eyes are webbed at the edges. She has aged. Her fingers dig into my shoulders. I want to bury myself in her arms and release a dam of tears on her shoulder.

"I lost my son," she says, as if I don't know.

Her grief-stricken eyes riffle through mine as if to unearth her son's fate, as if I am the reason she had to embark on this trip up the mountain.

I gently loosen her hands from my shoulders, holding them tight, searching for Cyrus in her. "Yaghout *khanom,* I am as despondent as you are. Believe me."

"Then do not stroll around as if we lost some wild weed."

I pull her into my arms and rest my head on her shoulder. "Yaghout *khanom,* you lost a grandchild, too, my baby."

Folded in her embrace, her wails in my ears, I know I am forgiven.

22

The ancient mirror in my bedroom reflects images of hair-brushes, face powders, ginger-tasting lip balm—delicious, he murmured—rouges for evenings, blushes to lighten freckles—his index finger tapped on each—small treasures—do not cover them. I pass the brush through the wondrous silver strip that runs through my hair. A sign from Cyrus? Will he reveal himself in the mirror if I stare long enough?

"Ghosts love mirrors," Mme Gabrielle has said. "Their past lives are reflected there." Is his soul with her now, she who believed I have the right eyes and ears to see and hear spirits?

Cyrus's suspenders are draped over the mirror—another emblem of defiance, as Persians find suspenders foreign. He refused to be threatened, refused to be forced into conformity.

Is this why he disappeared?

I drop the pouch Beard gave me on the bedspread I stitched together with bits of negligees, petticoats, and *soutiens-gorge*.

Cyrus would have wanted me to unravel this mystery on my own. He detested nothing more than exposing his private life, revealing details the world had no right to know. I empty the contents of the purse on the bedcover. A folded piece of paper flutters out and behind it shiny, round drops of blood. One gem rolls away to lodge in the seam of a stretch of crinoline stitched to a square of chiffon.

The thought occurs to me that Cyrus's red diamond must have planted him in the eye of danger, the earring that represented his first success. He wore his fortune on his earlobe.

And they robbed him, not of his life, I pray.

The twisted, venomous script in the note advises me: *Shaunce Banou: Leave Persia or you will join your dead husband. You were lucky once. It will not happen again. Take this wealth that will last the rest of your life, and flee.*

Shaunce Banou—Lady Fortune—I repeat over and over again. How am I fortunate? How could I abandon the home where Elijah's spirit roams? Into which Cyrus might walk at any moment? Despite the crowd of mourners in the other room, despite Beard's solemn assertion, despite the cut-off ear of the horse, Cyrus will not be dead as long as I do not see his body.

Shaunce Banou. Did he ever call me that? Lady Fortune.

And if I am not around, I will still find ways to be with you, he assured.

I jump to my feet and search for a sign.

Cyrus would have left a will, a document. I look under the bed, inspect closets and drawers, check behind the mirror. My eyes fall on the mantelpiece and his tallit bag, and I know he is here with me. Concealed in his Bible is the name of those who would aid me. I stroke the taffeta, slip one hand in and comb the tzitzit fringes. A note and a vellum envelope flutter out of his Bible. I lift the envelope flap and retrieve a

single sheet of paper with his bold handwriting, the ink of
certain characters bleeding into each other. I imagine sweat
on his fingers staining the script. He must have been fright-
ened.

Dear Simone:
If you are reading this letter I have been murdered. Do
not mourn my passing. You are the love of my life and I
would not have exchanged you for anyone or anything,
even my life. I, in return, brought you nothing but grief.
Do not remain in Persia. Raise our son a free man in
France. I regret not being at your side during your preg-
nancy, but what I found in Africa reinforced the suspi-
cions that sent me there. Do not be angry with me for not
sharing my finding with you. If you are ever interrogated,
an honest "I do not know" will save you.
Mention me to our son.
Teach him to value his integrity above everything else.

I fold and unfold the paper, smell and rub it to my cheek.
The revelation that he might have been murdered threatens to
smother the last flame of hope. I scoop up the gems and let
them shower down upon the impression of his body on our
bed. Are these garnets? Or pigeon blood rubies? I roll one
around, light bouncing off the seamless facets. They are as brilliant as Burmese rubies from the depleted region of Mugak. A
certain tremulous liquidity in their heart sends me for the loupe
on the bed stand. Drawing from the extensive lessons I had
from Cyrus, I pass the loupe over the gems and focus on the
scintillating drop of water that trembles in their cores, a trans-
parency rare in rubies.
I slump down, my womb tender, my head pounding. I am in
possession of a treasure of red diamonds—five to be exact. No!

Six. One embedded itself somewhere in the seams of the stitched-together petticoats. I search the ridges, folds, insets, and pluck from an eyelet Cyrus's red diamond earring in its original four-pronged setting, the post and back intact.

They were not after his red diamond after all.

23

The orange disk of the sun lies idle on the summits, biding its time until nightfall. In my stone garden, I pull out weeds and hack on wild plants that have sprouted in Cyrus's absence. I pour my grief into the earth, chop stubborn roots, plant seeds, and exterminate insects. My figure is settling back into its slim outline, my shell hardening with resentment.

Names Cyrus had mentioned in the past begin to gel in my mind. M. Jean Paul Dubois. M. Amir. M. Rouge. Mehrdad.

Yaghout came to visit. I asked her if she knew Mehrdad. She did not. What she knew was that the custom of keeping mourners company has its own wisdom. Left alone, a mourner's grief could lead to madness. She stirred rock-sugar in a teacup and handed me a plate of saffron halvah. "It will warm your womb, strengthen your heart. Do not tell anyone I gave you sweets." I drank the sweet tea. I ate the halvah. I want nothing more than to be left alone. Yaghout did leave. But Beard has become a permanent fixture outside my garden. I call out from behind the fence, "Beard, would you like to come in for a cup of tea?"

He lowers his head and murmurs that he is entirely comfortable where he is, an annoyed expression—maybe anger, but certainly apprehension—apparent on his face.

I open the gate and climb up and around one boulder, then another, avoiding the jagged edges to come face-to-face with him. I shift the gardening shovel he had procured for me from Tehran from one hand to the other, attempting to talk sense into my stubborn head. I am seconds away from demanding that he either share his concern or leave me alone—forever—because I don't need a chaperone. But this is not true. In the evenings, when I can't bear my grief, I seek his café and a few puffs from his hookah. Reluctant to hurt his feelings, I hesitate before I deposit my shovel at his feet. "What is it, Beard? Tell me?"

Then this man who is compelled to lower his eyes in my presence, who finds it difficult to address me directly, takes me by the arm. "*Beh harf man goosh bedeh!* Listen! They will murder you, too, if you do not go."

"Who?"

"It is better for you not to know." He unfolds a newspaper and smoothes it out on his knee. "Nothing here! No news of his death here, either. Nothing! There is a reason."

He is right. I, too, have wondered at the unusual silence as I comb through newspapers and eavesdrop on conversations in his café. I have even expected Beard himself to ask me a few questions about that night. But not a word. As if Cyrus, the shah's esteemed jeweler, had never existed. As if he was not worth one phrase in the news.

Beard bows his head. "Allah my witness, I loved Cyrus like a brother. I respect you, too, Simone *khanom*. Please go back to your country!"

"Then they will win. Then I will never find Cyrus's body."

With a regretful shake of his head, he murmurs that he understands I am French and innocent of Persian ways. "But this is a very dangerous world. A woman alone will not survive."

"Cyrus would have wanted me to demand his body," I try to convince Beard, to convince myself.

"No! He loved you. He would want you to live."

"But why would anyone want me dead, Beard?"

He lifts one atrophied leg and rests it on a rock. The backs of his cloth slippers are folded under callused heels immune to the ice underfoot. He digs his hand into his pants pocket, his tattooed tarantula crouching on his biceps. He retrieves an envelope and unfolds it on his thigh. Slipping a letter out, he flattens it with care.

He hands me the bluish litmus paper on which Cyrus once recorded our aborted history. His sensual script, the bold tip of his pen, the ink he created by combining lapis and algae green stare back at me. My womb shudders, complaining against its emptiness.

Beard averts his eyes from the hand pressed against my belly. His small, yellow teeth are visible beyond the twisted ropes of his beard. I tighten the knot of my headscarf and tuck in my hair. I lean against the snow-stricken body of the mountain. My husband's handwriting floats on the sheet.

If anything happens to me, take care of Simone and my son.

One sentence and Cyrus binds me to Beard in ways I cannot begin to fathom.

"Cyrus knew he was in danger!" I murmur out loud—a reassertion—knowing full well he did.

"He did, Simone *khanom*. Classified information is exchanged in my café. If I overhear something, I usually put it out of my mind. Do not ask more," Beard warns. "Do not talk to anyone. *Motevajeh hastid?* Understand?" He removes a manila envelope from his pocket. "Everything you will need to get you to Paris is here. *Khoda Hafiz,* Allah protect you."

"Tell me who gave you that pouch. What did he look like?"

"Nothing unusual about him, other than he wore a red diamond earring like Cyrus's."

24

❧

Paris
August 1900

"*Red diamonds are a bore, Grand-mère*. And I am not interested in the Persian jeweler," Simone said, facing Mme
Gabrielle across her writing desk.

A map of Paris was spread on the table. The grandmother
dipped her pen in an inkwell. She superimposed a red line on
the diagram of streets and avenues the Persian's carriage would
negotiate from the palace of the president to the château. She
dramatized her tracing with an exclamation mark at the point
where Château Gabrielle would have appeared on the map—his
destination. "The city is terribly congested these days," she exclaimed. "What do you think? Will he arrive in time for high tea
or for supper?"

"Does it really matter, *Grand-mère*? He is not coming for tea
or supper, but to enjoy your company."

Mme Gabrielle tried again. "You, too, will enjoy the company of this refined gentleman and might even want to know
him better. He has come all the way from Persia with the shah
and his royal entourage."

"Our exposition attracted fifty million," Simone interjected. "Another one does not matter. Haven't you gone out lately? From Champ de Mars all the way to Les Invalides and beyond is congested. So he will be late, too, as we all are these days."

"*Oui, oui, c'est vrais*. Nevertheless, cultivated ladies like us must impress our good manners upon foreigners, whatever the situation. It is only proper that all three of us Honoré hostesses welcome such a guest. You would do me a great favor, *chérie*, if we welcomed the Persian as a family."

Simone stepped closer to the writing desk and leaned over to take a better look at the map. She would, of course, rather study or roam the hills with Sabot Noir. On the other hand, wasting an hour or two would not make much of a difference to her, although it would please her grandmother enormously. "If that's what you want, *Grand-mère*, I will try to be there," she replied, planting a kiss on her grandmother's forehead.

Mme Gabrielle did not smile or reveal her delight. Red diamonds were known to elicit romantic reactions. Her stallions were beside themselves and in a state of constant arousal, the peacocks in a frenzy of mating. Françoise had canceled her appearance at Maxim's bar, the Omnibus, where she was to have met the Prince of Wales. Mme Gabrielle herself had given up her night at the opera, relinquishing her tickets for Balzac's *The Splendor and Misery of the Courtesan* to Sabot Noir's father and his wife, Effat, who blackmailed Françoise into lending her a leopard cape for the evening.

Simone went to her boudoir to try on the gown the seamstress had embroidered for the occasion and that had been left idle in her armoire. She gazed in the mirror, shocked at the horror facing her. The taffeta was too red and clashed with her hair, the tucks in the bodice were too tight, and the frills were exaggerated. She tore off the lace collar. Drove a finger into one of the flounces and ripped it off. About to tear off another flounce, she heard the clatter of faraway hooves. She left her quarters, crossed the corridor, and entered the balcony overlooking the park and the road that snaked toward her home.

The balcony was the vantage point from which she first glimpsed a suitor her mother anticipated, a caller her grandmother identified as an "old friend," and where she customarily welcomed Rabbi Abramowicz, he who kept her rooted in reality and reminded her of the surrounding decadence.

"The lust-tinged air you breathe is poisonous," he would repeatedly remind her. "Nothing but a cluster of tempting mirages."

He was the one who, without the slightest show of embarrassment, guided her regarding intimate matters. While her first menstrual period was occasion for her mother and grandmother to plan soirées to introduce her to wealthy supporters, her great-grandfather did not hesitate to impart sensible advice. A woman was to immerse herself in the mikvah on the seventh day of her menstrual cycle, before joining her husband. It was a compulsory mitzvah for a husband to bring gifts on Sabbath and satisfy his wife in bed—or she had a legal right to divorce. While Françoise and Mme Gabrielle found no place in their lives for Rabbi Abramowicz's tradition, he conveyed the importance of faith to anchor Simone in difficult times. He compared his deceased wife to the great Jewish matriarchs: Sarah, Rachel, and Rebekah. "Commitment and respect are the foundations of every relationship," he said. "This is the eleventh commandment."

The rumble of carriage wheels, at times broken, at times muffled by gathering winds, drew nearer and, for an instant, Simone wondered if red diamonds truly influenced the elements. She certainly detected greed on the wind, the sweat of horses, and the oily smell of worn leather. Would the Persian arrive in his ethnic attire, with funny cloth shoes and cone-shaped hat?

The carriage neared, and she bent low over the balustrade to take a better look. She lost her balance, her heart plunging.

She screamed. Her grandmother grabbed her from behind. Smoothing down her skirt, Mme Gabrielle wrapped her arm around the trembling shoulders.

A carriage thundered around the turn to the stampede of twelve white stallions coming into view and galloping toward Château Gabrielle. The grand gates were flung open to accommodate the entering carriage, which wheeled to a stop in front of the steps that led up to the terrace.

A swarm of fireflies flickered like tiny green flames, gathered in number, and descended upon the horses. The four coachmen on the front box lost control of the charging stallions whose nostrils flared and tails twitched to chase off fireflies that buzzed their way into the inner flesh of their ears.

The malicious M. Günter hissed in Mme Gabrielle's ear, warning that although fireflies seem harmless to the novice eye, in reality these harlot-flies lure each other's mates to gobble them up. Alarmed by this bad omen, she flipped her fan open with a flick of her wrist and waved the ghost off. She did not like this one bit. The fickle creatures had appeared out of thin air at the most inopportune time.

Having shooed the fireflies away, the footmen jumped down to unfold a footstool and open the door to the carriage.

A giant stepped out.

He raised massive arms tattooed with mythological warriors in hostile battle stance. From one hand, he dangled an iron box with a heavy lock. He checked his right and left, his clean-shaven head shining in the sun, his billowing pants flapping in the wind, the fireflies descending upon him. He belted out something in a strange language that startled Mme Gabrielle and Simone out of their skins and dispersed the fireflies.

Simone gasped, her hand springing to her mouth.

Mme Gabrielle, unable to believe her eyes, pressed her palm over her heart as if it would burst out of her chest and tumble down the balcony. *"Ce n'est pas vrai,"* she grumbled under her breath. What could have happened to the Persian jeweler? Who was this monstrous hulk? What kind of a crude monster had the devious minister of court dispatched to her house? She took Simone by the arm and led her inside.

Simone felt triumphant. The arrival her grandmother heralded with such fanfare had yielded a waking nightmare. She lingered at the threshold, directing a self-righteous expression toward her grandmother.

Mme Gabrielle heard the faint click of a bolt, glanced behind her, and with Simone in tow, stepped back onto the balcony.

The Persian jeweler sprinted out from the opposite side of the carriage. He stretched his long legs, shook his slim body like a grand cat, and closed the carriage door with a silver-tipped cane. His shoulder-length hair was pulled back in a ponytail, his nut-brown beard perfectly clipped. His black tunic was carelessly open to reveal a muscular chest darkened by the sun, defying Simone's image of a jeweler imprisoned in an atelier.

A red diamond gleamed in his earlobe.

Climbing the stairs two at a time, he rapped his cane against each step, then ambled across the terrace toward the house.

Simone followed his advance. Her revolver knocked against the wrought-iron balustrade as she fished out her lace handkerchief from her corset and set it fluttering down the balcony.

He heard the click of metal, aimed his hazel eyes at the two women overhead, and raised his cane to catch the handkerchief on the silver tip. He nodded his salutation, and disappeared inside.

25

Half illuminated in light filtering through muslin, half in mysterious shadows, Françoise had positioned herself by the windows. Encrusted with pearls, her organza neckline plunged low to reveal plump breasts.

Before Alphonse had occasion to announce the Persian, Mme Gabrielle stepped forward and blocked Françoise from view, presenting her hand to the jeweler.

Simone observed the fabled fingers bared for the occasion, the tapered tips, the ivory nails rise to the Persian's mouth. How long will he hold her hand? How long a kiss will he plant on those legendary fingers? His lips lingered for nine beats of Simone's heart.

Approaching Simone, he lowered his head, pressing his lips to her right hand and the handkerchief into her left.

His lips embracing her flesh, she counted to eighteen. Perspiration trickled down her back. He released her hand. Only then did she realize that she had not studied his palm, that for the first time she had failed to familiarize herself with a new acquaintance through the geography of his palm. Why would he kiss her hand twice as long as that celebrated hand? Why would hands that groomed horses, tackled revolvers, and traced palms merit such attention?

M. Gerard Fontanel, Françoise's protector, settled himself firmly next to her. A portly man, he strove to conceal his massive belly with double-breasted jackets and floppy bow ties. He sported a nervous mustache and a full head of tar-colored hair that resembled a felt wig. Behind his pince-nez, a pair of caramel eyes contradicted the rest of his shrewd expression. He stood up to greet the Persian, his arm resting on a serviette on the side table.

Mme Gabrielle wondered if he had come straight from the bank with his briefcase bursting at the seams with millions. She considered the possibility that, if not a bracelet of red diamonds, Françoise might receive another jewel of importance.

At the sight of her mother's suitor planted in the salon like a gaudy artifact, Simone's cheeks turned the color of pomegranate.

Alphonse, who hovered around making certain everything was in order, escorted her toward a chair and handed her a glass of iced water.

The Persian, surrounded by pale skin, blue, blonde, and red hair, turquoise, slate-gray, and yellow-green eyes, was mesmerized. Every detail about the Honoré women—their confidence, their refined etiquette, and the candid shock of their gaze—was foreign. But he was most captivated by Simone. Her perfume evoked the scent of spices—cinnamon, cumin, ginger from back home. Her tilt of the head, as if she was never quite certain what she would do or say next, stunned him. She did not seem part of this decadence, the defiant gesture of the ripped collar of her gown proof she did not belong here. Finding his thoughts stray to the question of when he would visit these enchanted grounds again, he reminded himself of the reason he was here.

Conscientious men—and much less the shah's private jeweler—would not enter such notorious premises except when business demanded.

Mme Gabrielle registered the jeweler's smitten look, Françoise's growing irritation, and M. Fontanel's efforts to redirect her attention. Mme Gabrielle addressed the Persian. *"Alors! Did you manage to locate a red diamond bracelet?"*

The giant picked up an armchair and placed it opposite the table, where he positioned the box in front of the Persian. To the utter amazement of all, the giant stretched out on the carpet at the jeweler's foot. He was now a human shield in case the diamonds were accidentally dropped, his upside-down glare an effective deterrent against theft.

Cyrus turned a key in the strongbox lock.

Françoise's skirts rustled as she collected them, spread her fan open, and came closer to settle on the settee next to the table.

Mme Gabrielle shot a reprimanding look at her daughter.

M. Fontanel's thin mustache twitched.

Cyrus set a loupe on the tabletop, retrieved a velvet pad, and unfurled it. He clicked a satin box open and slid it to the center of the table.

Françoise approached the Persian, squeezing his shoulder with one hand as the other fanned furiously above her trembling breasts. Leaning over his shoulder, she took a look at the object lounging on velvet, and a film of perspiration formed in her cleavage.

Eighteen one-carat red diamonds, set in an intricately designed platinum bracelet, shimmered and dazzled in resplendent shades of red, violet, and purple of unparalleled vitality.

Cyrus lifted the bracelet and, paying no attention to Françoise's extended arm, clasped the bracelet around Simone's wrist as if she were the potential buyer. Raising her arm to the glow of the chandelier first, he then led her to the window to further demonstrate the bracelet's magic, the unprecedented tricks of the sunlight that descended upon the gems and made them appear almost liquid.

M. Fontanel, having tolerated enough folly, especially since presumably he was the person to part with millions, marched to Simone and seized her wrist. He unclasped the bracelet with two flips of a connoisseur's fingers. Before he had grabbed the loupe to examine the first diamond, he was uprooted and dangling in the air from the giant's hands. In his shock and rage, he did not fight back, even as his bones groaned in the monster's grip.

"Put him down," Cyrus ordered calmly.

His face the color of ash, M. Fontanel was deposited back on the carpet. He adjusted his cravat, ignored Françoise's delighted squeals, and slumped into a chair Cyrus pushed behind him. Fontanel waited for his heart to settle, laid the bracelet back on the pad, and adjusted the gooseneck lamp downward. His cheeks ached, not only with the effort to control his anger but also at his astonishment at the treasure he faced. He took his time to examine each and every detail of the rarest of red diamonds he had ever encountered. Where in the world did they come from? Who was the supplier? How did the Persian come upon them?

Mme Gabrielle watched the relationship between Fontanel and the gemstones evolve into an obsessive affair. She evaluated his growing admiration, the leisurely manner in which he turned the bracelet around to check each stone, his caramel gaze softening and melting.

He set the bracelet down, passed a finger over each iridescent stone as if stroking the eyes of a lover. His gaze traveled up to the ceiling, toward the intricate faïence, and remained there for what seemed an eternity to Françoise. A tear of excitement formed in her eyes, slid to the tips of her lashes to tremble at the edges.

Mme Gabrielle, clutching her strand of pearls around her

neck like a noose, followed the path of Fontanel's gaze, imagining him reflecting upon both the extraordinary favors his generosity would induce and the painful consequences if he were to decline the purchase.

"*Non! Ce n'est pas vrai,*" Fontanel shouted, the vowels clashing against each other. "Impossible! Unconscionable!" He hurled the bracelet up.

The giant sprang up with agility rare for such a big man and caught the bracelet in midair.

"A disgrace," Fontanel hollered, "to attempt to feed me garnets in place of red diamonds!"

Françoise let out a shriek and fainted back into the satin waves of her skirts.

Mme Gabrielle was not the least bit disappointed. On the contrary, she admired M. Fontanel for having attained a well-deserved revenge.

Simone remained by the window, digging her teeth into her lip, the sinking sun blazing through her hair, her freckles the shade of amber.

Cyrus snapped the box open, collected the bracelet, and locked it back. As if nothing of importance had occurred, he addressed Mme Gabrielle and Françoise, who had regained consciousness with Alphonse's aid. "Mesdames," he said, bowing low, "I shall take my leave now." He retrieved his pocket watch, snapped the top open, and pressed the tip of one finger inside the concave lid. He touched the freckle at the side of Simone's neck. Raising her hand, he planted what felt like a grain of rice on her palm. He gathered her fingers into a fist. "I owe you twelve more, Mademoiselle. One for each freckle."

He strode out of Château Gabrielle. The gates clanked shut behind him. The echo of hooves died.

Simone opened her fist. A sliver of red diamond was lodged in the lifeline that ran the length of her palm.

He will come back. Another twelve visits.

26

Simone dug one hand into the pocket of her riding breeches; in the other she carried one of Alphonse's books of Persian history. She rolled the sliver of red diamond between her thumb and forefinger. When would Cyrus return? Would he conceal the next diamond in a white rose, in the hem of a Kurdish tunic, or between pages of a book of poetry? She pressed her mouth to the back of her hand where the imprint of his lips glowed. With delight, she recalled his indifference to her mother's flirtatious affectations and how he had ignored the dim-witted M. Fontanel. Unable to sleep, she decided to spend the better part of the day in the *bois* in back of the Valley of Civet Cats with Zola, the stallion named after Mme Gabrielle's comrade, Émile.

The red diamond earring—a mysterious universe of mesmerizing colors—Cyrus wore had prompted Alphonse to give her a book on the mythological significance of the gems and their geographical background. He had eavesdropped on the gossip of merchants and had discovered that discretion was essential in the trade, and merchants from as far as the Congo, Russia, and even India circulated about Paris with diamonds for a few elite clients.

She was captivated by the origin of diamonds—carbons created more than a hundred million years ago, under titanic pressure and tremendous underground heat until rain and erosion freed them from the earth's crust, washing them down across the landscape to lodge in the gravel of riverbeds, at the bottom of oceans, or in red Lunda Sul soil. Nature's selectiveness fascinated her. Why did certain carbons develop into diamonds while others remained ordinary graphite? She lost herself in tales of certain "named" gems that commanded a premium: Braganza, a fist-sized diamond named after the Portuguese royal house, had allegedly been robbed from the crown of Portugal and shipped to France in a casket with forty thousand gold coins.

Was the origin of red diamonds the blood of mistreated diggers, the blazing eyes of dragons guarding illicit mines, or the tears of children forced into hard labor? Might her grandmother's spirits impart nuggets of wisdom regarding Cyrus and his diamonds? "Cyrus!" she repeated over and over again, and then, "Simone," tasting their similarities.

Some distance from the château, she ran toward the stables, her boots sinking into the dew-heavy grass. She circled the stalls and entered Zola's stall from the back. She moved silently so as not to awaken the stable hands, especially Sabot Noir, who would not understand her desire to be alone with her stallion and without saddle or stirrups. She stroked Zola, the familiar silk-rough hide, checked the domesticated gaze—not her present preference. A horse that had not been tamed into submission was more suitable to her mood this morning. Entering one stall after another, she touched, smelled, and whispered to each horse. Restive in the saddling stall, hooves raising the scent of hay and earth, Molière demanded freedom. She rattled the lead rope, patted the Arab, and murmured in a low voice.

From behind the wooden partition, Sabot Noir watched Simone caress the horse's forelock, pat the crest, and press her cheek to its haunch. Everyone, including himself, had failed to tame this stud. Would Simone succeed? She was able to detect the emotional idiosyncrasies of animals, to make them heed, run, or gallop. Horses responded to her perfume as if she were a creature beyond human. But Molière was wild and untamable. At the sight of the disarmed Arab settling into a nuzzling snort, Sabot Noir's heartbeat slowed. For the first time since he had detected Simone at Françoise's window, his mind readjusted itself back into a place of relative clarity. Simone *did* prefer the company of animals to that of men, after all. Like him, she sheltered animal spirits and had a special bond with horses. With that epiphany, he consoled himself that the two of them were nothing short of soul mates in a twisted world that would never appreciate them.

Simone treaded the path behind the stables, leading the horse out of the compound. Daily water used for washing the stables streamed down the sloping trail and the damp earth stifled the clap of hooves.

Shoe pads he had devised to smother sound tied around his mare's hooves, a rag stuffed into its mouth to suppress noise, Sabot Noir followed Simone out of the stables. A stream of urine shot out of the snorting and stumping Arab. The familiar breeding dance assured Sabot Noir that Simone was on her way to copulate with horses.

Once out of the grounds of Château Gabrielle, she circled the surrounding Civet Cats Hills and galloped deep into the woods. She dug her heels into the flanks, her thighs gripping the animal as she stretched prostrate, clutching the mane, her body molding to the stallion's as it trotted around the winding path, under an awning of branches, in and out of sight.

Sabot Noir sent the mare into a trot behind the woman

with hair a deeper red than any animal's mane, even the plush-
est he groomed with linseed oil. He trailed her as she advanced
into the canopy of trees. He imagined—no, he expected her to
turn around and wink his way, step out of her skirts and, in her
corset and riding breeches, toss her revolver behind as a signal
for him to join her.

Unaware of Sabot Noir behind her, like a cleansing ritual,
Simone methodically exorcised from her consciousness the
many men who continued to pass through Château Gabrielle.
She was preparing herself for Cyrus—a man utterly different
from the horde of suitors who invaded her mother's and grandmother's boudoirs.

She yanked at the horse's mane and came to a stop under a
chestnut tree.

A pink robin fluttered back into its nest of cobwebs and
lichen. Insects ceased to chatter, taking shelter underground.
Civet cats scampered deep into their network of burrows. She
dismounted the stallion but did not tether it, certain it would
graze nearby. She settled down on a carpet of leaves and rested
her head against a tree trunk.

Farther away, Sabot Noir slowed behind a gathering of
trees. His muscles strung tight, his groin aching, he fixed his
wild eyes on her. He found it rather strange that she would ride
out to the *bois* in order to read.

Lost in Persian history, oblivious of thirst, hunger, or the
damp earth seeping into her riding breeches, Simone let a good
part of the afternoon slip away. She entered ancient Persia on
the arm of the triumphant Cyrus the Great, founder of the
Achaemenid Empire. They planned the town of Pasargadae in
the heart of a lush valley framed by the Persian mountains. He
whispered in her ear that none of his roses in the Paradise garden carried her scent. She told him she was the granddaughter
of a clairvoyant. "Don't campaign against the Massagetes," she
begged. "They will kill you."

"I promise," he replied, his gaze on her.

She laughed out loud, eager to share her historical findings with Alphonse.

Sabot Noir felt himself tense. Had she come to copulate with horses? And if so why did she waste time? He pulled his lorgnette out of the saddlebag and directed it toward her book. *The Comprehensive History of Persians*. The canopy of branches turned to hissing tentacles. It was the Persian jeweler, after all, and not the Arab, who occupied her mind. Stealing closer behind another tree, he watched her break a branch overhead and study the horizon, then brush leaves and crushed berries off her breeches. Vaulting onto Molière, she slapped the animal into full gallop. Sabot Noir dug his nails into his palms, his heels into the mare, the curb biting into the lips and shoving the fabric deeper. Gathering speed, hooves muted by pads, wet earth, and grass underfoot, he *clop-clopped* closer to the woman who was ignorant of his rage.

Dodging trees and struggling to untangle curls that snagged in low branches, she pushed deeper into the lush netting. A golden whistler flew out of the branches and got caught in her hair. She freed the flapping bird, turning to follow the swooping arc of its departure. She detected Sabot Noir, closer now that he felt betrayed. She waved him away, slowed down when his horse caught up to trot next to Molière. "I want to be alone," she called out.

Reins tight in one hand, he grabbed Molière by the mane and brought them all to an abrupt halt.

"Let go!" she shouted. "What are you doing?"

She noticed the rag in the horse's mouth; the pads tied to the hooves, the veins at his neck standing out like twisted cords. "What's wrong?" she asked.

He leaped off his horse, never releasing Molière's mane.

She grabbed a branch overhead, held on with all of her might, swayed, and sprinted off the stallion. Landing on her back on the undergrowth of fossilized foliage, pine needles, and berries, she scrambled to get up. A branch caught her chemise, tearing the fabric and stripping flesh off her shoulder.

He pressed on the stirrups, poised to hurl himself on top of her.

She aimed her revolver at his heart. "Go home!" she ordered, as if to a wayward dog. "What is wrong with you? It's me. Simone!"

He scratched the back of his neck, drawing blood. Tears rolled down his cheeks. "I thought you like animals, copulate with horses. We are soul mates. You want that Persian, don't you?" The next words tore out of him like bullets. "I cannot bear it. Shoot me."

She trembled at the sight of his chest presented to her as if to accept a medal. The outline of his thin shoulders visible from under his shirt, he seemed to beg her to save him from himself. The internal geography of a madman began to solidify in her mind. They had shared fantasies when they were children, fodder for dynamic imagination. The two of them played what seemed innocent games then. She would assume the part of a fox, he the hunter, or he would be a raging bull and she his matador. But she did not expect these fantasies to become his reality, to make him jealous and come undone. Why would he imagine she copulated with horses? Did her presumed affinity with the animals connect her in some manner to his dead mother?

Sabot Noir guzzled the surrounding air, every molecule of decomposing grass, dry bark, and sun-ripe chestnuts. Even from afar, perched on his horse, he tasted Simone's undertones of a female in heat. Did the Persian, like Simone, exude the scent of foxes, sticky as molasses, strong as cat piss? Was *he* her soul mate? Although Sabot Noir had an urge to suck her lips as pink as a kitten's nose, as soft as bear paws, although he was needled with jealousy, he came to realize that Simone's animal spirit would not rest until she had had the Persian.

Sabot Noir ceased fidgeting and scratching himself raw. "Maybe the Persian will make you happy. Hurry back. I saw his carriage speed toward the château."

Her heart squeezed for her friend.

Despite his sense of entitlement, he divulged this information as if offering a lump of sugar to his favorite stallion, a carrot to a gelding, or fatty buffalo meat to the winds that carried his mother's spirit.

"Will you forgive me now?" he murmured.

"Yes, my friend, I already have."

A strange plant took root in Sabot Noir's heart, spreading into his limbs, emitting a strong hallucinatory fragrance more potent than sunny fields of barley, freshly watered stables, and copulating foxes. He tossed the lorgnette at her feet. For the first time since he had lost his mother, he laughed aloud.

27

Alphonse, sporting tailcoat and top hat, appeared on the terrace and descended the stairs to welcome Cyrus and his giant into the park. Numerous stone stoves with glowing mouths surrounded Mme Gabrielle as if she were a Zoroastrian goddess. Limoges porcelain cups accented in gold were set for afternoon tea. *Le pâtissier* had prepared sugared almonds, rice cakes, and chickpea cookies.

The oddness of Mme Gabrielle's shock of blue curls, and the choker of beaten silver that coiled around her neck to turn into a snake that lodged in her cleavage, shook Cyrus's brains back into pragmatism. He had accepted her invitation simply because he had failed to purge himself of the girl's perfume. What would his pious Jewish mother think of Simone's wild hair, Françoise's shameless breasts, and Mme Gabrielle's erotic hands? His mother had put up a fierce fight when he had become the private jeweler of a Muslim king. But this was an altogether different matter, a personal affront to his mother, who refused to travel to France because women were lax, men tolerant, and the entire nation corrupt. And it would not matter one bit to her that Simone was the descendant of an observant rabbi.

Despite Cyrus's meticulous research, the Honoré women's pasts had proved elusive, until he was directed by a fellow jeweler named M. Rouge to 13 Rue des Rosiers in the Marais. He had walked straight into Rabbi Abramowicz's synagogue and, it being Sabbath, he was welcomed with psalms and baked goods. He learned that Mme Gabrielle was born in 1853 as Ester Abramowicz, an only daughter who broke free of the Marais. But as to his question regarding her butler, the rabbi had wiped a tear from the corner of his blue eyes and had gone mute like a golem.

The visit to the Marais further convinced Cyrus that Simone was pure and innocent, a descendant of rabbis and the Jewish Ester Abramowicz. Not of courtesans. Still, he would consider this trip a business opportunity. The royal entourage would return to Persia in two weeks. And the Honoré mirage would become just that.

Mme Gabrielle embraced Cyrus in layers of gossamer and perfume of lavender. "Welcome, welcome," she chirped before turning to her butler and gesturing to the giant. "Be a dear, Alphonse, and escort Monsieur inside for supper and refreshment."

"I shall return right away, Madame," Alphonse replied before he led the giant away.

And Mme Gabrielle had no doubt he would. He felt too impassioned regarding the subject at hand to leave it to providence, or to her discretion.

"We are alone here, *cher* Monsieur," Mme Gabrielle said, motioning Cyrus to a seat. "I would like to discuss a matter in private now."

Cyrus's gaze traveled past the manicured hedges, attempting to locate Simone across the magnificent vista of the gardens. She was nowhere to be found.

Peacocks strutted down the slope to congregate around Mme Gabrielle. The aroma of the mint tea she poured transported Cyrus to the teahouse he frequented up the Persian mountains at the outskirts of Tehran, a city at once beautiful and dilapidated.

"The truth, Monsieur Cyrus," Mme Gabrielle said, unfurling her ostrich fan, "is that I am not interested in the bracelet or any other jewelry. In fact, I intend to offer *you* a rare gem you will not find elsewhere." She stroked the fur trim of her gloves, tugged at the tips, and peeled off guipure as if to reveal the priceless jewel in question.

Taking note of the opalescent patina of the famous fingernails, Cyrus was puzzled. Was this woman short of money? Did she intend to sell her personal jewelry?

Mme Gabrielle, who never tired of the awe her hands elicited, laid them in full view on her lap. "I am a frank woman, *mon cher* Monsieur, so I shall come to the point. I have noticed your admiration for Simone—and hers for you. I intend to offer you a great honor, a great honor, indeed, Monsieur.

"The privilege of making love to my virgin granddaughter. But there are certain conditions attached. The first is that you make the experience as enjoyable for her as it will certainly prove to you. The second is that with no further ado you disappear from her life forever. Consider this a transaction that will benefit all of us, but you in particular."

His back stiffened against his chair. His fingers interlocked, the knuckles standing out like white hills. His mind whirled with possibilities and impossibilities. His first reaction was to stand up, and since he had not partaken of the delicacies set on the table, it would not be rude to leave without thanking the hostess. But then he would never know Simone. Nevertheless, he found it tasteless and unacceptable for anyone, especially a grandmother, to hand her granddaughter over in such a humiliating manner. He rose to his feet, turned to his hostess, and bowed. "I regret, Madame, you leave me no choice but to take my leave."

Mme Gabrielle was about to make another strategic move when Simone wrestled her way through the jasmine hedges. She brushed leaves off her mud-caked breeches and picked trapped foliage from her hair. A gash on her shoulder was visible through the ripped fabric of her blouse. One hand resting on her revolver, she marched toward Cyrus. "Do not leave yet, Monsieur, not before my grandmother apologizes for her unacceptable behavior. I could not help overhearing her. To think she would sell her granddaughter in this preposterous manner is beyond explanation."

The grandmother donned her gloves, bunched her skirts, and sailed into the château.

Simone took Cyrus by the hand. "Come, Monsieur, I promise to make it up to you."

28

Despite the scent of hay, civet, and berries, Cyrus was overwhelmed by the increasing hold of Simone's perfume, as she guided him through the park toward the château. In her anger, she was even more charming. Her response to her grandmother had impressed and further endeared her to him. He told himself that in France, not unlike back home, it must be essential for a girl to reserve intimacy for her husband. Then he remembered the calling card Mme Gabrielle gave him in the president's palace, an open invitation tucked in his wallet, ample proof France was a very different world from Persia. He found himself first challenging his mores and beliefs, then persuading himself that Simone would end up a courtesan despite her defiance.

He held her back. "Dear Mademoiselle, I intend to properly court you as befits a lady. But I am not certain I will have time, and I am afraid I will never have a chance to give you all the diamonds you deserve."

"There will be other occasions for diamonds," she whispered, "but never for another first kiss." She lifted herself on her toes and embraced his mouth in hers.

He dug his hand into her hair, her lashes sweeping across his face, her tongue seeking his. He eased her out of his hold. "Good evening for now. I will call upon you tomorrow."

She broke into laughter as she pulled him after her into the foyer. "What's wrong with now?"

He was mesmerized by the photograph at the foot of the Grand Staircase, a life-size version of the calling card in his wallet. Simone in riding breeches, a revolver tucked in her belt, her profile turned away. She rejected the camera as forcefully as the flesh-and-blood Simone rejected the life handed her.

Tugging at his arm, she coaxed him away from her image and led him up the stairs and toward the apartment Mme Gabrielle and Alphonse had prepared for them. Disoriented by her rising scent, his mind a mist of desire, he followed her into a Baudelaire-inspired opus of tempting colors.

She did not stop to wash dried mud off her face, nor care to undress behind the partitions. Raised by the Honoré women, she had few inhibitions to shed. She stepped out of her breeches, pulled her blouse over her head, and exposed the full youth of her proud breasts.

The Persian, discerning certain insolence, even vulgarity in her, had no difficulty shedding his own cultural taboos. He lifted her up in his arms and carried her to the carpet at the foot of the panel where cupids watched over the love-stricken Carmen. Surrounded by nightingales and cucumber bushels, he feasted on her nakedness as if he were breaking a lifelong fast. He drank in the intoxicating perfume of her alabaster skin that intensified with his tongue strokes on the freckles scattered between her pale thighs and higher up where they congregated like amber jewels. Lowering himself on her, he wet his finger in her mouth and stroked the outer shell of her ear. Easing himself into her, he kissed her pain off and swallowed her pleasure sighs. He licked her cheeks clean of mud and tears, loving her neither with the haste of a virgin nor with the nostalgia of age, but with the leisured assurance of a man who did not fear loss.

Her nipples blossomed in his mouth, her thighs warm honey folding about him, embracing the pain of her first time, the warm trickle of blood they washed later at the farthest end of the peacock-shaped lake, laughing and splashing in the water, unaware that Mme Gabrielle observed them from the clover hill, rejoicing that her granddaughter would belong to her, at last.

29

Mme Gabrielle slapped her hand down on the stack of travel documents Simone deposited on her writing desk—passports, Russian and Turkish visas, and a money belt containing Russian, Turkish, and Persian currency. While she had assumed Simone was wrapped up in the first stages of discovery and infatuation, she had gone out and fallen in love right under her sharp nose. To annoy her further, she intended to go to Persia with that jeweler, whose name the grandmother hardly remembered.

The evidence was piled in front of her. A map that traced their passage from Germany through Russia to Baku, and boat passes through the Caspian to the Persian port of Anzali The route was chosen wisely, she had to admit reluctantly, the shortest and easiest rather than the challenging course on horseback through tortuous mountain territory. The Orient Express running from Paris to Constantinople could even be fun if not for the fear of robbers. She had been one of the passengers on board the l'Orient Express , the very first official express train from Compagnie des Wagons-Lits. Being young and ignorant, the suggestion that travelers carry guns and rifles had excited her. Still, she had sat up in the cabin the entire first night, fully awake and with her rifle, which she hoped she had handy to point across her desk at Simone, who confronted her with eyes deeper than brass.

She brought her hand down again, scattering the documents around the desk. "*Non!* Unacceptable. You of all people, Simone! I considered you smarter than this. To turn your back on all this." The all-encompassing wave of her arm indicated the château and the grounds beyond. "I forbid this folly! If you as much as mention Persia again or entertain the thought of seeing that man again, I will take away your books, will not let you attend classes and, if necessary, cut you out of my will."

Rebellious by nature, in the last few weeks Simone had matured into a stubborn woman as calculating and as bold as Mme Gabrielle, whose disapproval she had expected. She challenged her glare with the same level of intensity. "*Grand-mère,* it is a fait accompli, so please give us your blessing."

Mme Gabrielle d'Honoré pressed her refined hand on her enraged heart. "Listen, *chérie.* He is a fine man, yes, good looking, *oui.* Charming, *bien sûr.* But you mistake your infatuation for love. I will not hear of it. You may not rot in a godforsaken Persian kitchen while sewing on the buttons of his fly. You seem to have no reply. Then go! And if you disobey me, you will be left with nothing but your revolver and lace handkerchief.

"And, *chérie,* do not ask my blessing, either. I am far from a saint."

Although her love did not require anyone's blessings, her grandmother's last words sparked an idea, and Simone cast her eyes down as if defeated into consent. She kissed Mme Gabrielle on both cheeks, planted an extra one on her forehead for good measure, and walked out of the *bureau.*

30

Rabbi Abramowicz rocked in the speeding carriage, Alphonse at his side, the coachman whipping the horses into frenzy. The rabbi's red beard, parted in the middle and turned up at the sides like inverted horns, exhibited no sign of gray due to the dye applied for the occasion. The scarlet bow tie around his neck felt like a noose, the brass medals on his lapels heavy, and the cape over his shoulders a burden he could not wait to discard. Assuming that dire circumstances must have warranted such an urgent note from Simone, and that sixteen was an age that demanded diplomacy, he set out to approach her as a friend rather than a voice of authority. Concluding that he had to dress in a manner she would relate to, and ignorant of contemporary fashion, he sought inspiration from a collection of photographs of young, progressive artists. Consequently, he now felt as if he had shed his true skin and squeezed himself into a stranger's.

"Alphonse," the rabbi said, turning to the butler at his side, "even after all these years, I have difficulty accepting Ester's conversion into, into, this . . ." He stammered, at a loss for a term to describe his daughter's lifestyle. Failing to come up with the proper term, and aware that no consolation was forthcoming from Alphonse, he began to pray.

Alphonse, who had learned to tolerate the touch of a Jew, still cringed at the mention of the name Gabrielle was given at birth. The many years in France, and his loyalty and admiration for her, made him question the belief that the touch of every Jew was *najes* and impure as the Koran warned. He had resigned himself to his love of the Jew and the necessity of preparing for the consequences in the next world. But he still struggled to be gracious to the rabbi and mindful of his never-ending sorrow.

The rabbi, frustrated at having to be cordial to the man who had had a part in, if not downright caused, his grief, slapped Alphonse on the back as if to awaken him from a nightmare. "My dear man, do you realize that if I choose to, I can still disown Ester?"

Alphonse continued to stare out the window. He had helped Gabrielle weave her tight web of lies and continued, even now, to hide her past from her daughter and granddaughter. He had become so entangled in the lie that he had difficulty believing that the pious man next to him was indeed Gabrielle's father, who insisted on reincarnating the past and shaking Alphonse's present.

The rabbi waved Simone's note that advised him that a carriage would be dispatched to transport him to the château. She was in dire need of him, she had asserted, red ink emphasizing the urgency of an undisclosed matter, the envelope fixed with Mme Gabrielle's seal. "What could be so urgent?"

"I do not know, Monsieur," Alphonse said. "The ladies do not share."

The rabbi, despite himself, took Alphonse's hand as if to comfort a member of his congregation and, in the process, caused Alphonse added consternation. "My dear old man, you and I both know more about these women than we are ready to own."

∽

Rabbi Abramowicz patted his beard into place, brushed his sleeves clean of the dust of the road, and stepped down from the carriage. He climbed the stairs up to the terrace and entered the foyer, crossing the expanse of marble floors that carried the imprint of his daughter's affectations. Every salon displayed a different motif of marble—cubes that resembled the *dreidel* Ester spun on Hanukkah, mosaic diamonds that shook him to the core because they bore a resemblance to Stars of David, and heart-shaped Verona marble the shade of prohibited ham. He chuckled at the folly of wasting money on stone that had no tangible use but to cover God's fertile earth and on which pompous people stepped, who perhaps never glanced down to appreciate the aesthetic value. Across the wall as he took the stairs to the second floor, "spirit photographs" castigated him. His daughter was fond of pointing out that even their dead ancestors had moved into Château Gabrielle to present themselves in family photographs so as to enjoy the peaceful ambience. These were far from family pictures, the rabbi sighed. His daughter had so thoroughly re-created her history that the only recognizable faces in the black-and-white photographs were Ester, Françoise, Simone, and himself—albeit forever slimmer, more elegant, his yarmulke absent, his pe'ot metamorphosed into smartly clipped sideburns.

Sprinting up the stairs as if he were a young gentleman caller rather than a sixty-eight-year-old rabbi, he called out, "Simone! Lovely Simone!" His voice echoed against the high ceilings and amplified his baritone, attracting curious servants from all corners of the house.

Mme Gabrielle peered out the door of her boudoir. Hardly recognizing the debonair figure of her father, she pursed her lips and shut the door behind her. What was her father up to? It was rather unusual for him to come uninvited and without notice. In fact, he had repeatedly refused her invitations to dinner. And why did he summon Simone as if he were accompanying her to a masquerade?

Simone, having caught sight of the carriage that transported her great-grandfather, abandoned her horse in the stables and ran into the château. Unable to control her amusement at the peculiar character who, despite his efforts, was still a rabbi, she tiptoed from behind, grabbed him from the back, and hugged him.

"*Alors!*" he cried out, "You nearly stopped my rusty heart."

"Nice topcoat. Chic bow tie." She flicked the medals on his lapel. "What's your rank? Joined the army, Papa?"

"Ah! *Ma chère,* lovely girl, your old man still holds some tricks up his sleeve. Isn't that why you summoned me with such fanfare? Red ink, and then Alphonse in person to fetch me. It must be important. Let's go out to enjoy the wonderful sun."

She accepted his arm but continued to climb up the stairs. She would not subject him to the *parc* with its fountain mermaids spewing water from between their legs and the clover hill with its galleries of sensual gloves and obscene portraits revealing Mme Gabrielle's most intimate horrors. Before she had occasion to coax him up to the landing, she was overwhelmed by another concern. What if he found the concept of her abandoning home for a Persian as unacceptable as his daughter did? He had never concealed his dislike of Alphonse and his country. "Fine, Papa," she said, turning around and following him down the stairs. "If you prefer, we will go outside."

She led him past the lake where she and Cyrus had bathed some days ago. Feeling wicked and corrupt, she guided her great-grandfather toward the clover hill.

He labored up the hill, finding the climb taxing but intent on holding fast to the youthful image adopted for the day. "Shoo!" he scolded a peacock that pecked at his cape, gathering the hem under his arm and continuing his ascent. "Where are we going, *ma chère*? Are these your grandmother's infamous galleries up there?"

She slowed, waiting for him to catch up. "Yes, Papa, they are. I know you have not seen them. I know it is not proper, and I apologize for bringing you here." Her mind whirled with potential arguments, with guilt, with her beloved great-grandfather's probable reaction to his daughter's life put on naked view.

He stopped at the top to catch his breath, stunned at the beauty of the flower-drenched galleries and their alarming decadence. "No, Simone, I refuse to go in."

"Please," she begged. "This once, for me."

"This is inappropriate."

"Yes, and cruel of me, but I have no recourse. Please, Papa, my future is at stake. And you won't realize why until you see the galleries for yourself."

He took a deep breath. Ester had never stopped inflicting painful surprises upon him, but it might prove otherwise with his adored granddaughter. He allowed himself to be steered into the gallery Simone considered the least offensive of the three: the gallery of kumquats.

Capes, foulards, and fans swayed on display. Turquoise velvet, sheer netting, leopard fur, and gossamer capes with feathers and nettings dyed the same shades. Swan, ostrich, and even osprey fans from beyond the edges of which Mme Gabrielle's eyes scintillated like jewels. *Drap d'or* shawls like liquid gold with corresponding diaphanous foulards as airy as snowflakes cascaded from branches.

The rabbi gazed around in wonder, touched the feathered tip of a fan, stealing his hand away as if electrocuted. He bent from the knees, craned his neck, and without touching, checked a white fan from the back to discover what it was made of. Perceiving the spines of feathers in back, he gave out a startled cry. "What poor bird was plucked for this?"

"You have no idea," Simone muttered in embarrassment. "So many swans, peacocks, and other dear birds are sacrificed for one fan—some plucked alive for healthier feathers." She removed the fan and startled the rabbi further by fluttering it. "Touch, it feels like human hair. *Grand-mère* flirts through the two slits."

The rabbi took the fan from Simone and, finding the sensation of its feathers quiet strange, dropped it like scorching sin.

Simone picked up the fan and blew on it to dust it off, put it back, and stepped aside to make sure it was properly replaced.

The rabbi, mesmerized by such exotic feathers and colors, felt uncomfortable at the revelation of this facet of his daughter's life. He turned on his heels and walked out.

"For my sake, bear with me just a little longer," Simone said, as much to herself as to him.

He sighed, closing his eyes, turning away from the gallery of kumquats, and entering the museum dedicated to gloves. His first reaction was surprise at Ester's need for so many pairs of gloves. Were these tools of her profession, and if so, why? Was the naked hand not more seductive than fabric, fur, and leather? His daughter concealed her hands the same way she concealed her past. But her hands, like her past, were beautiful. Nothing to be ashamed of. He realized with despair that his daughter was even more of a stranger than he had imagined.

Simone, too, did not comprehend why a contingent of prominent men made pilgrimages up the clover hill to pay homage to Mme Gabrielle's legendary hands. Gloves of black lace with tiny silk bows and diamond studs, golden tulle laced up to the elbow, camel kidskin with satin lining that flopped around her wrists, chinchilla mittens, and tip-cut organza that revealed fingernails as delicious as bonbons. She donned a pair of peek-a-boo gloves and imitating the seductive ballet of her grandmother's fingers, swept the glove under the rabbi's nose.

"Shoo, shoo!" He waved away the improper feel of velour and the scent of his daughter's perfume. "Pssht! What is this? What use for gloves with holes? Not even to keep warm in winter. Even Sara the beggar would not wear these *schmattehs*! Take them off, Simone, I insist. Right away!"

Simone wiggled her fingers out of the gloves and placed them back on the shelf, reassessing her plan. Did she have the heart to expose the rabbi to portraits of his daughter's corporeal poses with her lovers? The fans had disturbed him, the gloves clearly offended him. Still, they were here now, and she must forge ahead.

"Come! Come!" she said as if she were taking him to the Garden of Eden.

He did not budge. The gloves and fans had shocked him into paralysis. The concept of his daughter surrounded by such indecency broke him down. He did not intend to be humiliated further. "I have seen enough. You go in if you have to, Simone."

She rested her head on his shoulder, her sobs escaping. "I am sorry. I should not have. I will call for the carriage to take you home."

"You have not told me why you summoned me in the first place," he said, unable to bear her tears.

"I have caused you enough pain."

"All right, all right, you win. Show me this one, too, if it will stop your tears. But promise it will be the last."

They stood at the threshold of the gallery, holding each other by the hand, Simone as horrified as the rabbi. He fished a large handkerchief out of his pocket and wiped his damp forehead. Was this true, this spectacle that ambushed him? Had his daughter bedded all these men? What other transgressions had his Ester, the shy little girl who had listened to his stories, committed in her life?

He was about to lower his eyes when he saw a most prominently displayed portrait, and his stunned stare riveted to it. Did his eyes deceive him? Was his daughter so far gone, so mired in disgrace, that she would establish a relationship with the notorious Rasputin? The rabbi fell down on his knees in front of the image of his naked daughter in Rasputin's arms.

Simone knelt beside him, their sobs reverberating about the pergola. "I apologize, *Grand-père*. Will you ever forgive me for doing this to you? But you had to see my future."

They walked out to Mme Gabrielle's rattan chaise longue, sat side by side, and gazed into the lavender horizon peppered with chestnut trees.

He released the pe'ot he had tucked behind his ears. He who believed in the *tikkun olam*—repairing his world—had initiated a series of blunders that had fostered nothing but sinful indulgence. "*Ma pauvre chérie,* to have a great-grandfather like me, from the shtetl, alienated from everyone and everything. This is why I did not want Ester to be an outsider like me. But I never imagined she would stray this far." He indicated the galleries as he twisted a side curl around his finger. "I beg of you, Simone, to be aware of your surroundings, sniff the air and identify the various shades of greed and lust you must avoid."

"Precisely, *Grand-père,* this is why you had to observe this for yourself."

"Lust such as this poisons the soul. Passion that is the result of matrimonial love is desirable, but one created by corruption such as we observed in there must be avoided at all cost."

"Yes. This is why you must to talk to *Grand-mère*. Convince her that I deserve a different future. I am in love, Papa, with a wonderful Persian man. I plan to go to Persia with him."

"Now, now, wait a minute, my lovely. A Persian! Where in the world did you meet a Persian? This is quite startling. Not at all what I expected. Please do not cry again. Are you truly in love, or maybe curious? Have Frenchmen disappeared into our sewers such that you get involved with a Persian?"

"What's the use of explaining?" she said, holding on to the secure warmth of his eyes. "Like everyone else, you will not understand."

"Ah! Now I am like everyone else?" He released her hand, pretending offense. "Come! Come! What do you know about this backward desert, Persia? What do you know about this man? Will you give up your family? Did you think of the consequences? Would you banish yourself to a backward place of sheepskin-clad nomads?"

"Yes, because there I might have a chance at a different life. Or else temptation and *Grand-mère*'s influence will turn me into an adornment on the arm of one man or another, a *grande horizontale.*"

The rabbi listened not only to Simone but also to his heart, which refused to settle. He was aware of his daughter's intention to preserve her dynasty, aware that Françoise was incapable of managing such wealth, and aware that Simone was the anticipated heir. He stared into his lap as if the answer were inscribed there.

She squeezed his hand. "In any case, *Grand-père*, what future do I, the illegitimate daughter of a Bavarian perfumer, have in Paris?"

Rabbi Abramowicz struggled with his own failures. He had sinned in the face of the high heavens and the low earth. He had raised a daughter who had sprung off like an arrow from his bow and had landed in the eye of immorality. He might not have accepted but neither had he forcefully voiced his disapproval of Ester's way of living because he was a coward, afraid of losing her affection. Every single morning and night, when he recited the Shema, he struggled with his conscience. Did encouraging Ester to go out and experience life push her overboard? Would she have returned home if he had threatened to disown her? Should he not have stood his ground and fought with his every breath and with the last drop of his Jewish blood?

Now, at last, he was presented with the chance to redeem himself. He would talk sense into his daughter even if he lost her, even if forced to lie—small price to pay to safeguard Simone's integrity. He rested his hand on her head and recited the blessing of Kohanim—a great-grandfather's blessing upon his beloved granddaughter. *"Yevarekha Adonai v'ishmerekah. Yaer Adonai panav eleikha veikoneka."* May the Lord bless you and keep you safe. May the Lord's countenance shine upon you.

"Go, my child. Follow your dreams wherever they take you as long as it is away from here."

31

❧

Paris
Winter 1901

Simone left Persia fifteen days after the northern lights heralded the death of Cyrus. That night, unbeknownst to her, the people of Tehran were paralyzed by fear of the previously unobserved phenomenon of the aurora borealis, the hissing sky snakes, a chorus of soothsayers portending disaster.

Jews whispered among themselves that the vision blazing across the firmament warned of impending pogroms. Muslim fundamentalists wailed that the fires in heaven proved that infidels were congregating around the world and that the great Persian Empire would be attacked—this time, with far worse consequences than the Arab and Mongol invasions. Zoroastrians, certain that the forces of good and evil were colliding in the heavens, rejoiced at the inevitable outcome that the righteous prophet Ahura Mazdah would come to rule again.

To Simone, the aurora borealis had meant nothing. But Cyrus's numerous attempts to warn her from somewhere else had taken their toll. She decided to leave Persia before another catastrophe had a chance to develop.

She embarked on the first leg of her trip to France on board a postal carriage. After numerous stops for the coachman to puff on an opium pipe, Tehran was mercifully left behind, and she arrived at Anzali on the southwest coast of the Caspian Sea. From there, a Russian vessel crammed with sweating bodies and sun-baked faces, restless children, and nursing infants set off for Baku with hundreds of grumbling souls, whose blistering skins peeled off like old paint. The ship foamed ahead, misting her cheeks with tears. Hot winds from the south rushed into a purple horizon as she tried to vomit her grief into the sea. She did not succeed. Unwilling to postpone her journey, she immediately boarded a train from Baku to Tiflis, St. Petersburg, Warsaw, and finally Hamburg to arrive in Paris on a clear evening. A sky so lively, it seemed to levitate an arm's length overhead.

Only then, back in the familiar streets of her city, did she realize that while her red hair and white complexion had attracted attention and caused all sorts of people to stare her up and down, neither her belongings nor the handbag with the red diamonds had been inspected at the numerous checkpoints.

Were there people watching over her, assuring her safety, *Shaunce Banou*?

Françoise and Mme Gabrielle welcomed her with silent embraces, curtailed curiosity, and murmured condolences. She wondered if they had embraced her as their Simone or the foreigner she had become. When she told them she needed time to mend, they left her alone. Alphonse handed her a *Tehillim* from her great-grandfather, the mourner's prayer marked with a silver bookmark.

She settled into the Valley of Civet Cats, in the apartment where Cyrus had first loved her, and dropped wide-eyed on the rosewood bed. She turned away from her image in the bamboo-framed mirrors on either side. The cucumber bushels on the wall panels were reminders of the vines Cyrus had unsuccessfully tried to cultivate on the mountain. Baudelaire's "Invitation to a Voyage," her grandmother's attempt to initiate her into the Honoré lifestyle, had led to tragedy. Was her mother right, after all? Was love a woman's greatest downfall, marriage an alliance that legitimized grief?

Her wedding night was forever stamped into the rest of her life. The two of them in white. Beard their best man and bridesmaid in one. The sky their nuptial canopy, the crisp-scented air more intoxicating than the wine Beard smuggled up the mountains. Despite being Muslim, Beard, their improvised rabbi, married them with recitation of poetry. Later, wrapped in sheepskin, her skin prickled with goose bumps, she took shelter in her husband's arms, their sole spectator a mountain lion.

Now she opened a trunk and unpacked the minimum essentials—nightgown, underwear, combs, and riding breeches she had worn in Persia when Cyrus had introduced her to the mountains on horseback. She placed his tallit bag on the mantelpiece above the fireplace. Despite Beard's warning that excessive luggage would be an impediment and an invitation to robbers, more containers with Cyrus's belongings were scattered about the room.

She felt the weight of the pouch of red diamonds, slipped it under the mattress. So light. Untouchable blood money. And in her left earlobe, Cyrus's diamond had found a new home.

She leaned out the window to gaze at the château's park. From the same window, Cyrus had discovered the clover hill bathed in the sepia glow of delicious sins. She had shared his vision then, but the hill whirled in ash clouds now, the galleries ghostly against the silhouette of the Civet Cats Hills. Nothing but manicured hedges and artificiality. Would her great-grandfather's magic, the *Tehillim* with their psalms, bring back a semblance of normalcy into her days?

She riffled through one of the containers that held her belongings and selected two outfits she had worn to Beard's Café—wool skirts, brown sweater, a long-sleeved coat, and opaque stockings. She tossed them into the fireplace and watched them sizzle, curl into gray wisps and hiss into nothing.

She spooled out one colorful negligee after another—orange, gold, violet—held them up to the light, draped lace and satin about her shoulders, folded them around her waist, and let them fall down her thighs and ankles. Raising the hems, she inhaled his scent of love and lust woven into the fabrics. Scissoring off the top of a negligee, she held the cut-off material at the waist and ripped the rest. Sorting out diaphanous nothings, one after the other, she tore them with her hands, teeth, and scissors, cut them into strips, shredding each carefully and methodically. A ritual to commemorate an end.

She turned her back on the strips of gauze, grosgrain, and gossamer piled high. Releasing the black velvet ribbon from her hair, she slipped Cyrus's wedding band off her finger, strung the ribbon through the loop, and tied it around her neck. She touched his earring—*your delicious earlobes,* he murmured. And for him, she kept the earring on.

She would bury Cyrus's Simone, his sensual, sexual woman. She would close that chapter of her life forever. She would never allow another man her precious vulnerability. Never grant another man the intimacy she had shared with Cyrus.

Appraising herself in the mirror, the freckled pallor of her shoulders, the breasts fuller after her aborted pregnancy, she saw herself rolling around in sheets and pillows, enveloped in silk, moist and receptive, worshipped as no woman ever was. They were lovely, those hours behind closed doors with him, when she had unleashed her sexuality, plump with desire, wanted and adored. Stroking containers of his belongings, she opened one. She chose the white shirt he wore in a world of somber blackness. She stretched out upon it, enveloped herself in it atop the bed. Never reprimanding herself for wanting him so soon after his absence, for stroking herself with fingers familiar with the geography of her body, she took herself to the end and fell into exhausted sleep.

32

After five sleepless nights and days with little appetite, except for a glass or two of wine, and overwhelmed by the obsessive need to satisfy herself, as if to exorcise her body of Cyrus, she had slept at last.

Clasping a book of vellum leaves bound in brocade, Alphonse hovered over her like one of her grandmother's ghosts. Unable to come up with the proper conciliatory words, he placed a chocolate-filled Sèvres goblet and a bowl of fruit at the bedside. He opened the book he held to an earmarked section and laid it on the windowsill. "Your grandmother wants you to read this. You are terribly pale, Simone, you must eat something."

"*Merci,* maybe later."

"Do you need anything at all? Tell me, ask for something to make you feel better. I feel helpless."

"I feel the same way, helpless and hopeless."

Alphonse lowered his head and walked out the door.

Simone began to read Mme Gabrielle's flamboyant handwriting, which curled across the earmarked pages like gilded ballerinas.

∾

My darling Simone, when I first embarked on documenting my memoirs, I intended to hand them to you after you conceded to carry the Honoré mantle. But difficult times demand drastic measures. I have decided to tell you about the war I survived in the hope it will give you strength as you wage a battle of your own. Maybe exposing that part of my past will help speed your own healing. Maybe my story will make you appreciate why my fate took the turn it did. Maybe you will come to value the lifestyle you were afforded. And if nothing else, you will know that you are not alone.

Ma chérie, war is a pitiless beast. Especially for a young girl such as I was—adored by her magical father and raised in a miraculous house of dream-fed roses and love-soaked barrels of wine that held the Marais in their intoxicating grip.

Assaulted by the Franco-Prussian War, suddenly, instead of the soothing gurgle of fermenting wine, I was confronted by the rumble of hunger. Instead of Papa's perfume of orange blossoms, the acrid stench of gunpowder seeped through the window cracks. Instead of the comforting warmth of melting butter and burnt sugar, of freshly baked éclairs and Napoleon tarts, icicles formed in our veins.

And Papa's warm eyes, whose gaze had once sent my mother into a flurry of complaints over the curdling of her crème brûlée and the souring of wines in barrels, turned into bleak wells.

The stench of war in my nostrils and the growl of hunger in my belly, I walked from one local grocer to another searching for a piece of rotten fruit, a giblet, or a bare chicken bone for potato soup, if I was lucky. The landscape was shrouded in gray smoke, and nothing could be found in food stalls. What was most unsettling was the cloud of hopelessness that levitated above the Marais.

Two children ran past me. I followed, as they seemed to be chasing a ball and the thought of them engaged in a game gave me a glimmer of hope. They scuttled along, their thin legs moving like the puppets in the shows Papa organized on the feast of Purim. One of the boys stopped and waited for the other to catch up. Their skeletal forms scurried into the putrid duct leading into a sewer.

They were chasing rats to eat.

The grief I had concealed from my family flowed down my face. I wiped tears with my sleeves, my skirt, the back of my hand, freeing the loud sobs I had locked away for far too long. Torn by the guilt of having enough money to purchase a piece of rotten cabbage for soup while children caught rats in stinking sewers, I stood undecided as to where to go next.

A young girl, dark circles framing sunken eyes, approached a pedestrian farther down the road. The vision of his tall silhouette remains sharp in my memory, chère Simone; you will know why when you come to the last pages. He was an unusual and refreshing sight against the black-stained horizon of my neighborhood, a specter from a better world. In a wide-lapeled suit and silk cravat, he carried himself with grace, an aristocrat lost in the Marais. And then, the girl's shrill, pubescent voice yanked me back to my reality. "Un centime, s'il vous plaît, pour acheter du pain pour ma famille. Alors, j'irai avec vous." She was offering the gentleman her body in exchange for a loaf of bread for her family.

Without the slightest hesitation, he dug his fingers into his pocket and took out a fistful of coins, many more than I had seen at one time since the beginning of the Franco-Prussian War. He dropped them in her hand, sending her away with a kind pat on her back.

I clutched my stomach, bent over, and vomited my grief, hunger, and despair onto the roadside. His large, beautiful hands upon my shoulders sent me into panic. His intense eyes gazed down at me from his impressive height. "Are you sick?" he asked with a peculiar accent. "Are you, maybe, hungry?"

I quickly straightened up, wiped my mouth clean, and readjusted a semblance of pride across my face. "Yes," I said, shocked at the confession and embarrassed at the sour smell emanating from me.

"Mohammed, a native of Esfahan," he said, offering his hand in a patrician manner. "May I have the honor of inviting Mademoiselle to dinner?"

Despite my silence and awestruck expression, or because of it, he later confessed, he garnered the courage to take me by the arm and walk me away from the nearby sewers. We crossed the Rue des Rosiers, past Moses Kosher Butchery, Sabbath Bagels, and Goldstein Brothers Delicatessen, while he recounted fascinating details of his journey to France. He had traveled by train from Tehran to Tabriz, Badkoubeh, and Tiflis, then to Moscow by boat, and by horseback and coach to France.

"I left my hometown of Esfahan more than five months ago," he said, "in protest of the Qajar's pro-British policy. I could not bear to watch the shah sell my country and my faith to a ruthless empire." He looked down at me and smiled, his broad forehead widening further. "I survived floods, earthquakes, and highway robbers to come to you."

And I smiled back. I found it charming that he lied with such candor and ease, cared for his birthplace as much as I cared for mine, and considered Esfahan, which I had never heard of or even seen on maps, as "half the universe." His noble manner, the glamorous account of his trip, his chance encounter with me, and his pocketful of coins made him a hero and savior.

He walked me out of the Marais, straight into the heart of Paris and into a high-class boutique, where he bought me silk stockings and a crepe de chine gown an empress would have envied. He took me to a restaurant that served a complete menu with coeur d'artichaut, *fois* gras, noisette d'agneau, *and* pêche flambée. *There were many such meals and many more gifts to come. The best way I might explain our relationship is that Mohammed fell in love with me, and I fell in need with him. Throughout those years, our relationship, Mohammed's and mine, vacillated from that of lovers to trusted friends. We anchored each other. We remained indispensable to one another.*

Mohammed at my side, I plunged into Parisian society. My main concern during those first months was to save my family from starvation and death. And I did, as Mohammed developed a willingness to spend his wealth on me and my family.

We endured the cold winters of 1870 and '71, Mohammed and I, and reveled in the arrival of the Third Republic as Paris began to recover. I fell in love with a Paris that came back to life after the war. A Paris that reemerged with her voluptuous beauty intact to reluctantly lower her social barricades and allow me a taste of her dazzling decadence. I pursued pleasure and style, seeking to be part of le beau monde—the beautiful world and the fashionable society. I frequented the opera and les grands *boulevards and their outdoor cafés, engaged in discussions with the bohemians, artists, and libertines of Montmartre and Montparnasse.*

But even that did not suffice. I wished for fame and power. I wanted to own horses and cabriolets, and a château in my name. I wanted to drench myself in jewelry, dictate each season's fashion, and be crowned the grande dame of Paris.

I took wealthy, influential lovers with gilded uniforms and upturned noses. I frequented salons particulières *with kings and counts. And I drowned myself further in their excesses. I wanted to possess a wealth so great that wars and plagues could never rob or outlast it.*

Mohammed, on the other hand, was stunned by the unfolding events he encountered and saddened by the profound interior change I experienced. He was content at my side. He did not want more. He did not understand my propensity for careless abandon, the effect of the war on me, or my determination to remain independent, not only of him but of anything or anyone who might limit my freedom.

Ma chère Simone, now you know more about where I come from and who you can depend on at this difficult time. Your great-grandfather will always cast his magic upon you. The soul of your great-grandmother, whose heart was broken by the Franco-Prussian War, will always hover above you. Your grandfather, Mohammed, whom you have known as Alphonse, is a generous-hearted man with strong values who will continue to inject our lives with a healthy dose of realism. I will not elaborate beyond the little you know about your father. Men such as he are better left to providence. And your mother, Françoise, will enrich your life with her eternal joie de vivre. I love her more than life itself, but you are the kernel that has bloomed into a sturdy tree.

Shake yourself out of mourning. The survival of the Honoré name depends on you.

❦

Alphonse! Her grandfather! The revelation did not shock as much as surprise Simone. She should have guessed the truth earlier. To her, he was always a father figure on a par with her great-grandfather. No longer the illegitimate offspring of a de-spicable nobody, she now had a flesh-and-blood grandfather. Sturdy roots to survive future storms.

Despite Mme Gabrielle's markings, indicating which pages she should read, starved for more and enjoying her new-found status, Simone turned to another page.

A cup of *chocolat* in one hand and *jus de pamplemousse* in the other, Alphonse appeared at the threshold.

"Mohammed," Simone whispered and walked into his arms.

"My child, my sweet child," he murmured, hot chocolate spilling on one hand, grapefruit juice on the other. He set the refreshments down after Simone released him to pass her hands over the contours of his face, as if to verify the miracle of his existence.

"Come, my child, sit next to me. There's more to know, is-sues your *grand-mère,* bless her heart, cannot bring herself to confess, even to her memoirs. Have some *chocolat* while I speak. After your birth, your grandmother and I recorded a certificate of our secret marriage at the registrar's office, nam-ing you and Françoise our daughters. We believed that proof of legitimate parents would free you to operate within France's social hierarchy."

"That makes Françoise my sister," Simone said.

"On paper, yes; in reality she is your mother."

"And you are my father on paper and my grandfather by blood."

"Yes. As you see, around the Valley of Civet Cats things rarely are what they seem. Gabrielle, as you know, is a Jew and the daughter of a Polish rabbi, but she considers herself a French empress and you heir to her throne."

"An unlikely heir," Simone sighed.

"Yes, admittedly, our dear Gabrielle harbors elusive hopes of future grandeur for you. Still, as a family we all need to make concessions. I am doing my continuing share for your grandmother. Since she did not want to attach herself to anyone, wanted to be noticed for who she was, I became her butler. I also remained at her side to be close to my daughter, and then you. I kept my word to conceal my identity from society and even you and my daughter. And now I am doing everything in my power to ease the anxiety her ever-multiplying spirits instigate. She, I am certain, must often wonder how and why she ended up, and still remains, loyal to a Muslim from Esfahan. Even Françoise, with her endearingly vague temperament, appreciates the perils her mother suffered to become a self-made woman in a world where girls are assigned their place in society at birth. You, too, Simone, should learn to appreciate your grandmother and even learn from her as you find your own path in the world."

33

Mme Gabrielle pulled aside the curtains and flung open the windowpanes. Françoise fell into a comfortable chair. Five days was long enough for Simone to lock herself in her apartment, both women had concluded, and it was high time she faced the world—if not on her own, then with some assistance.

"Up! Up!" Mme Gabrielle chirped. "It is afternoon already. It would do you good, *ma chère,* to go out for a ride with Sabot Noir. He has always had a way of lifting your spirits."

Simone rubbed her eyes against the harsh light from the window. Despite being light-headed and not at all certain what day of the week it was, she would not mind a ride around the valley.

A trace of absinthe on her breath, Mme Gabrielle enfolded Simone in her scents of violet and powder. "Now that you have read my story, *chérie,* do you agree that all is not lost? Now collect yourself and get dressed. I will have Sabot Noir prepare a sure-footed mare."

"*Grand-mère,*" Simone whispered, "you once said that I, like you, have special eyes and ears to see and hear spirits. But Cyrus has not revealed himself to me."

"It is too early, *chérie*. Ghosts don't like to approach mourning relatives. It is too painful to them. In time, when you are ready, he will come to you," Mme Gabrielle replied, and with Günter's warning triggering a volcanic heartburn, she sailed out to conduct her séance.

Françoise rose to her feet and blew air through her mouth, sending Simone a kiss across the room. "I am terribly sorry about Cyrus. I had prayed for this love affair to work out for you. But love is always a pain, *chérie*. Now pick yourself up and move on with the rest of your life."

"I will, after I find out what happened to Cyrus."

"Is this truly necessary, Sweetfire? Do you have to torture yourself further?" The shards of anger in her daughter's eyes startled Françoise. "As always, you will do what you need to, I am certain, but do take care of yourself. Don't become another victim of love." She tossed back her fabulous hair and prepared to leave.

"Mama," Simone said, jumping out of bed, "don't go yet. Please. I need your advice."

Françoise's eyes swiveled to the right and left as if searching for another individual her daughter might be addressing. "Mine?" she asked.

"Yes, yours, but I owe you an apology first. I was young when I left for Persia. I refused to listen to you then, to respect your wisdom. I promise to be a diligent student now."

"*Je suis choquée!* What in the world could I teach you?"

Cheeks flushed, Simone glanced down. Her mother could teach her how to tap into men's vulnerabilities, how to make them receptive to her questions. Afraid of becoming undone, she met her mother's puzzled gaze. "Teach me how to satisfy a man without . . ."

"Well, Sweetfire, what exactly do you want?" Françoise

asked, adjusting her pearls. "You must never be ashamed of pleasuring a man."

"I want to know how to please," Simone murmured, "without allowing penetration."

Françoise turned on her delicate feet, her chiffon skirts foaming around her ankles as she stepped out of them. She lounged across sheets that had inherited Simone's perfume. Lifting a strawberry from the urn Alphonse had placed on the side table, she licked the shell to a glistening sheen, sucked on the melting flesh in her mouth. Her head thrown back, she demonstrated the fruit's journey down her throat, dropped the stem in a china goblet, her small finger wiping remnants of red from the corners of her mouth. "Your first lesson, *chérie,* is to enjoy your fruits."

Simone followed the curve of her mother's white throat, the stroke of dainty fingers at the corners of her mouth, the glide of her tongue across swollen lips. She was left with the awkward sense of having requested a favor she might regret. Captivated by the sensual dance of Françoise's mouth, Simone remembered a time when she was mortified at the sight of her mother thrusting a banana down her own throat. Her world had changed now. She was a changed woman. So much had transpired in less than two years since Cyrus had descended from the president's carriage, tapped his silver-tipped cane on the steps, and entered Château Gabrielle. Love had chosen to bless her, but not for long. Its flight had frayed the edges of her youth, left her with cynicism befitting a much older woman.

"Sex is an art. You want him to become mad with desire but never to find out what struck him. To achieve this, hold him in abeyance as long as possible—and do not give me that look, you know what I mean. Do not let him ejaculate. Keep him in a state of arousal, the longer the better. The more energy a man expends minding his baton, the more brain cells he burns in the process, making it easier to manipulate him. So, how do you keep him in this state? By arousing with your eyes, breath, toes—yes, toes are erotic, too. Then promise such sensual adventures, promise with such shameless innocence, that he will do everything in his power to control himself because the end promises to be more exciting than the journey."

Françoise gestured toward the velvet ribbon strung through Cyrus's wedding ring. "And replace this with pearls. Men gravitate to the opalescent roundness of pearls."

Simone's hand sprang to her neck, holding on to Cyrus's wedding band. The glare in her eyes forbade further discussion.

Françoise dangled a bunch of cherries from their stems. "Cherries are named after the Turkish town of Cerasus. They are the reason men seek women with 'lips like cherries.' " She rolled one in her mouth, the leisurely sway of her jaw demonstrating the graceful art of enjoying the nectar. "Do you know that Catherine de' Medici was considered scandalous for the way she ate artichokes? She was an exceptional woman, if a bit mercurial. She knew how to portray the image of a forbidden fruit, a jewel that might be possessed through great danger and cost. This is why an army of men—apart from horses—constantly licked her toes." A slender arm reached out, plucking a chocolate from the Sèvres goblet. "Undisputed queen of aphrodisiacs. Nourishment of the gods. Do not trust a woman who dislikes chocolate." She hugged the dark sweet in her mouth, picked another chocolate and revealed the center. "*Chérie*, look at the pink filling. Sumptuously lickable."

"Mama, it would certainly take more than chocolate to make a man give in to my most preposterous wishes."

"I am getting there, Sweetfire. Foreplay is more important than the actual play and must never be dismissed."

"This is the problem," Simone retorted. "Foreplay leads to penetration, and I intend to avoid that."

"What you must really avoid, *chérie,* is a kiss. Considerably more intimate than penetration and consequently more dangerous."

"Especially *my* kiss, which would poison any man."

"I am not concerned about the men, *you* are my concern. Now try to be patient and listen. It is vital to live up to a man's expectations. Remember the three magical words that swell a man's loins: 'I am yours.' And do not be afraid to break the rules and to use your earthy allure, which men find arousing. Never look down, but startle with your shameless stare. And do not forget the element of surprise. It is an important aphrodisiac.

"Now, to your main concern. Sex, contrary to what you might think, is not primarily a physical act but an illusion, *chérie,* the switching of fact with fancy created by witty women such as us. With the help of the finest silks and gossamers wrapped around your hands, under your armpits, across your buttocks, and between your legs as camouflage, you can create such an effective illusion he would never know, or care, about penetration, since he would have just experienced his most explosive orgasms. The truth is that in the throes of passion, a man is unable to differentiate between the soft touch of silk and inner thighs, the grip of muslin and the vagina."

Simone slid to the edge of the chair. This suggestion might be promising, even practical.

Françoise lifted herself from the ocean of satin, fluffed pillows behind, two pink pearls at the tips of her breasts. "Nearly everything I have told you so far might have been practiced, now and then, by one or another clever woman. But not what I shall reveal next. This is why men find me brilliantly ruinous. And the reason women consider me a sorceress. I never revealed this to anyone, not even to Mama.

"I have detected an additional sensual and sensory organ in the male anatomy. I call it the lust vein. It originates at the lowest part of the spine, where desire rests, and curves up to

the neck and the base of the brain, where illusions are created. Come, darling, lie on your back, and I will demonstrate
how you can locate the male lust vein, massage and awaken
his senses, and in the process enslave, without becoming a
slave."

34

Simone called for a meeting of the Honoré women.

Once again, mirrors were polished to a high sheen and maids in starched uniforms fixed flowers in their chignons. Once again, stableboys woke at the crack of dawn to groom horses and sponge down the stables. And in the excitement, Sabot Noir, forgotten and sulking, conspired to draw Simone's attention.

Françoise was instructed to retire early the night before. And Alphonse diluted Mme Gabrielle's afternoon absinthe. The servants prepared the Salon of *Women of Algiers,* a room named after Delacroix's celebrated painting. Here, Mme Gabrielle welcomed influential suitors to display her most cherished possession on an enamel pedestal.

The Honoré women entered the salon. Simone locked the doors behind them. Servants loitered around, hoping to catch a word or two that would reveal the reason for such tight secrecy.

"Have either of you come across a character known as Monsieur Rouge, or a certain Monsieur Amir?" Simone asked.

The two women gazed at one another, first with puzzlement, then with sparked memory. "Monsieur Rouge—yes, him I know," Françoise replied. "He is a *diamantaire.* His love affair with red diamonds is legendary. I had an interesting and not en-

tirely profitable encounter with him. At the time, he was searching for a saint, which I am not. And he is obsessed with redheads, which I am not. You, on the other hand, are. You can use
his obsession to your benefit as he is connected to most, if not
all, diamond merchants. I hear he's put a rare five-carat diamond on sale. But I must warn you. His home is off-limits to all
his women. Be prepared for that."

"I am prepared for anything," Simone replied. "And you,
Grand-mère, have you heard of a Monsieur Amir?"

"I am not certain," Mme Gabrielle mused.

At that moment, the ghost of Dr. Jacques Mercier material-
ized from behind Delacroix's painting. He tickled her soles and
swirled at her feet. Finding his vantage inappropriate, he stumbled up to squeeze between her breasts. A pest of a dwarf, he
constantly prescribed outlandish remedies to fortify her memory. Now, he insisted she consume a drink of *citron pressé* laced
with darkling beetles to strengthen her memory.

"Now that I think about it, *chérie,* I did have a fleeting liaison
with Monsieur Amir." At that, the triumphant dwarf popped his
head out of her cleavage. She squeezed her breasts together to
choke his chuckle. "I don't know much about his profession, so I
can't help you there. Although he did confess to loving his frigid
wife. He so wished she demonstrated some of my intellect and
passion. You could use his unhappy marriage to your benefit and
with a bit of skill drag out every one of his dearest secrets. You, on
the other hand, must never reveal your wiles, because their under-
lying simplicity invariably disappoints men. By the way, *chérie,*
would you be introducing yourself to these men as an Honoré?"

"How else, but as your granddaughter? This pleases you,
doesn't it?"

"Yes, it does, enormously. Don't be angry, *chérie, c'est pour
rire,* allow your grandmother a moment of diversion. You are
not ready now, of course, but one day you will be. On that day,
ma chère, although you must seem malleable like dough, you
must remain as unshapeable as iron."

"Thank you for your advice, *Grand-mère,*" Simone said. "Now, do you know of a certain Monsieur Jean Paul Dubois?" She had once asked how M. Jean Paul Dubois had come across so many red diamonds. Red diamonds, Cyrus had replied, are almost impossible to find. They are an aberration of nature, a distortion in their chemical structure affecting the manner in which they absorb light. The miner, Cyrus added, had come across a rare South African pipe that produced an extraordinary breed of red diamonds that not only survived the diamond wheel but were enhanced by it.

"No," Mme Gabrielle replied. "Do you know such a monsieur, Françoise?"

Françoise shook her head.

"Another matter, *ma chère,*" Mme Gabrielle said. "Now that you are looking everywhere, do not dismiss the possibility of the Persian minister of court's involvement in Cyrus's murder."

M. Jean Paul Dubois, Simone knew, had introduced Cyrus to the Persian minister of court. She had always wondered why, in a country where Jews were persecuted and forced to display identifying signs so Muslims would not come in contact and thereby defile themselves, the minister had selected a Jew as the royal jeweler. Was it easier to intimidate Jews into silence, to use them as pawns? "Why do you suspect him?" Simone asked her grandmother.

"I am a connoisseur of character, *ma chère.* When I met the minister in the president's palace, he seemed in control of affairs. Not only Cyrus's, but the shah's as well." Mme Gabrielle buttoned her gloves as she contemplated her next move, Simone's introduction to the Parisian society. "I have a brilliant idea," she said at last. "We shall organize a New Year's soirée. Invite eminent personalities, those we know and those we do not. This is the best way to introduce you to Amir, Rouge, and anyone else you suspect. We must dispatch an invitation to the president's palace, too, in case the minister of court is in town."

35

Flanked by four armed bodyguards on horses, the carriage wheeled through streets, tunnels, and bridges toward Place Vendôme and the Hotel Ritz. A cryptlike trunk lay on the carriage seat between Simone and M. Rouge. She had had difficulty persuading her mother and grandmother that she was equipped to take care of herself. To convince them, she had aimed her revolver up and shot a bird in flight. Finding them unmoved, she tapped a passing servant behind the knee with her heel. He shouted, staggering to regain his balance. "You see," she had said, "I know every vulnerable part of the body. Even the cluster of nerves behind the knees. A harder kick would have sent him to the ground."

Now she had no doubt that one of her kicks would injure the slender M. Rouge at her side. The graceful shape of his head and his fragile features reminded her of the castrato Luciano Barbutzzi, her grandmother's dead lover, who had once considered the clover hill his private opera house. His disjointed eyes, one narrow with a tormented expression, the other wide and observant, were depressive, if she were to give his eyes a name.

The carriage circled the Place Vendôme to stop at the grand entrance of the Hotel Ritz. Simone's flounced skirt sounded brash to her as she followed him through the lobby and into the plush silence of an upstairs suite.

M. Rouge, who imagined relieving her of the same skirt, stopped at the great mirror in the hall to adjust his cravat. At the sight of his image so close to her, she touched the velvet ribbon around her neck before stepping into the oak-paneled suite.

Silk drapes hugged a pair of French windows flanking a carved armoire. A mahogany desk sported an inkwell and a bronze sculpture of an Arab astride a stallion. A low table presented exotic delicacies—baklava, halvah, stuffed vine leaves, and honey-dipped cakes. M. Rouge had notified the management of their arrival.

He flipped two fingers, and the guards stepped out with the strongbox. Before the proper formalities were exchanged, his tragic eye narrowing, the other continuing to marvel, he asked, "Is this your natural hair color, Mademoiselle?"

"Of course not," she whispered in his ear. "And it is Madame."

He pointed to the silver strip of hair that had appeared after Cyrus's death. "This is the work of a *coiffeuse*? Madame is not a true redhead, then!"

Her gaze skimmed across his crestfallen expression, and she felt pity. "Pardon my banter, Monsieur. Of course, I *am* a natural redhead. In truth, nothing about me is artificial but this," she whispered, flipping her handkerchief out and wiping off the glitter Françoise had applied to her eyelids.

"Kindly show me the red diamond that is for sale," she said.

At the mention of his diamond, M. Rouge's eyes became dreamy. As if cataloguing the merits of a most beloved lover, he praised the color, girdle, and facets of the five-carat gem. When he was done, he stroked his cravat as if it were studded with the aforementioned diamond.

Simone combed her fingers through her curls. "Monsieur Rouge, please do not keep me in abeyance any longer."

"Dear Madame, the cost of safely transporting the diamond has been astronomical. I shouldered the cost assuming the client would accompany you. I might consider a viewing if you would trust me with his identity."

"I am sorry for the misunderstanding, Monsieur, but I am the client." She clapped him on the shoulder as if he were a male comrade, and in the process astonished and disarmed him further.

He had encountered many odd incidents in his trade and had carefully planned this meeting. But he did not expect her to appear on her own to conduct a transaction worth millions.

She stood up and presented her hand. "Monsieur, either you show me the diamond, or I shall take my leave." She felt his smooth palm, as blank as a slate. A forty-year-old man whose tragic youth had impressed itself upon his future, he continued to live in the past. But his little finger was rather straight; he might not be as devious as his eyes insinuated.

He scrambled to recover his bearing, calling out to the guards outside. They walked in with the strongbox on a rolling table, which they placed in front of her. One of the guards lay down at her feet.

M. Rouge tackled the lock and raised the cover. Unfurling a velvet fabric, he opened a pouch, retrieved a satin box, and snapped the lid open with a great flourish.

Simone slipped to the edge of her chair.

A five-carat gem of dazzling facets shimmered in resplendent shades of red and purple. Of more than ten thousand natural diamonds, only one becomes a fancy color, Cyrus had said. And among those, red was the rarest color. Connoisseurs would barter their souls for one glance of such a gem. How did M. Rouge come upon this diamond? She directed the gooseneck lamp down and studied the diamond under a loupe. The intensity, depth, and artfully executed facets did not seem to exhibit signs of heat treatment, although she could not be certain. She removed Cyrus's earring and compared the two. At first blush, they appeared similar in shade, cut, and lucidity, except that one was four carats larger. Was this the same red diamond Cyrus had acquired for M. Rouge's mistress the night of the inauguration of the Ritz Hotel? Why was it for sale? What would be the asking price in return for information about Cyrus? M. Rouge held the diamond up to the light, his disjointed eyes finding temporary relief in the course of adoration. "The two of us could work well together, Monsieur Rouge. As you can see, I have an obsessive, some would even say illogical love affair with diamonds," she said as she placed the earring back in her earlobe.

He circled the diamond between two fingers, locked it back in his fist, then opened his fist and presented the diamond to her.

She plucked the gem from his palm and raised her yellow gaze to meet his. "What is the price, Monsieur?"

His eyes snapped shut as if stabbed by her words. "My sweet, innocent dear, I am at a loss as to how to reply. By your own admission, you have an obsessive love affair with diamonds. Therefore, it is impossible for me to come up with a price. You, and only you, the lover, must decide upon its value." The answer to her question left dramatically implicit, he reclaimed his diamond. He had seduced famed courtesans for the sake of adding their names to his prestigious roster, but this redhead was an entirely different specimen. He had discovered her through the photograph in Château Gabrielle. Her voluptuous freckles and the tiny brass-colored hairs on her arms had made him wild with hope that he might, at last, encounter the woman of his dreams.

Now that his diamond had lured her, he did not intend to lose her. He appraised the evolving relationship between her and the gem, whether she would have to own the object of her desire no matter the price. He interpreted her every move— how long her finger remained on the diamond, how fast she let go, and how the glint of her tiger eyes diminished. Not a positive sign. She was losing interest and would soon leave him. He followed the path of her gaze toward a corner of the ceiling and found himself melting into her eyes, which were changing to the shade of diamonds, lost between her freckled thighs, wrapped in her sighs, and soaking in her feminine scent that permeated the room.

She set the diamond back on its velvet bed and passed a finger over its shimmering surface as if closing the eyes of a corpse. A thump of disappointment shook his chest. The words she uttered next sent him into a flutter.

"I want the diamond, Monsieur Rouge; I want it more than I have ever wanted anything."

He quickly dismissed the human shield at her feet, who twitched anxiously with every move of the hand in which she held the diamond. Left alone with her, M. Rouge grabbed her hands. "I expect nothing more than a quiet evening in your company, Madame."

36

M. Rouge gasped at the sight of Simone at his door, her burnished curls on fire, the silver streak of hair scintillating in the setting sun behind. Since their last visit five days ago, at the Ritz Hotel, he had remained in erotic anticipation, unable to contain his desire to thrust his face into her curls. "My lovely angel," he repeated over and over to the low cooing of pigeons on the awning overhead.

Inside, she was assaulted by scarlet drapes, maroon carpets, and red oak furniture with shiny coats of liver-hued lacquer. Feeling as if she were drowning in blood, she grabbed his arm. He guided her straight to his bedroom. Raising a strand of her hair to his nose, he inhaled its properties.

She thought of Cyrus, his face in her curls, the curve of her neck, the soft skin of her eyelids—*you smell divine, I had no idea it was possible to love like this.* She harnessed her memories to stopper her perfume. She would not prize this stranger's carnelian-shaded bedroom with her fragrance. A side table was set with cabbage, beet, and arugula salad—"rocket seed," Françoise had branded arugula, documented as an aphrodisiac since ancient times. Pomegranates were piled high on a red louro tray. Eve had tempted Adam with pomegranate, not apple, her mother believed. Cherrywood bowls held strawberries, raspberries, and a single artichoke. Simone sat at the table and prepared to indulge his senses. She gave her napkin a delicate shake, spread it on her lap, and poured herself a goblet of Bordeaux, sliding her tongue over the rim. Taking his breath away with the toss of her magnificent hair, she cupped the artichoke in her palm as if embracing her breast. She stripped each leaf with languorous fingers, dipped the leaf in melted butter, and scraped the flesh with her teeth.

M. Rouge imagined the same teeth grazing his most erogenous part.

But Simone was back in the Persian mountains, in her stone house, with Cyrus and his sheltering arms, the salty taste of his skin. She dipped her spoon into a goblet of strawberry mousse and imagined it as chocolate, nourishment of the gods. She swiveled her spoon in the cream, poured sugar, and watched it fizzle and dissolve in its silkiness, licked the mousse off the corners of her mouth.

M. Rouge longed to lick her cherry-bright fingernails, golden freckles, and tangerine mouth. But more than anything, he was impatient to lose himself in the red hair between her thighs, the ultimate proof of her authenticity. He had squandered millions on his fixation, on fake henna and sienna redheads. Now every fiber in his body screamed that Simone would not disappoint him.

Ever since his eighteenth birthday when he lost his beloved red-haired mother to a toppled carriage, her vivacious body a red stain on the mud-packed earth, his elusive quest to locate a redhead had robbed his appetite. He had encountered one artificial redhead after another with penciled freckles that told of dyes and lies. For years he had decorated his home in anticipation of the day he would find an honest woman.

And now she was here. In his bedroom.

He lifted her in his arms and carried her under a canopy of gauze, to the round bed of purple heartwood on which he had loved no one else.

Her eyes shut against the assault of wine-colored sheets.

His chest aching, he fumbled to unclasp, unbuckle, and unbutton her. In his eagerness, he further entangled the strings of her corset and skirts, lost patience, and crushed silk, satin, and her soft body under him. His roaming eyes gaped at the sight of the tiny copper hair on her arms, freckles that turned amber under his fingertips, and the strip of hair, silver to the very roots.

She turned her mouth away from his breath and whispered in his ear that she was on fire, that she had never enjoyed a man's touch as much, and that she was wet with desire.

"Show me your pubic hair," he insulted her ear.

"I need to free my breasts from the corset," she murmured, stepping down from the bed. She loosened the ribbon that crisscrossed the length of her corset, strung it out of each eyelet, and rolled it around her fingers. She released each breast from its cup as if offering him peaches. She stepped back into bed, smoothed her skirts down around her thighs, and directed the creamy gaze of her breasts at him. "*Mon amour,* do you happen to know a certain miner known as Monsieur Jean Paul Dubois?"

"What?" M. Rouge mumbled, staring at her blushing nipples.

"Who is Monsieur Jean Paul Dubois?" she repeated. "Do you deal with him?"

"No, I mean, yes," M. Rouge muttered, a tremor in his voice, a flicker of concern in one eye, terror in the other.

She wet a finger in her mouth and traced his lips. She coaxed him into a sitting position. Before he plunged into sexual hysteria, she whispered, "Didn't his son study at the Sorbonne?"

"Yes, yes, the Sorbonne . . . the poor boy . . . lost an arm."

Simone lifted her petticoats, spread her thighs, and allowed M. Rouge a glimpse of her pubis.

He thrust his hands under her skirts to cup her buttocks.

One hand on the headboard, she pushed him away with the other. "A lady must be fed first," she said sternly.

He spirited her into his dining room to be seated at his purple heartwood table with gold-trimmed napkins, crystal goblets, and crimson candles. He hovered over her, a hand folded behind, enjoying the role of her maître d'. "Sit back, lovely angel, and allow me to serve you." He turned a plate of steak tartare to face her. Settling on the opposite chair, he leaned back, soaking himself in her glorious vision. He did not touch his food.

Her insides surged at the sight of raw meat, the color enhanced with spices. She pressed the napkin to her mouth. "You dear, dear man, *merci* for the trouble you've gone through. But I am a vegetarian." She extended her plate over the table and pushed the meat into his plate, settling for *potage de tomate*.

Content that she had tasted his food, and presumably enjoyed it, he addressed his soup. "After many unsuccessful years of searching for the holy female, I have never felt so close to discovering her. During those years, my digestive system would not accept more than mere essentials for sustenance. And now, I want some soup."

She licked a chocolate into a glistening orb and popped it into her mouth as she waited for him to enjoy his repast, pausing now and then to communicate a tender word. Her red hair had won over an influential man in the closed world of diamonds. His newly found appetite, she hoped, would make him more receptive to her questions.

He folded his napkin and set it on the table. A tinge of alarm creeping into his voice, he invited her back to bed. Her fragrance of watermelon and berries, and her staggering capacity to locate his mysterious pleasure peaks, had held him in the throes of ecstasy. But he had been allowed nothing beyond a glimpse of her pubis. And he was beginning to question whether she was a redhead after all.

She rose, leaned against the high-backed chair, and lifted layers of skirts. "Come, kneel at my feet and find out for yourself whether I am a natural redhead."

He kissed the soft folds of her thighs, licked the pink flesh, and parted her pubic hair as if searching for jewels. The harder he explored the roots of her silky hair, the more convinced he became they were the same color as her curls. He had discovered a true redhead, at last!

Droplets of ecstasy dribbled into his veins, the initial tremors, the preliminary ripples that would surge into spasms. He braced himself, folding inward, delaying the eruption so as to enjoy the full force of a much-awaited release. He threw himself on the chair, his nose beaded with sweat. His eyes were on her, one tender, the other with eternal gratitude. "*Merci,* lovely angel, thank you very, very much. Please sit down now and enjoy dessert with me."

She had had enough of his obsession with red foods. What kind of decadent dessert would he offer her next?

He disappeared into a room and returned with a satin sachet. Its stark whiteness was as welcome as a white butterfly fluttering into a crimson garden. He held the sachet out to her.

She pried open the satin neck and dipped two fingers in.

His unhinged eyes gauging her every move, he said, "A small gift for being you."

She tossed her head back in astonishment at the red diamond she held, the five-carat gem she had seen at the Ritz Hotel. Any sane person would have appreciated such a generous gift, yet she was offended. Was this payment for sexual favors? Their encounter in bed was certainly not sexual on her part. She had been emotionally detached, had at no time removed her skirts, opened her legs or her heart to him.

She gazed down at the red diamond in the center of her

palm. No, she did not want his diamond. The only diamond she desired was the one in her earlobe. "I didn't know nature produced such large red diamonds," she said.

"A special mine in South Africa does," he replied.

"Do you own the mine?"

"Oh, no! I am a well-connected middleman with vast resources. I acquire raw diamonds and distribute them. I have a knack for whom to approach and whom to avoid."

"Do you personally know everyone you deal with?"

"I am on a first-name basis with most."

"Did you happen to visit Monsieur Jean Paul Dubois's mine?" she asked.

"No one has," he replied. "The man is a cartel unto himself. He sells by closed bids and private transactions."

"Where does he live?"

"Here! There! Everywhere! Egypt. Paris. Mostly Namaqualand." He broke off, passed his hand over his head and brushed his cravat clean of a bit of steak. "This can't be of consequence to you."

She closed her fingers around the diamond. "Thank you. It is truly stunning."

After a pause, she persevered. "Tell me, *mon amour,* does Monsieur Jean Paul Dubois have any shortcoming you know of?"

"His art collection," M. Rouge murmured. "He never leaves his art, except to seek new additions. Poor man . . . has no interest in women."

At that, Simone stood up from her chair. She turned her back to him in an attempt to isolate herself from the man who had lost his value to her. Adjusting her breasts into the cups of her corset, she fastened the upper hooks he had managed to disengage.

37

Simone gazed beyond her grandmother's shoulders to a gallery in the last stages of completion. Was it the influence of absinthe or that of her ghosts that had prompted her grandmother to squander her wealth on yet another gallery? This one, displaying portraits of prominent men who stood tall in their elegant coattails, proud to go down in history as having given the grande dame her most cherished jewelry.

Mme Gabrielle threw her head back and tossed a tumbler of absinthe into her mouth, taking pleasure in the searing trail of alcohol. Her hot breath startled her ghosts out of the folds of her tulles, gauzes, and chiffons. They had once limited their presence to the clover hill and, every now and then, to her boudoir to tease her particularly boisterous lovers. But lately, like her flowering guilt, they superimposed themselves everywhere, giggling in her lap at a formal dinner, wrapping their ethereal selves around her arms at the opera, and skipping across her shoulders as family matters were discussed.

Nevertheless, she was a content woman these days. M.

Rouge, having discovered a redhead, could not stop boasting about Simone's sexual sway, euphoric perfume, and erotic skills. To Mme Gabrielle's great delight, a flock of men from all corners of France descended upon the château to court Simone. They came from all ranks and positions, types and sensibilities, eager to meet the red-haired woman who had mesmerized the notorious M. Rouge.

The onerous task of sending these men away was left to Alphonse, who now that Simone knew of their familial ties, asserted his status as her grandfather. Defying Mme Gabrielle, he dispatched Simone's suitors in an icy manner without the promise of a future date. "Mademoiselle Simone is not and would never be interested," he would utter, his face a granite mask. But to his great dismay, the men left more eager than when they had arrived, their interest heightened by Simone's indifference.

Mme Gabrielle, who was appalled by Alphonse's behavior, could not believe the good fortune of her granddaughter's sudden fame. She had become the most mysterious and sought-after woman in Paris. Just as the fame of Mme Gabrielle's hands had become legendary, and the delicacy of Françoise's feet the talk of Paris, Simone's ability to arouse the infamous M. Rouge had made her an overnight sensation. Mme Gabrielle did not try to stifle the circulating rumors but rather helped to stoke them. Myths were essential to a courtesan's success. They were the sparks that kept her in the limelight.

Suddenly, she was shocked out of her gossamer cocoons as a newcomer joined her repertoire of spirits. Was it true? Had her teacher and lover, her *monstre sacré,* passed away in his sleep at the height of his fame? This was a tragedy beyond belief, a devastating loss to France. Her adored Émile Zola had died of asphyxiation from *un système de chauffage*—overcome by toxic fumes. His mustache tickled her earlobe as he whispered that he was murdered by his enemies who blocked the chimney and caused poisonous fumes to build up in his bedroom.

Simone, annoyed by her grandmother's incomprehensible gestures of affection for her spirits, knew better than to disturb her now that she seemed overcome with grief.

Mme Gabrielle reached out for another tumbler of absinthe. "I apologize, darling. I just found out that my dear Émile Zola has passed away."

"I am sorry," Simone replied, saddened by the news. "Do you want me to leave you alone?"

"No, not before you tell me what you want. But first, let me extend my congratulations on the occasion of being invited to Monsieur Rouge's home."

"*Grand-mère,* how else? His only choice was to invite me as a proper lady would expect because I am neither his mistress nor his whore."

"Whore! Ah, *quelle horreur!* Who taught you to reason like a man? Whore! Banish that despicable term from your vocabulary. This way of thinking proves that antiquated male reasoning is alive and well. Do not look down upon a mistress or, for that matter, a whore, your choice of words, *chérie,* not mine."

"I am sorry, *Grand-mère,*" Simone interjected. "I did not intend to offend you."

"Well, *chérie,* I *am* offended. Women like us are a force of nature and worthy of respect. We are ahead of our time with the courage to demand emotional and sexual autonomy. We are not just pretty faces who provide sex. To overlook our insight and resourcefulness and to brand us as whores is like calling successful businessmen pimps. Sex is the icing on our relationships. Men keep coming back to us for our complexity, political savvy, and wit. We are masters of our own fate, and this is more than can be said of those so called 'proper ladies' who don't even choose their husbands." She held up the tumbler of absinthe to Simone. "*Chérie,* a sip is essential to balance the humors. Do you know that absinthe is named in honor of

Artemis, the Greek goddess of chastity?" At this observation, she burst into hearty laughter.

Simone grabbed the tumbler of absinthe and raised it to her lips.

The grandmother shuffled her blue curls across her cheeks. "Respect your drink. Toss it up. Up!"

Simone grimaced at the bitter green liquid's searing course, which turned to radiating warmth in her belly, transforming the clover hill and its galleries into a better place. "*Pas mal*. What is it made of?"

"Wormwood, a strong-smelling plant that yields bitter oil, licorice, herbs, and alcohol—lots of it. All essential to our temperaments, *naturellement*."

In need of a favor she was almost certain Mme Gabrielle would turn down, and with her courage beginning to wane, Simone upturned the bottle of absinthe into her mouth. She had pleasured M. Rouge with the ancient rite of breathing, imagery, and massage, sustaining his ecstasy for prolonged periods, and without the need for penetration. Having located the lust vein that lay along his spine, she had awakened every one of his senses, rendering him powerless. But she required a different skill to persuade her grandmother to accept what she had come to ask of her.

"Be careful," Mme Gabrielle advised. "I am accustomed to the arsenic in absinthe. You, on the other hand, better start slowly. In the meantime, the arsenic will lighten your skin."

The roaming peacocks reminding him of his poverty-stricken days, when he ate sparrows trapped on his windowsill, Zola demanded his share of absinthe.

Now Émile, remember yourself, Mme Gabrielle reprimanded, the unspoken words flaming across her forehead. *If I recall correctly, it was you who criticized the consumption of alcohol with magnificent literary aptitude in* Les Rougon-Macquart. With a great huff, Zola slipped under her chin to take notes for his tetralogy, *Les Quatre Évangiles,* which he had left unfinished upon his death. Mme Gabrielle reminded him that her chin was not his notepad and that she would greatly appreciate his effort to treat her skin gently. "Tell me what you want," she asked Simone, after putting Zola in his place.

Simone staggered to her feet, struggling to bring her grandmother's image into focus. "*Grand-mère,* help me lure Monsieur Jean Paul Dubois to me."

"But of course, I will," Mme Gabrielle interjected. "Why are you so nervous about asking?"

"Because he is a shrewd man and rarely leaves his art collection, except to acquire new additions. You have one piece in your collection he would certainly covet. Your Delacroix. He will travel to the ends of the earth to acquire it. I know you cherish it beyond everything you possess, but please, *Grand-mère,* send him a letter saying your Delacroix is for sale. Invite him to the New Year's soirée to view it."

Mme Gabrielle was startled. "*Ma petite,* I cannot part with my Delacroix. But men do not need art. Women are enough temptation. He will happily accept an Honoré woman's invitation."

"Unfortunately, he is not interested in women. His son is the result of a marriage pursued for social advancement."

Mme Gabrielle had priceless works of art by masters she admired. Among them, Manet's *Olympia* with flowers in her hair; Cézanne's *Une Moderne Olympia,* innocent-looking but not quite, and Ingres's *Madame Marcotte,* the fashion maven. It was true that Delacroix's *Women of Algiers in Their Apartment* was her favorite. But she was not going to discourage the course of events that would aid Simone in finally accepting the Honoré legacy.

38

⟨❀⟩

Paris
New Year's Eve 1902

Carriages of all sizes, landaus, phaetons, barouches, and charabancs with silver fixtures and gilded bodies clattered and rumbled, snaking their way up and around small towns and villages toward the Valley of Civet Cats. They crowded the dirt road that twisted and curved into the cobblestone path ending at Château Gabrielle. Coachmen on high boxes wielded whips to keep horses in line. At the sound of cracking whips, villagers came out into the biting cold to congregate at the roadside and applaud carriages with shiny wheels and varnished coach panels carrying mink-, chinchilla-, and ermine-draped passengers.

Gates of Mme Gabrielle's *Parc Français* were wide open to accommodate the endless arrival of graceful tandems, tinkling victorias, and mail coaches transporting a contingent of curious, hopeful men, whom Alphonse turned away.

Footmen in festooned coats aided jewel-drenched women and tuxedoed men down from the carriages and into the park, where they stopped to check themselves in mirrors set outdoors. Gas lamps, candles, and tiny lightbulbs gleamed and sparkled outside. The château and the park shimmered golden under a massive tent that connected the house to the gardens, creating a sense of unity and keeping winter out. From the clover hill, which could not be covered, bursts of fireworks painted the skies above and cast magic upon the roof of the tent. Inside the warm tent, urns brimmed with roses that burst into bloom, their petals deepening into lewd shades under the astounded gaze of arriving guests. Champagne flutes in hand, the gathering crowd staggered about steeped in curiosity and intoxicated by the revelation that the exotic roses were imported from faraway Persia, a country inexplicably linked to the Honoré women.

A system of hydraulic motors shifted certain walls to transform the foyer, grand salon, parlor, and music room into one vast area. Silk-padded walls muffled the shimmying of restive horses and the bray of donkeys whose udders had not been emptied of milk in the earlier pandemonium. The peacocks, having sensed Mme Gabrielle's rare absence, waddled in dazed circles.

At midnight, the women of Château Gabrielle would usher in 1903.

Alphonse faced the unexpected arrival of charabancs and dogcarts loaded with passengers who had learned about tonight's soirée in the gossip column of *Le Figaro*. Trusting that M. Jean Paul Dubois and M. Amir would arrive in nothing less than elegant carriages, Alphonse turned away every mail coach or wretched cab that came burping along the road.

Mme Gabrielle glided around in layers of lace, the sheen of her blue hair visible wherever she was, welcoming her guests with diamond-trimmed gloves and a friendly tap of her ermine fan. Her indigo gaze sought M. Amir.

The tiara-clad Françoise had ingested blue pills to preserve her youth and arsenic to make her skin paler for the occasion. Her laughter rang out as her lovers pressed their mouths upon her white flesh as if licking cotton candy. In a silver-sequined gown of silk imported from the Persian city of Ormuz, she waltzed to chansons of Yvette Guilbert's lyrics. Her gaze never left Mme Gabrielle, who drifted in and out of ballooning skirts, embroidered bodices, and sheer flounces. Tonight, Mme Gabrielle had warned her daughter, belonged to Simone.

The festivities in full motion, guests mounted the steps to the terrace and entered the château, gathering in the expanded foyer at the foot of the grand staircase. There, the celebrated Simone d'Honoré was to present herself on the magnificent stage of her staircase. But there was no indication of her arrival.

Torch in hand, Alphonse shouted above the din, "It is only eleven-thirty. Mademoiselle Simone d'Honoré is not due until midnight. *S'il vous plaît,* clear a path or Mademoiselle will hurt herself." He attempted to redirect the crowd outside and toward the myriad stations serving peach-, lime-, and anise-flavored absinthe. Brandishing the torch above his head, he announced that pavilions in the gardens offered caviar, *escalopes de fois gras,* oysters, and much more. Palm readers, clairvoyant gypsies, and parrots fluent in Greek could be found in pergolas, along with virile monkeys that pleasured their mates at the speed of the newly inaugurated railway. But as hard as he tried, he failed to clear the dangerously congested foyer.

Men remained rooted in front of the large canvas of Simone's photograph, and the image of the inaccessible girl who, like Cassandra, seemed to read their most intimate longings. Anticipation of encountering the woman of their fantasies had caused embarrassing bulges in their trousers. Women, paralyzed by jealousy, could not tear themselves away from Mme Gabrielle's spirit photographs. Could it be true, the women wondered, that while they remained home, Mme Gabrielle flung her net wide and far to capture their men?

Midnight approaching, attendants at the gates locked the entrance to the park, abandoning a roaring crowd outside.

Alphonse, in a frenzy from the decisions of whom to allow in and whom to refuse, reassured himself that Simone had become an assertive woman, able to handle the crowd.

Mme Gabrielle and Françoise abandoned the gardens and crossed the terrace to join the crowd in welcoming Simone.

At the stroke of midnight, the orchestra ceased playing, and harps took over inside. A rising murmur echoed around the foyer. Eyes rose to the balcony. A sight more impressive than the grand opera's stage.

Simone stepped onto the balcony, rested her hands on the balustrade, and gazed at the crowd below.

Tucked behind her ears, her copper curls tumbled behind slender shoulders to sway down to her rounded derrière. She was not as plump as the women who gaped up at her, nor was she dressed in the ballooning silhouettes of the time. Saffron-colored crepe de chine hugged her curves, skimmed the marble underfoot, and trailed behind like liquid gold. A diaphanous foulard of the same shade fluttered behind like a breeze, transporting her perfume. What stupefied her guests most was her dewy complexion, the piercing alertness of her gold eyes, and the soft outline of her plump lips, which did not carry a trace of makeup. She was the image of aristocratic refinement, a woman who had stepped out of her bath, towel-dried her hair, shaken the curls loose, and emerged to welcome her guests in a delicious gown slightly lighter than the color of her hair. She did not wear a single piece of jewelry, save the black velvet ribbon with Cyrus's wedding band around her neck and his red diamond in her earlobe. Standing on her stage above the crowd, surrounded by the gilded décor of the château and bejeweled women below, her simplicity was striking.

A thunder of applause broke out, increasing in intensity with her rising scent of bergamot.

She descended the stairs, and the crowd parted to make way, coming together in her wake to capture the palette of her

scents. They cast spiteful glances at M. Rouge who, unable to
control his pleasure at her sight, tackled the crowd to make his
way to her. Women chattered among themselves, finding fault
with her passé style, her thin body, her too-pale skin, lifeless
lips, and loose hair like that of a madwoman. Men wondered
whether she wore undergarments under her skintight gown.
Unaware that she had trained her perfume to devastate the
most composed and cunning among them, men pressed their
mouths to the fragrant skin of her hand.

She wove her way around, murmuring her name to those
she did not know and exchanging niceties with those she did.
She continued her greetings, trying to reach Mme Gabrielle,
then M. Rouge. She hoped he would point out M. Jean Paul
Dubois, while her grandmother would introduce M. Amir in
the event the men had arrived.

"Is Monsieur Amir here?" she asked her grandmother, who
interrupted her conversation with M. Matin, a red-faced alco-
holic midget and a preeminent collector of Russian revolvers.

"I don't see him, *chérie,*" she whispered, her gaze searching.
"It is not too late. Both men will certainly come. Go, enjoy yourself."

Françoise adjusted her tiara and let out a sigh of exaspera-
tion. Simone's fragrance had lassoed her men. But it would be
temporary. Simone was a slippery illusion.

M. Rouge cupped Simone's elbow, trying to pull her away
from Mme Gabrielle. "A moment alone with you, please?"

She wiggled herself out of his grip and suggested he be a
darling and introduce her to individuals she did not know. "I
have been away for so long; I do not recognize half the crowd."

"My pleasure. Do you see Madame Fochone, who re-
arranges her tiara in front of the mirror? She is the ambassador's wife and Monsieur Rochefoucault's mistress. He just
put a canapé in his mouth. And that young girl with brown hair,
the one wearing a low-grade diamond necklace, is the daughter

of the great Madame and Monsieur Roland, who consider their daughter an angel. Well, far from it. She sleeps with anyone who gives her a piece of cheap jewelry. Now behind you, the man leaning against the chestnut tree. Yes, he is chatting with Madame Sorayan. He is Laban, an influential man who used to own Fouquet on Rue Royal but now has the jewelry store on Rue de l'Arcade."

"How does someone like *him* acquire diamonds?" Simone asked.

"From here and there. Most often from De Beers, although with the recent discovery of the Premier mine that is three times larger than the Kimberley pipes, De Beers's future seems unstable. There are other venues, of course."

"Suppliers such as Monsieur Jean Paul Dubois, I suppose." Her tone was flat, as if the matter were of no great consequence to her.

At the mention of M. Jean Paul Dubois, as if bitten by a snake, M. Rouge's eyes became more disjointed. "Is he in France? Keep away from him. Bad news however you look at him."

"My grandmother invited him," Simone said. "Do point him out so I will know whom to avoid."

Simone turned her gaze away from M. Rouge and toward couples waltzing to the thrilling notes of Strauss, toward the pungent scent of champagne in the air. She missed Cyrus. She missed him more than ever now that she was entrenched in uncovering the mystery of his murder, now that her intuition screamed she might be close to a resolution. The passing months had intensified the pain of her loss. Particularly tonight, as couples melted into each other and perfumes mingled with her longing to float up to the electric skies.

39

M. Jean Paul Dubois stepped down from the train, slowed his pace, his breathing, and the beat of his Medusa-handled umbrella on the cobblestones. The night was punctuated by the rumble of fireworks around the city, the constant cracking of whips, and drunken laughter. His black pupils bled into the irises and whites of his eyes, settling on the four clocks on the tower. They were not synchronized. Annoyed, he flicked open his pocket watch. Half past midnight. He did not like to be out this late, especially on New Year's Eve. He detested surprises and was rarely caught in them. Nonetheless, he had behaved like a shark trailing the scent of blood. He traveled to Paris, conscious of the risk of his presence here, where his every move might be monitored. He gave the Medusa handle a hard whack. He need not worry. He had calculated his every move. He was confident of his ability to maneuver within dangerous situations and walk away unscathed.

He was also accustomed to claiming the object of his desire. And he had come to claim *Women of Algiers in Their Apartment*.

Particulars about the Honoré women were imparted to him through numerous sources—his spies, those of his enemies, and individuals who had taken his bait, cash, diamonds, promises—the tempting payback impossible to refuse. The distillate of reports was that the granddaughter was stunning but not necessarily beautiful. The few men she tolerated failed to penetrate her surrounding barrier. The grandmother's rise to fame and fortune piqued his interest. And the daughter was a shallow courtesan he did not dwell on. His constantly buzzing brain had analyzed and reanalyzed the letter Mme Gabrielle d'Honoré had dispatched to him. But he failed to determine any ulterior motive for the invitation other than financial profit from the sale of the rare Delacroix.

Delacroix was a master artist with a significant flaw. The elements of chemistry and physics were foreign to him. He failed to distinguish between a good and bad canvas, between reliable paint and a pernicious one. Once he liked the grain of a canvas and the nuances of color, he would set to work. Despite the deterioration his paintings underwent, he continued to use combinations of wax, essences, and new colors with no solidity. But *Women of Algiers in Their Apartment* proved an exception. The artist had applied special care in his choice of oils and paint. And that had served the painting well. Consequently, for some time now, M. Jean Paul Dubois had been seeking to add it to his collection.

He waved at a passing troika, gathered his cape, and jumped in. He was tired from his long journey but remained wide-eyed and alert, his umbrella punctuating the carriage floor. The challenge of encountering *Women of Algiers in Their Apartment* energized his fifty-seven-year-old body. He threw one leg over the other and directed the coachman to the Valley of Civet Cats.

From her vantage on the terrace, Simone watched drunken men and flirtatious women sway in possessive embraces to chansons of Yvette Guilbert, the petite singer with a conversational voice. Beyond the dance floor, couples crowded pavilions where palm readers wove destinies with threads of lies, strolled into pergolas where clairvoyant gypsies gazed into glass globes that revealed nothing but trapped bubbles, and farther away, behind trees and bushes, men and women, men and men, or women and women fondled damp thighs and eager breasts and made love as if all were well in the universe.

Simone turned to the commotion outside. The rumble of carriage wheels, clatter of hooves, cracking whips. A carriage came to a halt at the gates. Guest list in hand, Alphonse hurried to inspect the just-arrived troika. The woolen-capped coachman, on his high seat behind the carriage hood, tugged at the reins, trying to control a lame mule.

With a tired wave, Simone gestured for Alphonse to turn the visitor away. She felt despondent. Her grandmother had failed to spot M. Amir. And M. Jean Paul Dubois would not arrive in such a shabby cab. Had Cyrus mentioned the miner's age? For all she knew, he might have died of old age. With Alphonse's frantic orders to leave and open the way for other carriages ringing in her ears, she prepared to join the crowd. A man stepped out of the troika wearing a silk vest, stylish top hat and cape, and the shadow of a beard.

Alphonse, whose head reeled with the many decisions left to him, planted himself in the man's way. The torch he wielded in the stranger's face sparked eyes that registered a rat scurrying under the carriage.

Simone rushed down the steps, signaling Alphonse to open the gates.

She came face-to-face with the enlarged pupils and white-ringed irises that gave the appearance of a nocturnal bird of prey. Her immediate reaction was to turn back and flee. But tonight's soirée was organized to lure M. Jean Paul Dubois. And she had a strong sense he had just arrived.

Alphonse struggled to draw her attention, warn her of the man's danger-charged aura. Finding her oblivious of his gesticulation, he raised himself to his full height and waved the torch in the stranger's face. He did not care if he was one of the much-expected guests. He did not want this man near Simone. "This is a private event, Monsieur."

A semblance of a smile hovering around his mouth, the man aimed his Medusa-handled umbrella like a loaded revolver at Alphonse.

"Thank you, Alphonse. I believe Monsieur received a formal invitation." Simone rose on her toes, planted a kiss on both cheeks of the man who might be Cyrus's murderer and, in the process, pearled his pulse with her dark fragrance. "Simone d'Honoré," she whispered.

"Of course," he said, towering over her and raising her hand to his mouth for the expected kiss. "Jean Paul Dubois."

In no hurry to reclaim her hand, Simone tested his palm—the square that straddled his lifeline indicating long periods of confinement. Exile? Prison? His line of Mars crossed parallel to the lifeline—nothing incapacitated him. No worry lines to suggest concern. The crooked formation of his little finger spoke of dishonesty—a past intentionally erased, for which he was not held accountable. His intelligence had soured into slyness, his dealings into plots. She detected an arrogance she would exploit to her benefit and his downfall. She held on to his hand, afraid he would disappear and leave her in limbo. She had anticipated him with the eagerness of a child awaiting a gift, and she would not now leave it unwrapped. She turned away from his insolent, hunting eyes. "Do come in, Monsieur Dubois. Festivities are in full force."

He absorbed the crowd, Yvette Guilbert's song "Jeux d'Eau," and the exploding fireworks above. "Could Madame Gabrielle meet me in a quieter place?"

"Come, come, Monsieur, I will certainly inform my grandmother of your arrival."

He followed her as she steered him past the crowd, up the terrace steps, and into the Salon of *Women of Algiers* that the system of hydraulic jacks had not connected to the grand foyer. She indicated a settee with a wave of her hand. "Please make yourself comfortable. Madame Gabrielle will join us momentarily."

He bypassed the settee for a stiff-backed chair, added protection from any danger behind, rested his hands on the armchair, and reassessed his surroundings. His tar-pit pupils dilated at the sight of Delacroix's painting on the easel. The painting was in far better shape than he had expected. It did not suffer from the excessive use of bitumen, the cracks were minimal, and the women had not lost their shocking brilliance.

"Monsieur Dubois," Simone said, struggling to meet his eyes, "I am thrilled you came. I, like everyone else in Paris, know that you are not the type to freely travel. *J'espère bien,* Monsieur,

we will be able to do business together. How much is this painting worth to you?"

The abacus of his mind clicked to calculate how best to answer this forthright woman, uncommon in his circle and more
so in his presence. He concluded that nothing less than an
honest reply, or one that was at least partially true, would do. At
that moment, he noticed Simone's eyes flicker past his shoulders to the door behind him, and his grip tightened on the arm
of the chair.

Warned by her collectively distressed ghosts of the arrival of
an eerie-eyed, umbrella-flourishing man, Mme Gabrielle breezed
into the salon. She raised the slippery-smooth satin of her glove
to M. Jean Paul Dubois's mouth and introduced herself.

"Madame Gabrielle d'Honoré," M. Jean Paul Dubois said.
"Which one of the ladies am I conducting business with?"

"With me," Simone interjected. She approached him and
swept her hand under his nose with a wave that turned into a
final, voluptuous spray on his wrist, directly where the vein
pulsed. "You now had the chance to admire *Women of Algiers* up
close, and in the intimate setting of my home, no less. If you
need more time to decide on the price, you may join me outside
for a waltz or two, if you desire."

His eyes closed for a fraction of a second, as all five senses
converged into his olfactory cells. Her perfume was as pure as
diamonds, as crisp as recently printed francs. His jaws tightened
at having lowered his shield. But she would not allow him composure. She pressed against him as if to drag him out onto the
dance floor. His senses reeled under her essence that exploded
against his olfactory bulbs and composed a work of art. Was it
her perfume, he wondered, that startled him? He lost track of
time and place as he separated, analyzed, and filed her various
bouquets. What might cause such an effect—aged wine, cognac,
or absinthe? He shook himself back to full awareness. There was
a reason he had abstained from alcohol his entire life. He dis-

liked anything that meddled with his brain. And then, to his horror, he heard himself say, "Madame, in addition to an offer of five million francs for *Women of Algiers* without further formalities, I would like you to accompany me on a trip you would certainly enjoy. Your comfort will be assured in my residence, where you will find the diverse cultures fascinating. The only caveat is that we must depart as soon as possible. You may stay as long, or as little, as you wish, of course."

Simone, who had burst upon M. Jean Paul Dubois like a fragrant whirlwind, tried to reclaim her scent.

Mme Gabrielle looked up with an incredulous expression. Her fingers tapped on her thighs, sending Émile Zola skipping. Günter flew back and forth like a postal carriage, swelling her ears with the warning to put this man in his place. At the sight of M. Jean Paul Dubois's giant hulk hovering over the women, Franz Liszt dropped his baton and fainted.

⁓∞⁓

Fireworks were winding down outside. The crackling sparks of alcohol, neighing of horses, and tinkle of crystal began to settle. The last notes of Francis Planté's languorous tune for the piano pealed in the gardens. Winds began to gather force around the Valley of Civet Cats, tearing chestnuts off trees and felling them with the thud of a thousand rounds of ammunition. The yowling of civet cats reverberated around the hills.

Françoise stood at the gates, bidding farewell to the last guests, wondering where her mother and daughter were. She was unaware of M. Amir, who, unwilling to attract attention, had arrived in a nondescript carriage pulled by a pair of gray horses. Lingering in the shadow of the large mirror, he was dressed unremarkably, in a dirt-brown suit and without his prayer beads.

Earlier, having noticed Simone guide M. Jean Paul Dubois

into the château, and Mme Gabrielle follow, M. Amir had composed a hasty note. Once the last carriages began to roll down the cobblestone road, on his way out, he handed Françoise an envelope.

⊸∞⊶

Mme Gabrielle yanked up her gloves, rose to her feet, and strode to the windows. Nature raged and winds transported cries of wandering ghosts. Émile Zola at the helm, her fretful spirits pecked at her cheeks, insisting she drill sense into Simone. "Since *Women of Algiers,* Monsieur Jean Paul Dubois, is worth twice your offer, we cannot do business. I am afraid a storm is on its way. You will have to start back or you might be detained."

M. Jean Paul Dubois, having made an offer he had not anticipated, was startled by his lack of restraint. And by his uncharacteristic need to possess this woman, Simone. No other woman had piqued his interest in this manner. She was a find, like unearthing a rare diamond, like discovering a precious Vermeer. "Madame d'Honoré," he said, "I offer ten million for *Women of Algiers,* then."

Simone shivered in her crepe de chine. Her words echoed above the winds. "Now that the *Women* are yours, Monsieur, where do you intend to take *me*?"

"To Namaqualand," he replied.

Mme Gabrielle breathed a sigh of relief. Simone had succeeded in enhancing the Honoré wealth by ten million. And she would never travel to a godforsaken place such as Namaqualand. But the dwarfish ghost of Dr. Jacques Mercier would not allow Mme Gabrielle a second of relief. He checked her heartbeat and suggested a tonic of dandelion leaves for her heart, which would be taxed further before the end of the night.

Simone was at a loss as to why a calculating man such as

M. Jean Paul Dubois would risk striking up a relationship with the widow of a murdered colleague. She surveyed him, first with uncertainty, then with disbelief. The appearance of his eyes seemed to change, the pupils shrinking and losing their blade-like glint, the edges softening, the whites more pronounced, and his earlier unwavering focus somewhat unhinged. She was aware of the aphrodisiacal effect of her perfume. But in light of M. Jean Paul Dubois's behavior, she wondered whether her fragrance possessed other properties.

"I apologize, Monsieur," Mme Gabrielle broke in, "but I must remind you of the dangers of traveling through the Valley of Civet Cats during a storm. Many lives have been lost to cyclones trapped in the valley. Alphonse will direct you to the safest route back."

Simone raised her hand to M. Jean Paul Dubois's mouth for a farewell kiss. "I accept your invitation."

41

The storm had dotted the lavender horizon with chestnuts and white clouds stacked high like cotton puffs. The carriage wheeled its way out of the château toward Bougival on the riverside of the Seine, leaving behind last night's tent, half collapsed. Servants scuttled about in the park, collecting empty bottles, embroidered bloomers abandoned in the heat of love, gold-enameled heroin syringes stuffed into pockets when Alphonse was not looking.

The New Year's soirée had been a success. Simone had unleashed her erotic perfume and captivated the infamous M. Jean Paul Dubois. But with the heady waltz and fireworks a distant memory, she acknowledged the risk she would be taking. Still, she would not remain here luxuriating in solitude as the monotonous wheels of her existence continued to grind ahead as if Cyrus and her son were at her side.

Since it was the season of electrical storms, danger of thunder and lightning loomed, and Simone could not have embarked on the trip back and forth to Bougival in one day.

But this was where Cyrus had wanted her to start, and so she would.

After Françoise's erotic lesson the previous week, Simone had retrieved the two notes from the silk folds of Cyrus's tallit and held them against sunlight at the window. Her eyes stung at the sight of the litmus ink, no longer bright, the inscriptions bleeding, his thumbprint fading—*do not mourn my passing* . . . One note held the name of Mehrdad, his address in Persia, the other M. Amir's address in Bougival. She would have much rather met M. Amir in person on New Year's Eve. But she was left with a note he had handed Françoise.

The whole matter was a complicated maze. She suspected no one and everyone—the shah; his minister of court; Mehrdad, whom Cyrus had trusted; and, for a second, even Beard, to whom she owed her life. As of now, having no concrete proof, M. Amir was her only lead.

She had twisted her hair on top of her head, the strip of silver striking among orange curls. Her reflection in the mirror evoked Cyrus's memory: the amber, violet, and gold negligees that aroused him—*succulent,* he said; intimacies she flaunted for him—*zaneh khoshgeleh man,* my very own gorgeous wife.

She had wrapped his prayer shawl around her shoulders, sinking into his scent of cardamom and tobacco, and had sat down at her writing desk with his bold-tipped pen to compose a reply to M. Amir. She wrote that she would accept his invitation. And she had agreed that the distance and frequent electrical storms would require that she spend the weekend with his family.

The carriage gathered speed, lavender fields fading in the background. Mme Gabrielle and Alphonse had packed the carriage with food, blankets, and drinks. A flask of absinthe was tucked in the back pocket of the seat. Anticipating electrical storms, Françoise had left a parasol on the backseat. A breeze fanning her face, Simone rested her head on the leather couch.

Not minding the smell of man and horse, she shut her eyes to return to Cyrus.

She had spent an entire afternoon with him on the clearing of the carriage just left behind. Depending on the shape and gesture of the hands of strangers who came to observe Mme Gabrielle's galleries, she fabricated their sexual proclivities, adding intimate details she embellished. Soon, her language of hands metamorphosed into foreplay. They abandoned the un-corked wine bottle and unpacked lunch to melt and mold into each other. Afterward, he had pulled her close on the blanket as the setting sun transformed the horizon into violet waves. Wicked sparks in his eyes, he had promised her an apartment on Rue de l'Arcade close to the Place Vendôme—*so you can walk out and purchase jewelry nearby,* he said. And Simone, aware he re-ferred to Françoise and Mme Gabrielle, whose protectors had once settled them in expensive apartments in that area, pro-posed that he marry her and take her to Persia.

Persia is the end of the world, he said, *you might not like it there.*

"I've always longed to see the end of the world," she had as-sured him.

She walked him through her own Paris, under archways and across bridges. He kissed her beneath the Arc de Triomphe as she pointed out the twelve avenues that radiated from the arc, an architect's obsession with geometry.

Genius lies in tiny details and the insight to recognize good enough and let it be, he had said.

The murderers had done away with good enough.

"Mademoiselle, Mademoiselle, *c'est ici? Oui?* The road nar-rows. The carriage will not go farther."

Her eyes sprang open. She was in Bougival. She had spent the better part of the day without feeling thirst or hunger. She gave directions to the coachman to find lodging for the night and expect her on Monday in the same place. She gripped the handle of the small valise with her nightgown and a change of clothes. Her revolver secure in her corset, she stepped down from the carriage.

She walked along heights that rose above the Seine, hills immortalized in Monet, Renoir, and Pissarro paintings. Sunlight flickered on roofs of country cottages scattered around the sleepy Voisins village. The hills resounded with the metal clang of tables dragged onto terrace cafés. The voluptuous scent of *boulangeries* laced the air. She braced herself, forging ahead to follow the winding Rue des Voisins and cross Rue de la Machine, where Louis XIV's Machine de Marly pumped water from the Seine to Versailles. Mme Gabrielle had tried to reproduce Versailles's grandeur in Château Gabrielle, Simone thought, and she had triumphed, as with every project she had ever tackled. But when it came to her effort to transform her granddaughter into an Honoré, her grandmother had failed on a royal scale. She had gone out and fallen in love with a Persian, only to return a widow with nothing on her mind but vengeance.

She cut through a corridor of ancient trees across the riverbank. People were already congregating for the evening's dance on the small island in the center of the river, known as Camembert because it resembled a cake of cheese. Dances would begin in a few hours in riverside dance halls, at boating parties, and floating cafés.

The evening chill crept inland and water lapped against the shore. The buzz of insects and chatter of nocturnal birds crowded the falling dusk. She draped Cyrus's tallit and his scent of cardamom tightly around her shoulders. What about his clients had made him chew on cardamom?

To ward off their smell of corruption, he had said, *to hold on to a semblance of decency in a trade rife with greed.*

Who was M. Amir? Why did he live in hills populated by painters, poets, and writers? Here, artists unleashed their eccentricities, and the intoxication of fame and desolation of anonymity ruled the day.

Bougival was her mother's favorite stage. Even if she was unwelcome elsewhere, Bougival remained her haven. Decked in jewelry and opulent gowns, her enameled landau chiming to announce her arrival, she would come here to soak in the compliments of avant-garde artists.

The house Simone sought tumbled four stories down to lower slopes hard to make out from her vantage. Children's laughter rose from the adjacent courtyards. She pressed her hand to her stomach. Reluctant to accept their loss, her muscles were slow to regain strength. Her son would have been six months old today.

She held the tiger-head knocker in her hand and meditated on its forbidding feel. Was she stepping into the mouth of a wide-jawed creature that would snap shut behind her? She reasoned that no one would dare harm the daughter of the famous Françoise, granddaughter of Mme Gabrielle, confidante of the president of the Third Republic. Before she had occasion to deliberate further, she let go of the knocker and pounded on the door with her revolver.

The click of high heels could be heard from behind the door.

The rough-knuckled hand of a middle-aged woman held on to the half-open door. Her gray hair, parted in the center, was covered with a kerchief with a colorful design of perfume bottles. Her thighs flared out against a tight skirt, the chemise straining around ample breasts. An elegant hand-me-down, Simone concluded. She adjusted her revolver in her corset. Touching her petticoat, she raised her hand to inhale Cyrus's scent woven into the silken fiber. Plump and pregnant, she had worn the same petticoat on the day he came back from South Africa. "I would like to speak with Monsieur Amir."

"Who may I say is calling?" the woman asked, nudging the door with the tip of her shoe. The door swiveled on its hinges.

"Simone d'Honoré," she replied. She wanted to flip the

woman's palm up and decipher the geometry of her character, find out why her knuckles turned pale against the doorframe. The speed and silence with which she thrust the door open startled Simone, who scrambled to reclaim her composure. At a loss for words, she extended her hand. "Nightshade," the woman introduced herself as Simone's fingers grazed her palm, the deeper line that curved above her thumb, proof she was slow to trust, the shallow line that ran half the length of her palm that foretold of an aborted life.

"The family is expecting you," she said, stepping aside to let Simone into the vestibule.

The café au lait marble floor inlaid with geometrical designs reflected her legs on its shiny surface. Overhead, a chandelier encrusted with turquoise evoked memories of Yaghout. Was forgiveness so difficult? Did Yaghout have to suffer two painful losses before she could forgive Simone? A set of kingwood bombé commodes displayed Persian pottery horses. An inlaid mahogany cabinet held porcelain chador-clad women and sitar-playing musicians. Family portraits on a grand piano re- vealed a vast ethnic diversity of strong features, black hair and full mouths next to pale-skinned, blue-eyed individuals.

She followed Nightshade to the threshold of a salon crowded with oversized Aubusson-covered canapés and settees. A suite of four chairs with embroidered cushions surrounded a table with images of hunting animals carved along the legs.

"We have been expecting you."

"Yes, we certainly have."

The first voice, a woman's, floated to Simone from the left; the second, a baritone, came from the right.

Framed by a high-backed chair of magnolia green velvet, the woman sat in front of a tall window, the panorama of the hills her backdrop. A faint fragrance wafted through the win- dow from almond trees, lacing her surroundings with the cyanide scent of bitter almonds. Seated as she was, slim legs folded at an angle against the chair, black skirt falling around her ankles, her starched collar embracing a graceful neck, hair the shade of corn and braided from the crown with a strand of pearls, she gave the impression of a Nordic horse.

Simone had an urge to cover up her red hair, out of place in the presence of this woman who appeared hardly thirty-five. Remaining at the threshold, Simone turned her attention to the man on the other end of the salon. Wrapped in a silk robe de chambre, his muscular body leaned back in a leather chair the color of his sun-baked skin, his cravat loose around his neck. The lush vegetation of the hills outside the French windows behind him tumbled down as if to spill into the room. The eyes in his leather-dark face settled on her, inspecting her as if she were a thrilling mystery he would unravel in no time.

She fought with all her might not to turn away from the fire of his blue gaze, to disarm him with the poison in her own yellow stare. She would not allow him to triumph before she had even introduced herself.

A smile spread down from his eyes and quivered on his lips beneath his waxed mustache. He pinched snuff from a silver filigreed box and fixed a bit into each nostril. A couple of sneezes followed, as if to free him of some contagion. He gave off the smell of the brilliantine applied to his mustache, the spicy cologne on his black hair, and the Elburz Mountains. Amber worry beads clicked and flickered, snaking around his fingers, from one hand to the other, then pooled in the center of his large palm like drops of honey. "This is my wife, Madame Zizi Amir. We are pleased you accepted our invitation."

Zizi Amir rose from her seat, her ankles wobbling slightly to support her tall, slim body. Her face was the hue of white oleander, as if milk and not blood pumped in her veins. She shook her skirt as if to rid herself of some undesirable particles that might have settled on her. She extended her hand to Simone, who hardly reached the woman's unadorned earlobes. "It was nice meeting you, Madame. I will leave the two of you alone for now. Nightshade will show you to your room when you are ready."

Simone tightened her grip around Zizi Amir's fingers, grazed the thumb and the slightly protruded knuckles, analyzed the rigidity of the handshake, the frail bones, the hardly noticeable mound of Venus, and the scars across her palm. The woman's painful, almost mournful vulnerability touched her.

Zizi Amir's gaze flickered up, and she pressed her thumb against Simone's palm to release her hold. She crossed the salon toward the door. Hesitating at the threshold, she reached behind and tossed her braid over one shoulder. A clasp in the form of a rose composed of pearls held the tip of her braid together.

A red diamond dazzled in the center of the flower.

⌒∞⌒

"Enter," M. Amir said, gesturing to a chair opposite a marble-topped side table—close enough to sense his aloofness, far enough to impress distance. "Do not stand on ceremony. It is a long trip from the Valley of Civet Cats to Bougival. Are you hungry? Yes, yes, of course. Nightshade! Nightshade! Prepare supper for our guest."

Nightshade arrived with a teapot and cups, bowls of dates, dried mulberries, fresh cucumbers, plates, and knives.

"I am not hungry," Simone said. "I want to speak to you about—"

"About your husband's murder. I know. But do you have to remain standing there like that? Make yourself at home." He raised the cup of steaming tea to his lips and sipped the dark liquid, the lining of his mouth, like that of many Persians, numb from consumption of hot liquids. He selected a large date from the bowl and, his eyes married to hers, sucked the flesh off, then held the pit up between his thumb and forefinger as if displaying a bullet. "This is how he was killed! Right? Of course! Point-blank in the chest. You see, I know."

Simone clasped her trembling hands behind her. A trickle of perspiration rolled down her neck. She leaned against the door-sill for support. She did not know if and how Cyrus was mur-dered. How could she know when she did not see his body?

M. Amir held a cucumber between his brown fingers and with the flip of a knife sent the tip flying at her feet on the car-pet. "And I know of his horse."

She staggered back, sought the doorjamb to steady herself. Her arteries drummed in her ears. Because of the silence of the newspapers, only those who had seen his body or were involved in his murder would have known about the manner of his death, or about the cut-off ear of his horse.

So it was true. Cyrus would not come back to her then. He was shot in the chest—his heart shattered to pieces. And he was not even allowed the respect of a proper burial.

"I apologize for startling you. Would you like a glass of water? You are pale. Will you sit now?"

She slowly walked in, sat, and rested her arms on her knees, holding her head in her hands.

"Forgive me for being abrupt," he said, "but it is not in my nature, nor do I have the time or patience, to exchange trivia. Do you believe me now? I might add that Cyrus's murder is rather unusual, since knives are the preferred means of killing in Persia." The worry beads screeching between his palms, he shouted, "Nightshade! Food! Come before our lovely guest finds us inhospitable."

Simone glanced at the prayer beads he tossed from one hand to another. "How do you know about Cyrus and his horse?"

"In good time, my dear," he said, concealing the beads in his fist. "You and I will have to earn each other's trust. I nearly shocked you out of your skin trying to earn yours."

"Far from earning my trust, Monsieur, you made me more

suspicious. How did you come across the details of Cyrus's murder? And how did he come to know *you*?"

M. Amir settled back in his chair and gazed into the distance. "I am chargé d'affaires of court. I came to know Cyrus as the royal jeweler. Traveling often between France and Persia makes me privy to confidential matters. Unfortunately, I happened to leave for France the day Cyrus was murdered."

Considering that for now her only hope lay with M. Amir, she decided to be forthright. "Cyrus suggested I come to you if I needed help in France."

"I am not surprised. He knew that my wife is French and that we spend a large part of the year here. He found me unbiased, more tolerant than most Persians, someone to depend on when he eventually settled here with you. You know, of course, that he was considering a move."

Simone did not show her surprise. Cyrus had never discussed this matter with her. Was this another betrayal, or another attempt to protect her? Sidestepping this last revelation, she said, "I intend to find Cyrus's murderer. Do you happen to know who would want him dead?"

M. Amir pursed his caramel-colored lips. "You are a brave lady and must be rewarded with honesty. You know that I attended your New Year's Eve soirée. I noticed Monsieur Jean Paul Dubois's presence and am impressed that you lured him to Paris. I must assume then that you, too, suspect him. But I strongly advise you to leave the matter of Cyrus's murder alone. I promised Cyrus to watch over you. I shall do everything in my power to fulfill that promise."

"Monsieur Amir, I am capable of protecting myself. In fact, Monsieur Dubois invited me to Namaqualand and I accepted. If you want to protect me, tell me everything you know about him. Then I'll be better equipped to deal with him."

"Do not go, Simone. He is dangerous. Leave this unsolvable matter alone."

With his unexpected role as her guardian, her life was taking an unwelcome turn. She was in dire need of his cooperation, and he seemed immune to her seductive wiles. But his wife might not be. The woman had the essential canvas—blank, bare, and willing. A few simple strokes would prove miraculous. "Monsieur Amir, I will make a deal with you. I will attempt to cure your wife of her frigidity. If I fail, I'll forget about Cyrus's murder. If I succeed, you must promise to reveal all you know about Monsieur Jean Paul Dubois."

M. Amir's eyes flashed toward the entrance. "An interesting offer indeed. We all need each other. You need me, I need you, and Madame Amir needs us all." He joined his thumbs and index fingers in a circle. "We are connected. Nothing is accomplished in the Amir household if my wife is unhappy. Do what you can, but know that it will not be easy." Rising to his full height, he tightened the belt around his *robe de chambre* and bowed ceremoniously. "You must be tired. Nightshade will show you to your room. Good night." He sent his worry beads into wild circles around his finger.

Simone, mesmerized by the dizzying path of the chain, was left speechless.

The light from the chandelier exploded against facets of a red diamond at the tip of the knot that secured the thread of his amber beads.

42

Nightshade escorted Simone through a corridor with Persian carpets and miniature paintings of mythological figures. Open doors revealed bedrooms as still as tombs. The boudoir assigned to her, with its Kashan carpet, wooden backgammon set, and decorative water pipe, reminded her of Yaghout's home.

The housekeeper hurried to lock up the windows. "A storm is expected after midnight." She pulled at a rope draped over the bed's headboard. "This will ring downstairs in my room if you need anything."

"I will be very quiet," Simone replied. "I don't want to disturb Madame and Monsieur next door."

A low sound rumbled in the woman's throat, and her lips pursed as if to give her words time to ripen. "Madame and Monsieur won't hear you. They have separate bedrooms at the far ends of the corridor."

Left alone in her room, Simone locked the door, retrieved the revolver she had cleaned and loaded back home, and slipped it under the pillow. Fully dressed, she curled on top of the blankets to wander through the convoluted maze of her grief, the routine of loneliness she was settling into. An appealing alliance was beginning to shape between her memories and her reality. The question was, how many men and women could she accommodate, how many groping hands could she tolerate? Many, she concluded, many if the answer lay with them. She scrambled out of bed and stepped into the bathroom to splash cold water on her face. She changed from the skirt and sweater she had arrived in into a peignoir embroidered down the front with eyelets. Wrapping her revolver in her lace handkerchief, she tucked it in her corset, unlocked her door, and crossed the vestibule.

ᶜ∞ᵓ

The light was on in Zizi Amir's bedroom. Simone peered through the half-open door. The woman sat upright in a chair facing her dressing table. Her bone-deep sadness and desolate expression sent a shiver up Simone's spine. Her aborted love had once fulfilled her every need. For Cyrus, she had readily abandoned her country, family, and every other accoutrement of civilization to which she was accustomed. And she had never regretted that move. Zizi Amir did not realize she was more fortunate than Simone. Her dilemma had a solution; death had none.

Zizi picked up a pair of scissors from the dressing table and observed it with a detached, somewhat puzzled gaze. Pointing the tip down, with methodical and calculated agility, she slashed one cross after another into her palm.

Alarmed, Simone knocked and stepped into the room.

Her features set as granite, Zizi replaced the scissors on the tabletop. Finding the placement uneven, she relocated it to the center. She turned to Simone. "Madame! *Avez-vous besoin de quelque chose?*"

"No, no, I don't need anything. My room is quite comfortable." She strode across the room, flung the curtains back, and opened the windows to chase out the stagnant air. "I am here to seduce you."

A look of utter alarm flashed across Zizi's eyes.

Simone laughed softly as she came to stand over the woman. "What I mean is that I intend to teach you the art of seduction and how to win your husband back."

Zizi forced a chilly whisper from between her lips. "I don't understand."

"I can tell that you have not been intimate with your husband for some time. I can help you. You must have heard about my mother and grandmother, of course, her hands, the galleries."

"And her bed," Zizi Amir murmured. "What is it called?"

" 'Seraglio.' "

"Does it truly have aphrodisiac powers?"

"The women who occupy it do. You see! You are in good hands. Cooperate with me so that before sunrise you will have tapped into your femininity to do with as you please." She slowly, tentatively coaxed Zizi out of her flannel gown. Surprised to find her in *soutien-gorge* and bloomers, Simone decided to leave them alone for now. "Come, come, how long since you let yourself go with nothing between you and the sheets, nothing in your head but lust?" She squeezed Zizi's calves, thighs, and arms. "You feel like rock. Who would want to make love to a mannequin?" She hesitated for a moment, then tucked her hand behind Zizi's back and freed her breasts from her *soutien-gorge*. "Do not hide your lovely breasts. Let them breathe. Draw a deep breath yourself. Now, come and lie on the bed. Good. I want you to fantasize shamelessly, without care for how you will be regarded. No one will know. Not even me. You will never share your fantasies with anyone, unless you want to, until you want your husband to enjoy them too. Now close your eyes and conjure up the most delicious images you can picture."

Simone turned her back on Zizi, praying that the woman's fantasies had not atrophied like the rest of her body, hoping her voice from across the room could awaken the woman's dormant emotions.

Beyond the window and the Bougival hills, the ghost of a crescent moon was imprisoned among steely clouds. The midnight chill was beginning to lift, and humid winds were gathering. Simone's voice flowed like warm honey: "Saturate yourself with lust and desire until your skin tingles and vibrates. Lick your lips; pass your tongue over the moist flesh. Blow through the cool wetness. Coax your senses onto the surface of your skin, the tips of your fingers, between your legs. Adore yourself. Love him."

She felt Cyrus's face in her hair, his hands sliding down her back to stroke the two dimples above her buttocks: *intoxicating—how is it possible to love like this, to desire like this, to become drunk like this with your perfume?* Thunder cracked across the skies. Plump drops of rain fell on the windowsill. Beads of perspiration glowed on her neck. She turned around. Zizi lay on the bed like a corpse. Her hands stiff at her sides, her blank eyes stared at the ceiling. Simone approached to stand over her, wondering if by removing her bloomers she might succeed in peeling off her inhibitions, too, or if she would thrust her into further shock. She gently slipped the bloomers off. Zizi threw a sidelong glance her way, then returned to the chandelier as if it were her potential lover.

Simone rubbed her hands together to warm them up. Administering fast, tiny slaps, she began from Zizi's toes, skipping up and around her waist, under her breasts and around the areolae. Turning her over on her stomach, she continued to stimulate blood to the surface of the skin, up and down the thighs, across the buttocks and shoulders, kneading and cajoling the muscles into submission. Zizi's breathing quickened; her chest rose and fell to empty her lungs. Simone adjusted a pillow.

"Come, turn over and slide up. Rest against the headboard. Are you comfortable?" She gave a soft whack with the palm of her hand on each of Zizi's thighs. "Now try to fantasize again. Watch me and do not be embarrassed to go wherever you want."

Zizi leaned against the pillow, her eyes riveted on Simone, her heartbeat quickening, goose bumps rising on breasts as firm as those of a pubescent girl.

Simone slipped out of her peignoir and stretched out next to the woman. She was doing this for Cyrus, whose breath warmed her, weight anchored her, scent of tobacco and cardamom blended with her longing, his desire, her sighs, his moans. She unleashed the burning sparks of her perfume, honeyed the room with her fragrance, with her scent of quince and peaches. Yes, yes. Now? Yes! Now!

She experienced a tinge of joy at the palpable mantle of her perfume woven with his threads of passion. But then she reassembled the scattered leftovers of her dreams and corked her perfume. Where had Zizi gone while she was away with Cyrus?

Her head thrown back on the pillow, her nostrils flaring, her mouth slightly ajar to drink Simone's perfume, Zizi's hand was tucked between her legs, the stroking gathering speed as if to make up for lost time.

Simone cupped the woman's breast and squeezed the nipple, registering the shudder, the hardening. A drop of moisture appeared at the tip. "He will want you like this. Soft and moist and wanting."

❧

"Dear Simone," M. Amir gushed the next morning. "You performed a miracle. I could not believe my eyes when Zizi appeared in my bedroom. I do not know how to thank you."

"By answering my question," Simone said, lightly tapping

him on the hand. "Who is Mehrdad? And is he involved in the murder?"

"Mehrdad," M. Amir mused, raising the screech of his worry beads. "He is, or rather was, Cyrus's most ardent supporter in court. I have not heard of him since Cyrus's death. His disappearance, I admit, seems suspicious."

Simone studied her palm. Yes, she would have to find her way to Mehrdad too. He would not have gone missing if he was not guilty. But M. Amir did not know, or did not want to reveal, more about Mehrdad. "Now, Monsieur Amir, you may further thank me by keeping your promise."

"Yes, certainly, I will help you if you agree to help me. I, too, am in a bind and require your expertise in an important matter."

"Monsieur Amir, how could *I* possibly help *you*?"

"You and I, you see, are after the same individual. Namely, your husband's murderer. And we both want justice. I have good reason to believe that the responsible parties are linked to additional atrocities in my country."

"You are the chargé d'affaires. Why would you need my assistance?"

He kept his gaze on her, inventing, reinventing, and piecing her together, creating the partner who with experience and feminine wiles would lure criminals out of hiding. Her single-mindedness and grief might come in handy where others had failed. He knew how difficult his request would prove. He had employed other means, other spies, all to no effect. "Hundreds of Persians are being deceived with outrageous promises and shipped away to slave under dictatorial cartels and ruthless miners. The responsible parties are elusive. I have failed to track them down on my own. It is hard to infiltrate their mines, but more than anything, their psyches."

Cyrus had mentioned the tragic situation of Persians in South African mines. Africans, he had said, were not impressed by the recent eruption of gold and diamond mining. The majority preferred farming to disrupting the earth by digging for diamonds. The shortage of laborers had encouraged the trade of slaves from other countries.

It is dangerous to meddle with these people, jounam. *For now the responsibility of fixing the problem rests with others.*

"You are the only woman Monsieur Jean Paul Dubois has ever shown such interest in. But I doubt he would allow you to get close to him. No woman has. And no man has witnessed what goes on in his mines and lived to tell. Yet an eyewitness is essential to convince the shah of Dubois's guilt."

"Monsieur Amir," Simone interjected, "you equip me with the proper ammunition, and I will promise to not only infiltrate his mines but also deliver an eyewitness."

43

❦

South Africa
January 1903

M. Jean Paul Dubois's residence in Namaqualand—
a windy stretch of land along the northwestern coast of
South Africa—is reminiscent of medieval forts. High stone
walls make access into the compound impossible for
strangers. The flagstone floors are the shade of burnt ocher,
the coal-mouthed fireplaces cavernous, the velvet drapes
confining, and the air troubled with the faint scent of sulfur
and mold.

A gallery on a grand scale, the mansion celebrates female
grandeur and speaks of its owner's obsession with collecting.
Austere frames exhibit, among other masterpieces, François
Boucher's *Venus Asleep, The Toilet of Venus,* and *Venus Adorning
Herself,* Jean-Marc Nattier's *Portrait of Mathilde de Canisy* in pearl
taffeta, and Louise-Elisabeth Vigée-Lebrun's *Portrait of Countess
Skavronskaia* in a magnolia-green ball gown. The splashes of

color afford relief from the stark backdrop. Frames lean on walls for labeling or subsequent rotation, I am not certain which.

We landed in South Africa late last night, after more than fifteen days of traveling. My focus was to slowly and methodically ensnare M. Jean Paul Dubois in my perfume. His sole intent was to convince me to share his cabin. I refused. Escorted to a bedroom of suffocating colors and grave starkness, I was unable to sleep. Wandering from one room to another now, I thread an imaginary rope behind to retrace my steps back from these vaults and catacombs.

In a large bedroom, a life-sized portrait looms above a fireplace. A young man with a melancholy face, bottomless pupils, and protruding lips glares down at me. The resemblance to M. Jean Paul Dubois is unmistakable. This must be his son, Cyrus's roommate at the Sorbonne, the boy who had lost his arm in a duel.

The missing arm is painted in.

Monsieur Jean Paul Dubois detests handicaps, Cyrus said on our first and last Persian New Year together. Noruz, *the Festival of Spring, symbolizes the triumph of light over darkness—come closer my lovely wife, I won't be done with the past until we walk through it together.*

What essentials did he trust to unreliable memory? What did he withhold? My eyes well up at the memory of that night, the call to prayer from blue-tiled minarets. I lean on the stone mantelpiece under the portrait and plead with Cyrus to send me another sign. Why does he forget me now that I need him most? Perhaps he blames me for being suspicious of his friend Mehrdad. How can I trust him when all evidence points to him? Perhaps Cyrus is angry with me for coming to Namaqualand. But we have separate bedrooms, M. Jean Paul Dubois and I. I try to suppress my rising scent of longing—amber slick, honey gold, and fierce.

"You did not sleep well!" M. Jean Paul Dubois thunders behind me.

Startled, I step away from his son's portrait. Wiping my eyes, I fumble for words. "No, not at all. On the contrary, I slept very well. And you?"

His reptilian tongue darts out to lick my earlobe. "Not enough. And not well."

I turn around to face him, wrap my arms around his neck, my pores tiny atomizers spraying him with the fragrance of valerian. Beyond his shoulders, I am riveted to a plaque: BEDROOM OF PERSIAN NUNS. Surrounding the plaque are paintings of nuns with faces as pure as dew, mouths as shiny as polished apples, rosaries as sensual as pearls.

I am in Cyrus's room.

These frames, canvases, and images shared the same space with him. I gesture toward the plaque. "Do you name all your rooms?"

"No! This is my son's room when he comes to town. His friends spend a night or two here, too. Didn't you live in Persia once? You must appreciate the analogy between habits and chadors."

I tilt my head up like a question mark.

"The veil, as you know, conceals a woman from all men except her husband. The habit, too, conceals a nun from other men, save God, *her* husband."

"I don't trust nuns, the way they hide under their habits," I lash back, freeing my wrist from his grip. "In fact, I don't trust women under chadors, either."

"You are an exemplary *morceau d'art*," he says, his nostrils flaring. "Mysterious and stimulating. You *must* come to me tonight."

Cyrus's rage palpable in the room, in my chest, in my fragrance that sprays M. Jean Paul Dubois, I whisper, "I am not ready yet, *mon cher*. Perhaps tomorrow night."

He tears himself away from me, or my ripened scent, shaking his head as if to readjust his brain into its habitual niche. His eyelid shutters down over the dark window of one eye. "Yes, yes, indulge me. Even if it is not so, make me think I am the first to discover you—pristine, virgin, and welcoming—like Namaqualand upon my arrival. Take your time. Delay is a most powerful aphrodisiac."

Namibia, M. Jean Paul Dubois's soft-spoken servant, with his deerlike eyes and skin the sheen of chocolate, is in awe of me. He mumbles something under his breath as he fidgets with his oil-stained apron. "Permission, ma'am, to ask if your hair is yours."

"You think I have a wig on?"

"Yes, ma'am. No one is born with hair this color."

He must rarely leave the premises, or perhaps has never come across red-haired women. I lower my head for him to rub a curl between his fingers. "I was born like this, I promise."

He throws his shoulders up as if unable to process this informality. Slowly, he passes a finger over a lock of her hair.

After a moment, I gently say, "I am very hungry."

"Yes, Ma'am Simone, yes. I will set the table right away."

"Not necessary. I will come to the kitchen. It will be warmer, I am sure."

We walk through a maze of stairs and hallways that open into salons and dank corridors that resemble underground tunnels. I would never find my way back if I was alone. Still, I stop to admire the work of masters my grandmother is fond of: Manet's *Lola de Valence Danseuse Espagnole,* Cézanne's *Une Moderne Olympia,* Ingres's *Madame Marcotte,* Delacroix's *Étude de Femme Nue, Couchée sur un Divan.* For ten million francs, *Women of Algiers in Their Apartment* will soon join this museum.

Namibia removes four portraits from their hooks, carrying them to the adjoining room. "Master likes to move his women around him."

A chill creeps up my vertebrae to lodge somewhere in my brain. M. Jean Paul Dubois is more than obsessed. He is a possessed collector. His lack of interest in women must stem from the impracticality of imprisoning them. Have I stepped into the frame of his home to become an *objet d'art,* something to own forever?

"You are colorful, ma'am," Namibia says when he is done rearranging his master's women. "Very nice to my eyes."

"Thank you, Namibia. It is nice for my ears to hear this."

The kitchen is hot with soot-blackened stone walls covered with African art depicting women toiling in fields, slaving over cauldrons, or chopping vegetables on cutting boards. A saucepan simmers on a firewood stove, raising spirals of strong-smelling steam. On a wood table in the center is a spread of strong spices and condiments—red peppers, purple garlic, black radishes. Bottles of vinegars exude the pungent odor of Alise-Sainte-Reine cheese or some fermented curd. Namibia lifts the lid off the saucepan. The sharp odor sends me reeling. "What are you cooking?"

"Sheep brains, beetroot, black-eyed peas, and celeriac in Cachat d'Entrechaux sauce. I do not think it is for you. Master likes spicy food. But I will prepare a meal to your liking, ma'am." He glances my way and whispers, "Spicy food would certainly strip the color off your hair." His expression pensive, he adds, "You are very delicate, ma'am. You must take care of yourself."

"I promise to do so, if you do me a favor, Namibia."

"Yes, anything, ma'am, anything," he replies in his sweet Afrikaner accent.

"Take me to Master's mine."

His skin darkens further by a spreading blush. He gestures toward the unfamiliar universe outside. "I do not desire to take you there. You should not go, either."

"We will keep this our secret."

"No, not even then, please. I am an honest servant, not a diamond stealer. I respect the earth," he says as if to declare his loyalty to his ancestors.

The metallic clang of the gates sends him running out to greet his master.

I leave the biting steam behind to follow Namibia, cross the corridor of dancing women, and enter an unfamiliar vestibule. I remain standing petrified with fear, still as the surrounding portraits. I call out to Namibia.

"Here, Ma'am Simone, on your left first, then an immediate right, a half turn now . . ." I grab the thread of his voice and walk toward the source. "Come quick! Right at the bedroom of nuns and straight to the main foyer. Master is waiting."

I stagger into the foyer and am confronted with M. Jean Paul Dubois's dilated pupils overtaking his eye sockets. His hands are shaking, his sweat-soaked shirt plastered to his chest hair.

I run to him, alarmed but slightly hopeful. I have been praying for this change in him—the trembling, the excessive sweating, and the unhinged eyes. He waves me off, mumbling something about having to take a bath first. He stumbles toward the hall to disappear into the *salle de bains*.

Namibia glances my way. "What is wrong with Master, Simone Ma'am?"

"I don't know, Namibia."

"Simone! Simone!" M. Jean Paul Dubois calls out, his voice

bouncing off walls and echoing against the high ceilings. "Come! Now!"

The *salle de bains* is all stone and steam and limestone counters. An ample-hipped Medusa is etched onto a marble panel in the center of the steaming arena. A free-standing basin of pure gold gleams under a skylight. At my sight, M. Jean Paul Dubois rises out of a lion-pawed onyx tub. He shakes water off himself, his pectoral muscles coiled like Aigaion, the sea god. He tosses away the towel I hand him. His chest expanding and contracting, his limbs trembling, he lifts me up in his arms and settles on a counter. Droplets of steam cluster on the domed ceiling, burst, and drop on our shoulders. In the surrounding silence, the rhythmical *pit-pat* of water echoes the drumbeats of my heart. His erection firm against my back, his arms tight around my waist, the omnipotent M. Jean Paul Dubois is at his most vulnerable. I turn to face him and wrap my thighs around his midriff. I unleash my perfume. Impregnate the steaming air. Water his thirsty irises, plump his arid cells. My fingers start from the nape of his neck, massage the lust vein that snakes down his vertebrae, fondle the ladder of sensory knobs, and knead kernels no other woman has accessed. The delicate atomizers at the tips of my fingers intoxicate him, a purple perfume to sail him to a place where I will steadily claim him.

My scent unleashed, my fingers running wild, I slip to another world, to another man, to a delicious abandon, wrapped in succulent perfumes of nutmeg and cardamom, and in the midst of the Persian mountains, flanked by earth and sky as intimate as the two of us.

M. Jean Paul Dubois murmurs incomprehensibly in my ear, his heartbeat an insult against mine. His pupils lose their iron glint, the whites frame kinder eyes.

45

Missteps unacceptable to M. Jean Paul Dubois in the past suddenly occur. He is indifferent to the drumming of a woodpecker outside the window. He failed to check the lock before retiring last night. He seems to have lost some of his obsessive skepticism. At eight in the morning, still asleep at my side, he is late for work.

I swing my legs off the bed and toss a peignoir over my shoulders.

He shakes himself into full consciousness. A look of utter alarm contorts his face. "Namibia! A cup of pepper tea. Now!" He steps into his pants, pulls on his shirt, and tosses a cravat around his neck. Stomping toward the door, he spins on his heels, grabs my scent-soaked handkerchief from under his pillow, and stuffs it in his pocket. He turns the key in the lock. Horror flashes across his eyes. "Why is the door open? Who else is here?"

"You did not lock the door."

"Impossible!" He storms out, his keys left behind in the

lock. Marching back, he disengages and stares at the keys as if they, not he, had committed an inexcusable faux pas.

I walk him out to the courtyard, my arms bare, the peignoir swinging around perfumed hips, indulging his senses, stirring up sensory and anticipatory cues, tapping into his well of olfactory memories, and tempting him further from the reality of his here and now.

He hesitates at the gates as if he might walk back into my arms. "Simone, prepare to retire early tonight."

Before the dust of his retreating carriage settles, I run back in. I pull on a pair of riding breeches, boots, and a man's shirt. I tuck my hair into one of his hats.

"Where, Ma'am Simone, are you going?" Namibia asks as I am about to step out of the gate.

"Master suggested I take a walk in the bazaar."

"Yes, yes, you could, of course, but not the way you are dressed. Please come in. I will give you the proper clothing."

∽∾

The busy thoroughfare outside M. Jean Paul Dubois's home is filled with the cries of vendors, begging sad-eyed children, sun-baked faces, and dust-filled lungs. Women balance fruit baskets on colorful headgear. Hanging from dark, sweat-slick necks, leather-strapped wooden trays hold cigarettes, nuts, and animal-shaped candies for sale. Baked potatoes, fried bananas, and boiled pumpkins are piled on crude counters. The air is sticky with the scent of spice and molasses. A number of fair-skinned peddlers wander among the natives.

Winter rains, I am told, could bring wondrous flower fields during the brief Namaqualand springtime. But the surrounding landscape of sandy plains and granite mountains speaks of a dry winter. M. Jean Paul Dubois's fort is the only sign of wealth among makeshift shacks.

Flickering glances, a shrug here, a nod there, and the covert exchange of cash warn of illegal dealings. The major source of income in the poverty-stricken region of Namaqualand is stolen diamonds. And the steady traffic of contraband is going on right in front of my eyes.

I solicit a harmless-looking pedestrian to direct me to the town's mine. He points past my shoulders as if the entire never-ending horizon is a vast mine. He continues on his way without as much as a farewell nod. I approach a short, white-haired elderly man behind a stall piled high with coconuts. He pierces the shell of one and empties the juice in cups stacked into a pyramid.

"Good morning," I say. "Could you direct me to the diamond mine?"

He cracks open the coconut, quartering it into small segments. His branchlike fingers shoot toward a boundless hazy desert. "This here and beyond is the Diamond Coast, from where we stand all the way to the Atlantic Ocean. Monsieur Jean Paul Dubois's territory."

Shading my eyes, I squint through the reverberating heat, past a deserted plateau strewn with thornbushes and sand hills. "Is it possible to walk there?"

"The sun will melt your skin off if you do. A carriage is better." A series of coughs rattles his hairless chest, and he shoots out a wad of blood-stained spittle into his palm. "Diamonds," he grumbles, "are a curse we cannot do without."

46

The Atlantic Ocean foams and crashes against the shore. Dry tongues of fire, the sun slaps down on my face and on the sweat-sleek torsos of diggers. Crude sandbags push back the ocean, a colossal wall stripping vast stretches of sand down to bedrock to uncover diamonds washed up from the Atlantic. Kilometers of invaluable ocean bed rich in alluvial deposits produce hundreds of carats of diamonds. A fleet of boats pitches and rocks on the heaving waves, suctioning gravel from the ocean. Debris is washed then sieved in search of rough diamonds caught in large strainers—hundreds of white, sparkling stars seeded in sand. Close to shore, thousands of men dig gravel with shovels and pails, sifting through dirt, mud, and pebbles. Farther down, air hoses clamped between their teeth, divers plunge off boats to collect diamond-laced gravel from the deep.

Moaning and creaking, a rickety wagon and a stubborn mule abandon me on the bleak shores of the Diamond Coast. I stand in front of a large placard that informs the world of

DUBOIS ENTERPRISES. NO TRESPASSING. I send a silent thank you to Namibia. Dressed as I am, in a threadbare shirt and pleated skirt, my hair pulled back in a headscarf, and a brown concoction that Namibia swore would protect me against the sun smeared on my face and arms, I might be mistaken for a native.

The cracking of a whip startles me. A digger, under persistent flogging, vomits a stomach full of precious cargo onto the shore. A baton-wielding man chases him off the premises. A fist forms in my stomach. Sweat drips down my face. In the tempting proximity of diamonds, the robbing of gems on beach mines is easy. Getting caught is dangerous. What did Cyrus witness here that might have led to his death? There is evidence of hard work under difficult conditions—not even a makeshift awning to protect against the sun—but this is not illegal. And there is no discernible suggestion of slavery, as M. Amir had implied.

The excited shouts of a digger attract my attention. Waves foaming and hissing about his ankles, he steps out of the ocean and runs toward the shore. Feet beating down on the blistering sand, he jumps up and down. Gravel showers down on him from the uplifted sieve he brandishes above his head. The entire ocean and its men metamorphose into an anticipatory seascape. Four men run toward the digger. They shout orders for the others to resume work. Like preprogrammed marionettes, the diggers turn their attention back to sand and mud.

A supervisor plucks a fist-sized raw diamond out of the sieve and holds up the gem. Fiery sparks glint under the sun. I squint at the sight of this inexplicable phenomenon. A red diamond of exceptional size!

Cyrus's words crystallize—*M. Jean Paul Dubois's underground mine produces red diamonds, a rare breed that survives the cutting wheel.* Yet today, at this very moment, in front of my incredulous eyes, a white diamond ocean mine has yielded a red diamond.

Cyrus's fourth sign.

His murder, he reminds me, is connected to red diamonds from an underground mine. I am facing the wrong mine. Since diamond pipes occur in clusters, the underground mine must not be far off. I turn my back to the ocean and come upon a panoramic view of kilometers of sand dunes depositing loads of sand into the ocean to be thrown up again. Harsh winds craft smooth, curvy paths into the bleak landscape farther inland, the surface as reflective as powdered glass.

In the distance, a baton-wielding supervisor marches in my direction. I wait. There is nowhere to go, nowhere to hide in this sweeping landscape. He passes me and continues toward the shore, giving orders to a gathering of diggers who deposit their shovels, pails, and sieves to follow him. I wait for my heart to settle and then follow the men at a distance. The ocean crashes behind, a vista of undulating haze in front, the exhausting heat everywhere. The men stop at the edge of what resembles a makeshift roof of soldered tin sheets laid flat on a large stretch of sand. Halfway around this vast tin field, a square panel is raised. The diggers step down and disappear from sight. The supervisor drops the panel back into place behind his men. He points his baton at me like a shotgun. I remain paralyzed. Helpless as a visible ghost plunked into the humdrum of life.

He circles the roof, plows toward me. Above the pounding in my chest and rush of blood in my ears, muffled noises rise from gaps between the tin sheets. He approaches to appraise me as if evaluating a rough diamond he might toss in his pocket. He nods toward the roofed area where the men had stepped down. He says something I do not understand. I shake my head. In broken French, he says, "Are you here for the job?"

"No! No!" I blurt out, a mere intuitive reaction, not knowing how else to answer, sweat stinging my eyes.

"Go then! Right now! This is forbidden territory."

I turn around and walk away, but not too far before the clang of tin attracts my attention. I glance back to catch the top of the man's head disappear underground. Clinging to my source of courage—the image of the hand brandishing the red diamond—I walk to the opposite edge of the roof where the men stepped down. My wisest course, I conclude, is to disengage and lift another tin panel, opting for a different entryway. I tuck both hands under the seam of two overlapping sheets. Nothing gives. I pull my revolver out of my corset and, using the barrel, widen and disengage two panels around the edges. Tucking the revolver back, I slide one slab to overlap the other, enough space to squeeze through without letting in much light. I glance up at the sky, the blanket of mist about to descend on the ocean in the distance. I fill my lungs with air and ease myself down.

My feet dangle in the void below, my hands clinging to the sandy edge above, as I search for solid ground. Carefully planting my feet down, I let go of the world above. Making a mental note of the exact location of the tin sheet, my point of exit, I slide it back overhead. Thrust into tar-heavy darkness, my mouth fills with dust. I struggle to suppress a cough. Although I am blind to the surroundings, the odor of mud and the echoing voices below give a sense of space. I fear I may fall with the slightest misstep. I press my back to a rough wall behind.

My eyes slowly adjust and a reluctant vista of shadows opens at my feet. Silhouettes take shape against a mud-caked background to congeal before my startled gaze. I am perched above an abyss, on a ledge as narrow as the length of my feet. A step forward, the slightest miscalculation, and I will topple to my death. I flatten myself against the wall, anchor my legs, and observe the chaos below, somewhat relieved that I must not be conspicuous this high above ground and concealed in darkness. An underground cave has been hollowed deep into the earth, past sand and stone and into water. A rough staircase is hewn into the stone precipice on the other side of the arena. The roof consists of crude overlapping tin sheets roughly sol-

dered. Walls of rock and earth rise high, threatening to collapse
and bury hundreds of diggers who work knee-high in an im-
mense muddy pond in the center. Men supervise from a gravel
ridge half a meter above and around the pond. Makeshift stalls
make up the outer boundary of the arena. In the ghostly halo of
gas lamps, clusters of three or four men crouch, lie, and sit in
the stalls.

M. Jean Paul Dubois is nowhere to be seen.

From my vantage, it is difficult to detect evidence of red diamonds.

A supervisor steps down into the arena and draws a leather
whip from a pail of water. He approaches a man who is leaning
down toward the ground, as if searching for a lost object. The
whip cracks down on his back, breaking the skin, every lash
leaving a trail of blood—to discourage theft, Cyrus said, it is forbidden to touch the ground in mines. The digger stumbles back
gasping, his mouth foaming, rolling in an epileptic fit. He struggles on all fours, attempts to wobble to his feet, only to cringe
back at the whip that snaps down across his shoulder. His arms
thrash about to ward off the continuous blows.

"*Nakon! Nakon!*" he shouts in Farsi. Don't! Don't!

A brutal kick silences him.

Mouth dry, hair sweat-soaked; my hands spring back to the
wall to regain my balance. Did Cyrus beg for mercy, shout
Nakon! Nakon! with his last breath? Or was the bullet too fast
for words? Did he know that M. Jean Paul Dubois imports
slaves from Persia to dig the diamonds he then exports to the
Persian markets?

M. Amir was right, after all. Even about the difficult task of
gathering the necessary evidence with which to confront the
shah.

A group of girls files down the stone steps, the oldest hardly
seventeen; they cling to each other like orphans, their fear palpable. At the order of a supervisor, a gathering of fifteen men

deposits their sieves and shovels. Each digger is supplied with an object I am unable to identify. Retreating into the cubicles, three or four men huddle close, settling down cross-legged to fidget with the item. Leaning against each other, they draw deeply from what I now recognize as a pipe. Smoke and the smell of opium spiral upward, stinging my nose. The girls adjust their skirts, comb fingers through matted hair. With a sad, juvenile sway of the hips, they enter the cubicles.

A hellish scene unfolds in the stalls below, more hallucinatory than real. Swiftly, without fanfare, the men roll down their pants. Enveloped in opium smoke, mud, and the promise of what will never come, they take their turns with the girls. Guts surging, I turn away from the scene of human desperation. An opium den. An underground whorehouse. Means of shackling Persian and African slaves.

This, I realize now, is "the job" the supervisor had assumed I was soliciting.

Is this what Cyrus would have revealed to the world?

47

M. Jean Paul Dubois shudders in sweat-soaked sheets. His broad shoulders quiver in a nightshirt glued to his chest. He reaches out to me. Quickly draws back. "Something is terribly wrong, Simone."

"You are running a fever," I offer.

"No. I have never been ill in my life, never missed a day of work."

I approach the bed to feel his forehead.

"Stay where you are. Do not come closer."

I remain standing at his bedside, unable to believe the speed with which he has been transformed. Could spending one night in my company affect him so? Despite murmuring that I do not understand what is happening, I have some idea of what plagues him.

He rises on one elbow, squirms as if in pain, his voice unnatural. "Simone, come to me."

I walk toward his outstretched arms, not at all certain how

to react, how far I have gone, whether I miscalculated his olfactory response.

He wipes his face with the corner of the sheet and gazes at the wet mark. "Look how I sweat. This is unacceptable."

"I will call Namibia. You need medical attention."

His glazed-over eyes hollow as pits, he says, "Why can't I breathe when I am away from you?"

I do not tell him that he is exhibiting the signs of addiction. I do not tell him that I am stunned, too, because my fragrance has not affected any other man in this manner. I do not tell him that from the very first day we left Paris, I gradually increased the dosage to keep him afloat in a morphine haze. That since his fragrance-induced orgasm in the bath, I have been withholding my scent. I could, of course, alleviate his misery with a few perfumed mists. But I fear his dependence has spiraled out of control, fear he will never free me, the opiate he so badly craves. Above all else, I am afraid he will transform me into his personal artifact, a curiosity to be locked away, framed, and rotated at will.

He pulls himself together with a great heave of his large frame and comes up to rest against the headboard. His black pupils invade the eyes as if spilling beyond to stain his cheeks. His voice is a monotone. "I will find the solution. I always do."

Arms folded over my breasts, my eyes turn to poisonous cobras. Whatever his solution, it will not be good. I unplug the pores of my skin. Release a voluptuous mist—dusky, warm, and mysterious to rattle his intellect.

His nostrils flare to absorb the meager handout. He lets out a couple of harsh-sounding breaths. He slaps himself on the side of his head. His arms shoot up in front of him to keep me at bay. "I know now what must be done. You must leave! Pack up and go back to Paris."

I stare at him in disbelief. He must have detected me in his underground mine. He will order my murder on the journey back home. He will not allow his addiction to walk away. I settle at the edge of the bed, my voice full of concern. "Let me nurse you back to health before I leave."

An artery along his neck stands out. His cheek twitches, a spasm visible under one eye. At once livid and helpless, he points an accusatory forefinger at me. "You do not understand, do you? I am a different person with you around. I have had my moment of madness and want no part of it. Go!"

His sangfroid leaves no question but that I must comply. With the inevitability of dismissal, I decide to risk asking, "Monsieur Jean Paul Dubois, I am alone and at your mercy. Why are you letting me go?"

He strokes the sheets as if to soothe a lover, fixes his gaze to a corner of the ceiling, and a soft expression butters his eyes. To my surprise, he seems to struggle to compose an honest reply.

"Simone," he says, without tearing his gaze from the vaulted ceiling, "you are the only woman I ever desired. You have proved more precious than any art I own. Far more remarkable than any museum treasure. It would be unforgivable to harm such a flawless artifact."

I feel a certain pride but also added trepidation. Even as he speaks, a scheme must be hatching in the convoluted maze of his mind.

"But in the end, this is not why I am releasing you. My son has become a fine gentleman. I owe his transformation to your husband. I have never been indebted to anyone, nor do I intend to be. This is my payment to him. Now go away before my obsession degenerates into resentment."

48

Namibia lowers his head and checks his chapped hands, his sigh hovering above us like an ominous breeze. His crest-fallen expression carries a warning I cannot place. He extends his hand. "Farewell, Ma'am Simone."

I hold his hands in mine. "You have something to tell me, Namibia. What is it? I will be off in an hour and we'll never see each other again."

He lifts my valise, straightens himself as if all is said and done. "I will show you to the carriage now."

"Master is lucky to have you. How long have you worked here?"

"Many, many years, ma'am."

"Master tells me Cyrus stayed in the bedroom of Persian nuns."

"Yes, yes, he did, many times. Do you know him?"

"I am his wife."

Namibia averts his eyes in a gesture that pierces my heart.

"But, ma'am, you and master . . . ," he stammers, unable to voice his shock.

"Cyrus is dead, Namibia."

He silently turns his back to me, his shoulders heaving.

"Namibia, please listen to me. I am not betraying my husband. I am fulfilling his wish."

He knocks his head to the wall once, then again, and again. I embrace him, letting my tears flow upon his shoulder. "Cyrus was murdered, Namibia," I say with urgency. "Tell me everything you know."

"What is the use, ma'am? There is no point to put you in danger, too."

"Tell me, my friend. I can take care of myself, I promise."

"He wanted to close the mines and end slavery. But some people would not have it."

I raise his chin and force him to meet my gaze. "How do you know these things?"

"Everything is in his book. Everything. You must give it to the proper people."

A flicker of hope materializes. Maybe I will not leave empty-handed, after all. "What book? Do you have it?"

"The Old Testament, ma'am. He took notes there."

I grab his arm. "Are you certain? Do you know for a fact that Cyrus took notes in his Bible?"

"Yes, Ma'am Simone. Late at night and early every morning, I would find him bent over his Bible, writing in the margins, anywhere there was space."

The Old Testament, I muse, as I follow Namibia through corridors, past vaults and portrait-filled rooms. It never occurred to me to look in Cyrus's Bible.

I gather speed to catch up with Namibia, pass by the master collector's precious artifacts. Would he honor his promise or, even as I prepare to leave, is he rallying his men to follow me? Trailing Namibia closely, I descend a steep staircase into a basementlike corridor flanked on both sides by locked doors. We are in an unfamiliar wing of the house. "This is not the way out," I protest.

"There are many ways out, but you will not find them alone," Namibia murmurs, eyes flickering up to meet mine. He points to a door, from behind which I can hear machines whirring. Flipping the handle, he pushes the door slightly open with his sandaled foot. A finger to his lips, he gestures for me to take a look.

I nudge the door further and peek in. My eyes stab shut at light so bright, I might have stepped wide-eyed into the sun. Fires roar in high-temperature ovens. Giant machines bearing what look like enormous lightbulbs surround men with goggles. They are bent over steam engines that drive a grinding wheel. Rough diamonds, partly exposed from lead wrappers, are being cut by horizontal blades rotating with such velocity they seem motionless to the eyes. Every diamond as red as a dragon eye.

I steal my head back and quietly shut the door.

Why would an accomplished miner and exporter shoulder the expense and trouble of hiring cutters to polish diamonds in his home? And why the intensely artificial lighting? Cyrus never described such a practice.

Namibia and I retrace our steps in a silence rendered loud by the blood pounding in my ears. "What is going on in there, Namibia?"

"There is more to diamonds than polishing, Ma'am Simone," he murmurs acrimoniously. "Suspicious things happen outside the mine, too. God placed great beauty inside the earth, yet man enslaves us to rob it."

With this, Namibia ushers me outside where dry winds blister across my face. A carriage is ready to transport me to the Cape of Good Hope. A young driver and a pair of robust horses give hope that the trip will not be too uncomfortable or too long. I extend my hand to the servant with the anxious eyes and soft voice. I have come to like him. "Come with me to Paris, Namibia. I won't be able to stop slavery without an eyewitness."

"Farewell, Ma'am Simone. I have arranged for a young girl to meet you at the side of the road. She will accompany you and take care of your needs. She worked in the master's mines. Maybe she could be an eyewitness. It is best I do not bring my bad luck to your home."

49

Paris

Simone wanted to scream, declare her happiness to the fragrant cats, the blushing lavender, whoever or whatever would listen. She was free. Back home from Namaqualand. She pressed Cyrus's Old Testament to her chest. The Valley of Civet Cats was bursting with purple exuberance, the lavender in full bloom, the air intoxicated with civet. Men abandoned the fields to join their women, stallions grew skittish in their stalls, and mares emitted copious streams of urine announcing their unseasonal willingness.

Simone wondered whether it was she, and not the château and its surroundings, who had changed. A woman now, she had come to appreciate the charm of the valley, the home that would be hers.

In the distance, Françoise stepped out of the château to take a walk. A vibrant illusion, as aimless as Mme Gabrielle's ghosts, she uprooted lavender blooms and tossed them to the breeze. She had sought the valley and its surrounding hills after detecting the first signs of age at the corners of her eyes and a slight dullness of the skin after an especially taxing evening.

"Age arrives in sudden spurts," Mme Gabrielle had suggested when Françoise sought her advice this morning. "One day you wake up and the supple skin of your neck turns into an accordion. Or a round chin of thirty-five years becomes pointed and harsh, and a strong back refuses to straighten. But *prendre courage,* Françoise. A period of no change invariably follows— nature's way of shocking us into submission, then allowing us to accept each phase before the cycle begins anew. Consider time your ally, because every wrinkle is an experience won, and every experience makes you a more interesting woman. Go out and enjoy the hills." Mme Gabrielle had then tapped her fan on her daughter's shoulder and advised her to study the masters— Molière, Baudelaire, Balzac, Zola—even if she disliked reading. Soon enough, she would require an extra mélange of lures to enchant her protectors.

Françoise flung her lovely shoulders up. "While you may think I enjoy only physical beauty, a secret knowledge I possess will continue to attract new protectors." And murmuring something about a lust vein, she had practically skipped out of the salon.

Now, from high on top of one of the Civet Cat hills, the grandmother watched Simone on the clover hill and Françoise mourning the onset of age in the valley below. Her daughter was beautiful and sensual but self-centered and vain. Traits that had their advantages and disadvantages. A seductress at heart, she had elevated the *caprice d'une jolie femme*—the right of a beautiful woman to an occasional folly—to an art. And that was an invaluable talent. Any man who won her favors felt infinitely more special than the others. And ready to toss gold at her feet. Still her vanity had taken over. Lately, she spent a large part of the day searching for the latest potion of youth. But Françoise was not Mme Gabrielle's main concern.

The matter of Cyrus's murder remained a mystery, and Simone remained detached from her familial responsibilities. At nineteen, she had grown into a glorious woman whose intricate sensibilities and fierce determination had led her to Persia and then to South Africa. Having failed to discourage her from going away, Mme Gabrielle had beseeched her spirits to spread themselves across turbulent oceans and scorching deserts to look after her granddaughter. They brought back stories about a flood of refugees from the Zulu developments, the contention between agents of the London Missionary Society and the Cape Colony Boers, and the intrusion of Cecil Rhodes and Paul Kruger into the British Protectorate of Bechuanaland. And they delivered her granddaughter safely home.

Mme Gabrielle, assuming Simone had come around and was prepared to shoulder her responsibilities, had paid a visit to the Marais. She had invited her father to settle into the newly completed wing of the château with an inoffensive view of the hills and, to persuade him further, had argued that the Valley of Civet Cats was too lovely a place for Jew haters to infest.

Upon hearing her invitation, Rabbi Abramowicz had grabbed his fur hat and tossed it upon the chandelier as if he were preparing to burst into a dance to the tune of Sabbath psalms. Taking that as a sign of consent, she had planted a kiss on his forehead and, a much happier woman, sailed out of 13 Rue des Rosiers.

Her father had followed her in silence across the sun-soaked rose garden, stood at the wooden gateway, and waved farewell. Then she felt, more than heard, the words that came next.

"Esterleh, my home is my temple. I offer a mikvah for spiritual cleansing here; the *bet din* and rabbinical court convene here. It is a home of spiritual healing into which I am not embarrassed to invite the Lord. I am a Jew, neither below nor above anyone else, and 13 Rue des Rosiers is an integral part of my identity. I will never, ever abandon my home . . . and turn my back on my people." At the sight of his daughter's crest-fallen expression, the rabbi had adjusted his yarmulke. "Ester-leh, wait. If you promise to prepare a kosher meal, I might come to dinner."

Although her father had rejected her most ardent wish, an-other one might come true now—the survival of the Honoré empire. Why else would Simone decide to spend the afternoon on the clover hill, but to test the weight of the Honoré mantle? Mme Gabrielle yanked off her gloves and slapped them against one shoulder, startling the flamboyant castrato, who had mo-mentarily climbed out of her armpit for a few gulps of fresh air. She tossed a tumbler of absinthe down her throat and, finding it unsatisfying, gulped down another, sending Zola's spirit into a huff. She shaded her eyes to shield her delicate lids from the flutter of her agitated ghosts. In their effort to convey the ur-gency of the moment, their frantic flailing whipped a torrential breeze against her cheeks. In the ensuing commotion, she hardly heard Günter's excited hiccups at the opportunity of another brewing scandal, or Franz Liszt's nervous tapping on her finger-nails to warn her of the arrival of uninvited guests.

She squinted toward the gates and, to her utter bewilder-ment, found not one but two parked carriages. She patted her blue curls into place, smoothed her skirts, and solicited Émile Zola: "What boorish animal do you think, *mon cher monsieur,* would call upon us without prior notice and at such a ghastly hour of the afternoon?" And the echo of her heart behind her eardrums was loud and clear: *Not for you,* chère *Gabrielle, not for you.* "For who then? For Simone, do you think?"

This you must find out for yourself, her collective ghosts advised.

50

Simone stepped into the recently completed Gallery of Jewels. The wild jasmine branches wound tentacles around trellises that kept the roaming peacocks away and muffled their shrieks. Portraits of men her grandmother had found deserving of honorable mention—due, of course, to their enormous wealth—adorned the gallery. Each man exhibited the specific gift with which he had successfully tempted the celebrated Mme Gabrielle. A turbaned sultan wore a striking suite of emeralds around his neck, wrists, and fingers, heavy earrings weighing his earlobes. A deposed Bavarian king, whose name she failed to find in the archives, exhibited a crown he had inherited from the queen mother but that he had willingly offered to Mme Gabrielle. A Russian prince wore boots he gave to her, the left one raised to show a ruby-encrusted sole. Simone recognized M. Rouge's likeness, the same floppy cravat and the once-emaciated frame. Ornate lapis lazuli script on a certificate notified the world that he had presented her grandmother with the infamous Braganza, a fist-sized, blue-white diamond named after the Portuguese royal house, which had disappeared for years until discovered in a casket stuffed with forty thousand gold coins.

Simone settled on a stone bench and opened Cyrus's Old Testament. The margins throughout were flooded with his annotations, the same rushed curvy letters that bled into each other as if to chase the words off the pages.

Jounam, I am writing this for you
in the safest place I know,
should anything happen to me.

הים
ארץ
בהו
פני

GENESIS

מים
אור
ויה

For some time now, I have been noticing an
alarming and inexplicable variation in the
chemistry of red diamonds around the globe.
From looking closely at their structure, I can tell
that ninety-nine percent of these red diamonds
originate from Jean Paul Dubois's newly acquired
mine.
As you know, I am deeply involved in the
importation of red diamonds to Persia.
I am afraid I might be part of a fraud,
unwittingly and unwillingly.
I fear the diamonds I acquired for the royal
bracelet and scepter might reveal the same
peculiar chemical variation.
I am alone in the royal atelier now.
Alone, but you are always with me, my lovely wife.

הים
בין
חשך
יום
ערב
אחד
קיע
בין
מים
קיע
תחת
מעל
כן
קיע
בקר
שני
מים
קום

וי או
שרץ
על-כ
ויבר
ואת
כי-כ
ויבר
פרו ו
ויהי
וי או
נפש
למינ
כה
וירא
וי או
בצלו
ובבו
ויבר
בצלו
ברא
ויבר
להם
השב
וי או
לכם
ואת
לאכ
ולכנ
השב
חיה.
וירא
עשה
יום ו

I am examining the bracelet I once delivered to Château Gabrielle to impress you.

Comparing my earring with the diamonds in the shah's bracelet.

My earring first.

Miniature, brilliant worlds explode under the loupe.

Breathtaking!

A crystal universe.

Fragile. Fluid.

Resplendent shades.

Now the bracelet.

Again the same perfection.

Vivid red with no trace of brown.

Even color distribution.

Equal intensity when viewed from either side.

But wait.

These are not the same.

There is a puzzling difference.

The core of my diamond reveals a deeper brilliance.

Intense red layers burst through the facets.

This is absent from the royal diamonds.

Simone!

My suspicions must be true.

I have stumbled upon fraudulence of a grand scale.

A cartel is tampering with red diamonds.

Distributing them into the markets.

Some mysterious method of interference.

The diamonds originate from the same mine.

Then why are they not all doctored?

Although my earring is from the same mine, it seems untouched.

Pray with me that the diamonds in the bracelet
and scepter are clean.
I must return to South Africa to find out.
I hate to leave you alone, jounam.
But the answer, I am certain, lies in Namaqua-
land.

אחד
בשה
ארץ
מים
טוב
דשא
זרע

EXODUS

It is midmorning in Namaqualand.
Earlier, Namibia, Dubois's servant, directed me
to a strange basement with blinding lights and
high-temperature ovens.
Diamond cutters were at work.
Steam engines drove grinding wheels.
Suspicious paraphernalia scattered on tables.
Why would cutters polish gems in such bright
light?
And extreme heat!
I will return at night.

It is two in the morning.
Am back in the room of Persian nuns.
This is what happened.
I visited the basement again.
The door was unlocked.
Inside, the reason for lack of security became
evident.
The room was clear of all evidence.
Tidy. Spotless. Silent.
Ovens boarded. Tables cleared, scrubbed.

ראל
את
באו
ודה
ימן
אשר
ירך
וסף
רים
וכל
הוא
רצו
מאד
אתם
חדש
ידע
וסף
הנה
צום
מנו
כמה
אנה
הוא

וילד Cutting engines nowhere to be found.
ותהו Not one gas or oil lamp in sight.
ולא
ותש Loupe in hand. I searched to
ותת confirm the scene I encountered in the morning.
ותרו Passed my hands over chairs. Over the surfaces of
הסון tables.
ותפו
ות א Around edges and down the legs.
הילז Examined the stone floors.
ות א I noticed an almost colorless residue.
ות א Resembled a sprinkling of gray. crystalline
הילז particles.
ויגדי Not a dried stain or coagulated blood from a nick
משי from the cutting blade.
מכה
ויפן No adhesive consistency.
ויצא No perceptible odor.
וי או I leaned forward to take a better look.
מ שו I was alarmed.
וישנ
מדין Afraid of contact with a toxic element. I gathered
ולכ ו the substance between folds of my handkerchief to
ויב ז bring back home.

Simone plucked a jasmine from a branch that coiled itself around the trellis. She dropped the flower in her mouth. The aroma dissolved on her tongue, evoking the jasmine tea she and Cyrus had enjoyed the night before he left for Namaqualand. They had created their own history—an aborted history she hoped would be revived in his Bible.

Keeping his suspicions to himself, she realized, was the cautious move at the time. The minister of court and M. Jean Paul Dubois would not have hesitated to silence her had they found out she had knowledge of the doctored diamonds.

LEVITICUS

Back in Persia!   לין

Back in your fragrant embrace.   לאמ

You are pregnant!   אדם

What a wonderful welcome!   יבו

Thank you.   נכם

You are asleep in the other room.   ריב

I do not know if you suspect anything.   הוה

Suspect why I went to South Africa.   לין

I apologize for keeping the truth from you.   -על

It is for your protection, you must understand.   ועד

I will now test the trace element I brought from   חיה

Namaqualand.   האש

                                                           אשר

Must try to identify it before you wake up.   זבח

Unbelievable!   הוה

Beryllium!   בנו

Yes! It is beryllium!   דמו

The lightest of elements.   ביב

I know beryllium from an experiment some years   האש

ago in school.   זבח

Traces of it accidentally diffused into sapphires,   אשה

triggering a change in color.   בני

But this is puzzling.   בנו

Beryllium cannot be diffused into a hard and   קיר

dense stone such as a diamond.   זבח

What, then, is occurring?   ליד

I apologize, Simone.   קום

To solve the mystery, I must risk our entire   דשן

wealth.   צים

                                                           הוה

ונפש *This next experiment might shatter our red diamond.*
והבי *The diamond is set in a jeweler's tongs.*
הניב *Fixed on a three-pronged device to hold steadfast.*
מסל *With my makeshift drilling device I created a path*
ליהו *into the center of our diamond.*
והנו *Opened a window.*
וכי ר
מנחו *Our diamond did not shatter!*

The day Cyrus returned from Namaqualand was sharp in her mind. His scent of cardamom and smoke on her, she had slept for the better part of the day, to wake up to a magnificent sunset splashing across the mountaintops. She had detected him in the other room, bent over the table, engrossed in the work at hand. He had refused to give her answers. They had had their first fight that night. The cut-off ear of his horse had been delivered to her the next night.

NUMBERS

וידבו *You are still asleep.*
באח *I assault the diamond with magnifying lenses and*
לצאו *loupe.*
שאו,
לבית *Amplify the light that hits the heart of the diamond.*
במסו *This is painful. Simone.*
לגלגי *My worst fears are coming true before my eyes.*
מבן י *The intense magnified light is robbing our diamond*
כל-י *of layer after layer of color.*
בישר
אתה *A pinkish facet is spreading around the edges.*
ואהו *Bleeding into another.*

And another.
Stripping the vibrancy.
Unbelievable!
Our diamond now resembles the gems in the royal
bracelet.
Apparently, all the diamonds have been tampered
with.
This is the reason for the inconsistency I detected.
The diamonds in the bracelet and scepter must
have been mined earlier than our diamond.
They have been exposed to light and the elements
for a longer period of time.
The window cut in our diamond made it more
vulnerable to light.
A process that might have required years to reveal the diamond's flaw took place in one
afternoon.
Nature is not always perfect, of course.
The African amethyst and certain sapphires
are known to fade when exposed to severe heat
and excessive sunlight.
But unlike amethysts and sapphires, the carbon
atoms of diamonds are dense and tightly packed,
keeping light and other elements from diffusing in
them.
This is what I know now.
An abnormality in the constitution and chemistry
of Jean Paul Dubois's diamonds causes them to respond to light like certain amethysts and sapphires.

הוּא
יְאֹר
יִשַׁדָּי
וְנָדָב
צוֹעַר
ן-חָל
הַצוּר
-גְדַע
יַעְזֵר
וְשֶׁר
וְלִיס
דָּתְלִי
עֵדָה
תוֹת
הֵם
שִׂים
וַשֶׁר
שָׁפְח
שָׁנָה
מְדַבֵּר
רִים
צָבָא
אֶלֶף
שָׁנָה
זְעָלָה
וְשָׁעָה
זֵאוֹת
תוֹלֵד
יוּמַת
מַדְּגְלוּ

וידב	*Exposed to the elements, his red diamonds weaken,*
איש	*lose density, and become vulnerable to light.*
והח	*Dubois must have discovered his misfortune at the*
וצבא	*height of the popularity of his gems.*
והח	
וצבא	*They had found homes in royal coffers and bank*
מטר	*vaults.*
וצבא	*A man such as he would never give in to bankruptcy.*
כל-ן	*Instead, he chose to tamper with an imperfect na-*
ראש	*ture.*
דגל	*This explains the illegal laboratory in his mansion.*
וצבא	*First, he stripped the color from the red diamonds*
והחו	*with the aid of intense light.*
וצבא	
ומט	*Then he added natural chrysoberyl, a source of*
וצבא	*beryllium, to borate and phosphate, and coated the*
כל-ן	*diamonds with the powder.*
ושני	
ונסע	*Then he heated the powder-diffused diamonds in*
דגל	*high-temperature ovens for hours to bake in and*
וצבא	*restore a uniform and vibrant shade.*
ועלי	*An effective but, of course, illegal process.*

Simone brushed moisture beads from her neck. She could write the rest herself. Once artificiality is introduced—once the belief that the brilliant colors are a product of nature alone is shattered—the magic and romance disappear. And the market topples.

M. Jean Paul Dubois, who commanded a premium for doctored diamonds, would do anything to stop this information from leaking, and so would the minister of court, who had merged his company with M. Jean Paul Dubois's cartel and was pocketing billions. The shah, who presumably owned an invaluable bracelet of red diamonds and another eight-carat diamond in his scepter, would not react well to this discovery. And smaller players such as M. Rouge and M. Amir and his wife, whose wealth was wrapped up in the red diamonds they either purchased or received as payment, would be thrust into bankruptcy.

She stroked the pages, the margins seeded with his cardamom breath. His lines were shorter now, more urgent. His fear and sense of danger drove his pen, slashing through the pages of the fifth book of Moses.

DEUTERONOMY

Visited the shah today.	מ שה
Informed him of the illegal diffusion.	ירדן
Promised not to do anything with my knowledge	ף בין
until he has a chance to act.	־פאר
On condition he affords us immunity	־ודי
and orders the diffusion halted.	עשׂר
He was furious at his minister.	שֶׂעיר
He gave me his word.	עים
	שה

Simone's gaze skipped over the next page, to Cyrus's last words—his testament to her.

	להם
Jounam, I love you more than the pupils of my	וֹשב
eyes.	רדן
But I will die before I will have you, or my son,	לאמ
question my integrity.	דבר
	הזה

She tucked the Bible under her arm and stepped out of the gallery to find Alphonse leaving the château and negotiating his way toward her. The last two years had left their imprint in the deeper lines across his forehead, the sunken cheeks, and the tremor in his elegant fingers. But he carried his pretenses with the same indignation, colored his hair with the same tint, and strode around in the same affected manner. His most significant transformation was the gradual, almost imperceptible shift away from his butler façade to behave more as husband to Mme Gabrielle, father to Françoise, and grandfather to herself. She would hear him tease Mme Gabrielle that he intended to return to his Persian roots, back to when he was Mohammed and before she had converted him into a butler. He would point out that an essential prerequisite to the full revival of his old self, which he missed terribly, would be to introduce his daughter and granddaughter to their Persian lineage. At that, her grandmother would whack him on the hand with her gloves and remind him that she did not find his remarks as amusing as he seemed to find them.

Breathless in his effort to reach her and visibly shaken, he said, "Half an hour ago, Monsieur Amir and Monsieur Rouge arrived in separate carriages. Rather distressed, they both asked for you. Monsieur Rouge clutches a copy of *Le Figaro* as if wielding his death warrant."

Before Alphonse had occasion for elaboration, she adjusted her revolver in the holster and ran toward the château.

51

Her head reeling, Simone stumbled into the salon.

M. Rouge, *Figaro* in hand, paced back and forth, his disjointed eyes darting, unable to settle on anyone or anything.

M. Amir sat in one of the high-backed chairs, his composure out of place in the tense atmosphere.

At the sight of Simone, M. Rouge brandished the rolled newspaper above his head and began to rant incoherently. M. Amir gazed around in amusement, a smile fluttering under his waxed mustache as he tapped his own copy against his thigh.

"Monsieur Rouge, calm down, *s'il vous plaît,*" Simone shouted. "You are making me quite nervous."

"It is a tragedy, dear Simone, a tragedy of unimaginable proportions. I am bankrupt. We all are," he added, nodding toward M. Amir and flicking *Le Figaro* open with a dramatic gesture of one hand. "Here, read for yourself."

She clenched the newspaper in both hands and read:

264 *Dora Levy Mossanen*

REPORT OF TREATED GEMS
STUNS DIAMOND INDUSTRY

International diamond markets are stunned by the news that an influential cartel is manipulating the internal structures of red diamonds.

A gem alert was issued, and the trade of red diamonds halted.

Monsieur Jean Paul Dubois, the main suspect, is in custody pending further investigation.

Mme Gabrielle, followed by her ghosts and accompanied by Françoise, glided into the salon. She was poised to chase the men off at Simone's slightest indication. She was reminded of another time when, *Le Monde* in hand, the president's couriers had burst upon her with news of the foiled assassination attempt on the Persian king. That incident had unleashed a string of tragic events that had altered the course of her granddaughter's life and consequently her own. And now Günter, eager to supply specifics that scared her curls stiff, predicted that she was about to lose Simone again. Zola's constant prying about who and what had brought the visitors swelled her ears like hot-air balloons. And Franz Liszt, his feral curls bouncing in the midst of this mayhem, skipped on her white-gloved fingers as if on his private piano keys. Having heard more than her fair share of doom, Mme Gabrielle slapped Luciano Barbutzzi out of her armpit and demanded Oscar Wilde halt the exercise regimen that had made her breasts blessedly firm. She aimed an accusing forefinger at M. Rouge. "I am tired of diamonds and gems and these endless scandals! *Messieurs,* I demand that you take your charade elsewhere."

"*Chère* Madame," M. Rouge replied, tossing a pleading eye toward Simone and ignoring the grandmother's finger, on which sparkled a valuable cushion-cut emerald. "You must remember the red diamond I gave you not long ago. The police tracked it to me and demanded that I produce it. If I fail, I will be taken into custody and tried as a conspirator."

"I have the diamond, Monsieur Rouge," Simone assured. "But I need to know if this diamond is doctored, too. And if so, is it possible to detect such a diamond with the naked eye?"

M. Rouge rushed to Simone, and for an instant she feared he would fall to his knees to beg for a gem she had never wanted in the first place. "I promise you, dear Simone, I do not have the answer. This is the first I have learned about the possibility of tampering with diamonds. I would not know how to detect them. As for whether the diamond is doctored, I believe so, since the police tracked it down due to complaints from a chain of sellers and buyers."

She waved him back to his chair. "You will have your diamond back, Monsieur, I assure you." Her least concern at the moment was the red diamond he had given her in the throes of his crimson madness. Her mind was preoccupied with the red diamonds in the pouch tucked away in her armoire. Were they doctored? And if so, the man who had given them to Beard must be the man she was looking for.

"And what, may I ask, troubles *you*, Monsieur Amir?" Mme Gabrielle asked.

"I am not troubled, Madame. On the contrary, I am enormously relieved that the law has caught up with Monsieur Jean Paul Dubois at last. It was just a coincidence that I arrived at the same time as Monsieur Rouge. Our intentions are entirely different, I assure you."

Despite her utter ignorance regarding the unfolding matters, Françoise fluttered her fan, her breasts heaving as she stole shy glances toward Alphonse. She struggled to adjust her expectations and accept him, the butler of many years, as her Persian father. She crossed her delicate ankles and studied him through pearl gray eyes, trying to grasp the full impact of her newfound legitimacy and how it would better her future. The prestige of having a father, she hoped, would welcome her into the elite arms of a higher society. Now, away from the limelight for far too long, she snapped at her mink-trimmed neckline to reveal two pearls at the tip of her rouged nipples.

M. Amir coughed twice, pinched snuff into each nostril, and sneezed. All heads turned to him. "I came here, Simone, to extend my heartfelt gratitude to you. Because of you, Monsieur Jean Paul Dubois, the longtime enslaver of Persians, is no longer a free man."

"I don't deserve to be thanked, Monsieur Amir. You knew all along that he was your man."

"True, true, but what you don't know is that after you left Namaqualand, he pursued you to Paris, straight into the arms of the police. Such a careful man, who calculated his every move precisely and mathematically, acted so foolishly when he lost his heart to you. Even I could not have guessed the extent of his obsession."

Simone was furious. Cyrus had trusted M. Amir, yet he seemed indifferent to her plight. "You knew that Monsieur Jean Paul Dubois was this dangerous, yet you encouraged me to go to Namaqualand. And do you care about Cyrus? Does it matter to you who murdered him? I honored my end of the agreement; I hope you will honor yours."

"I have not forgotten my promise, not for a moment. But first things first. You promised to deliver something else, too. Incontrovertible evidence regarding Monsieur Jean Paul Dubois's use of Persian slaves."

"But he is already in the hands of the French authorities. Why do you need evidence now, Monsieur Amir?"

"Monsieur Dubois will spend a short time behind bars for tampering with diamonds. Far from being deterred by incarceration, he will grow more dangerous when freed. Persia will have to impose her own solution. If the shah is presented with con-

COURTESAN   267

crete evidence, the French authorities are legally responsible to
hand Monsieur Jean Paul Dubois to the Persian court."

"A runaway prostitute, who witnessed the atrocities in the
mines, traveled to Paris with me from Namaqualand," Simone
said. "She would be happy to serve as eyewitness."

M. Amir rose to his full height and crossed the salon. "In
return, Simone, I will deliver Mehrdad to you."

She swallowed the burgeoning scream that threatened to
escape into the surrounding silence. She had been seeking for
an eternity now, it seemed, the identity of the murderer—the
deliverance of Cyrus's body—yet now she was terrified of the
revelation. And then, even as hope and fear tugged at her heart,
she cried out, "Mehrdad! He is in Paris? Was he here all along?
You waited until your own goals were achieved, didn't you, before revealing his whereabouts."

M. Amir adjusted his cravat. "I am extremely fond of you,
and of Cyrus, too. But the survival of my country takes precedence over any individual. I am eternally indebted to you for all
you did and know that one day you will agree that I made a difference, too."

52

A horse and its rider sped toward Château Gabrielle, whipping dust gales at the last bend of the road. Simone followed the course of the advancing stallion, the silver mane gleaming in the sun, the lush tail and proud neck reminding her of Cyrus's horse. She pressed her eyes shut to scare away the image. The cut-off ear of his stallion in Beard's hand. The northern lights wreaking havoc across the Persian skies. Such senseless brutality. To crack his chest open. To steal his body. But life continued. Her mother was expecting another gentleman caller. Her grandmother continued to flirt with her spirits.

The stallion came to an abrupt stop at the gates. The horseman sprinted off the saddle, tied the reins to the wrought-iron bars, and strode to the knocker.

It was not the dark color of his shoulder-grazing hair, his slim silhouette, or his seeking gaze through the vertical bars that convinced Simone this was not a gentleman caller. It was the red glint in his left ear that made her run across the terrace and call out to Alphonse. Grabbing the keys he produced, she dashed to the gates.

The stranger struggled with the lock from the outside as she fumbled for the keyhole, until Alphonse came to their aid.

She reached out her hand and, when the man embraced it, she no longer saw the astonished Alphonse or heard the hubbub in the park behind her. Cyrus stood in front of her with a quizzical expression on his face, his peculiar half smile there, but not quite, those inquisitive eyes that at once covered and undressed her, the unbuttoned shirt that heralded his defiance. And the red diamond on his left ear. He held her hand for longer than she could bear, but she did not release him for she had searched for him forever and would not let go now. She fought not to walk into his arms when, in a Persian accent, he said, "Simone." In silence and with a tearful heart, she led him into Château Gabrielle, negotiated a path through the park and up the isolated clover hill, a flock of peacocks pecking at his coat.

"I am tired," he said. "I traveled a long way to come here."

Feeling vulnerable to his composure, she sat next to him on the chaise longue. Assaulted by a hundred questions, she shivered in her crepe blouse. He removed his jacket and draped it around her shoulders. The faint scent of tobacco and cardamom sent her reeling. She drew the jacket closer. She seemed to have rediscovered her husband the moment this man had leaped down from his horse, seeking her eyes from beyond the wrought iron bars. He symbolized everything she had admired in Cyrus—his compassionate eyes, the careless, almost insulting disinterest in himself, and the unpredictable way he burst into her home. He appeared slightly older than Cyrus, and the thought occurred to her that if Cyrus were alive he would have aged like this man.

Offering his mélange of a quizzical smile, he said, "Monsieur Amir said you were expecting me."

"Mehrdad!" she exclaimed, reaching for her revolver and finding her lace handkerchief instead. She was at the mercy of a man who might be Cyrus's murderer, yet she was not carrying her revolver; a man she had hastily let in simply because he reminded her of Cyrus. She removed his coat from around her and handed it back.

He tossed his coat over one shoulder with a nonchalance that pierced her to the marrow. "I will go if you wish," he said, crossing the hill and ambling down the slope.

His tall silhouette retreating farther from view, he called out, "*Shaunce Banou.*" And the valley echoed, "*Shaunce Banou. Shaunce Banou.*"

Her pulse skipping, she jumped to her feet and rushed down the clover hill. "Why did you call me *Shaunce Banou*?"

"Because I knew you would respond." He held her arms with both hands as if he had known her for a long time or even felt a sense of ownership. "Listen, you owe your life to a streak of luck. *Shaunce Banou* means 'Lady Fortune' in Farsi, but is a double entendre. It could mean either that you are charmed, or that you are a sorceress. It can be used as a compliment or a threat. An attempt was made in Persia to warn you, make you understand that despite being lucky once, you must not try fate again. You are in great danger. I want to help."

She stepped back, freeing her arms. "I do not trust you."

"How could you with all you've gone through? But we don't have the luxury of time. I am being watched, too, you see, and might be ordered back to Persia any day now." He gazed up at the sky and at the puffed-up clouds. "Cyrus and I came to rely on each other. We were innocent players in a cruel game."

"What game is that?" she asked, moving down the hill to seek the château and her revolver.

His jaw tight, mouth a tense line, his tone was defiant. "The mess of diamonds! Jews and Muslims. The world has gone mad."

Cyrus's voice rang around the Civet Cat hills—*Muslims per-*

secuted us again and again—they do not like us—there will be no end to this insanity. Unreliable wisps of memory congealed. Mehrdad was the colleague her husband trusted in the dishonest world of diamonds. He was the man Cyrus wanted her to meet, a role model for their son. But he was also the prime suspect months of investigation pointed to; the person she feared would pull out a knife.

And then she heard Beard's voice, clear and resonant, every word fresh in her mind—how could it not be, with her raw feelings and stinging heart grasping at anything that might explain the horror of her loss? An expression, an act, a simple word from Beard was tantamount to a lifeboat in her dim horizon. A man with a red diamond earring like Cyrus had handed Beard the pouch of diamonds.

"You gave Beard the red diamonds with that note," she said, stepping away from him.

"Yes, I did. I hoped it would encourage you to leave Persia," he said, passing his hand over his hair.

She noticed a streak of gray in his hair. Her own strip of gray—the Red Sea for grief to cross—had appeared soon after Cyrus's death. "Why did you disappear after Cyrus's murder?"

"I was dispatched by the shah to Paris," he replied. "To investigate the cold-blooded murder of his jeweler."

⌒◯⌒

She led him toward the clearing where she had loved Cyrus. Not because she would be safe with Mehrdad there. In truth, she did not feel safe anywhere. She simply had to distance herself from the galleries, virile studs, and wandering souls. She did not notice the arriving carriages deposit spectators outside the château walls. She was next to Cyrus. It was Cyrus she talked to, his eyes lighting up with the smile that was there one moment and gone the next.

Mehrdad gestured to the crowd. "What are they watching?"

"My grandmother's galleries have become a place of pilgrimage. Quite silly, I think."

He turned toward the clover hill. "Up there, where we were?"

"Yes, the myth surrounding them is far more interesting. The moment you see something it loses its charm."

"You are more charming in person. And you even read palms."

"He told you?"

"Yes. The first time he pulled out your photograph from his breast pocket and passed his thumb over your profile to introduce the running-away woman in the photograph as his new Parisian wife, I was captivated by your wide-eyed curiosity and audacious posture. You were striking with your revolver, your boots pushing against the stirrups as if to fly off the saddle."

Simone remembered the day a photographer had come to the château with his bulky cameras and attendants in tow. Her grandmother had fussed over him as if he were the president himself. Hardly sixteen, Simone was on her way to the valley for her morning ride when she was called back. She had tried to accommodate the photographer, who had the air of an important artist. But she could not tolerate the instructions to turn on the saddle in such and such a manner and to gaze at the despised camera eye as if at a lover. "Cyrus never told me about this photograph."

"He did not want you to be angry with your grandmother. She had fashioned calling cards with your image. She gave one to Cyrus. That prompted his visit with that red diamond bracelet."

Simone cast her eyes down at her grandmother's betrayal. She had no right doing this without her knowledge. On the other hand, she longed to witness the calling card, the catalyst that had brought Cyrus to her. Had he left it somewhere for her, perhaps as another sign?

Mehrdad was back with Cyrus in Persia. "The entire royal court was abuzz with Cyrus's recent acquisition, an eight-carat red diamond that enormously pleased the shah. A celebration was held, dignitaries invited. The diamond was displayed for a week in a gold-framed glass case in the Museum of Royal Jewelry."

The red diamond was set in the shah's scepter.

The next week, in the royal atelier, Cyrus retrieved the calling card, laid it on his palm, and blew on it as if clearing Simone's image of dust particles. His Parisian wife was struggling with this uncompromising culture, he informed Mehrdad. And his mother caused her intolerable grief. The next day, he slipped the photograph out and rubbed it against his sleeve as if to polish her image. He had arrived at a difficult decision. They would move to his mountain house, even if his family disowned him.

He placed her photograph on a table in the shah's palace one day when they were sorting raw diamonds. Gathering diamonds around the four edges, he fashioned a frame. "She is stitching a bedcover out of her petticoats."

Mehrdad became an active spectator in the unfolding events, a voyeur of sorts. He anticipated milestones, anything that would make Cyrus retrieve her photograph from his coat pocket and add another bit of information to illuminate her further. He began to live his dreams through Cyrus—dress like him, grow his hair like him, wear a red diamond like him.

And unaware of this growing fascination, Cyrus continued to stun Mehrdad with Simone's capacity to reinvent herself. She slowly cast off her earthly qualities and took on mythical traits.

After Cyrus returned from South Africa, his eyes evasive, an artery racing at his temples, he folded the calling card in his handkerchief and handed it to Mehrdad. One day, it might come handy as a reference rather than a calling card,

he said. Just in case. He inscribed the back and marched out
the door.

Suddenly, despite everything revealed to her, the calling
card appeared the spark that might clear the stubborn cobwebs
of doubt. "Where is the card?"

Mehrdad retrieved his wallet from his coat pocket. Tucked
in the frayed leather flaps, her image was folded in Cyrus's
handkerchief. A rush of sorrow, anger, and shame deepened
her freckles into tiny flames. The calling card was complete
with her image, name, and address. As far as she was concerned, this made her grandmother her official pimp.

And she was angry with Cyrus. He had no right to keep
such essential matters to himself. She gazed at the back of the
calling card: *To Simone, just in case.* In case of what, she wondered, although she had a distinct feeling that this, her husband's most important sign, was an endorsement of Mehrdad.

He pressed his hand to his chest pocket, into which he hur-
riedly tucked the card she returned to him. "I felt, more than
noticed, the signs of trouble in Mozaffar Ed-Din Shah's court. I
was aware, of course, that Mirza Mahmud Khan controlled the
political reins of the country. But since the foiled assassination
attempt on the shah in France, he was a changed man. No
longer the impotent king we had known." Suppressing a smile,
Mehrdad flipped a sprig of lavender between two fingers.
"Rumor has it that the king owes his newfound confidence to
your grandmother's ministrations."

Simone plucked the sprig from his hand and tucked it behind her ear. "Yes, she is an exceptional woman."

"Anyway, Cyrus, with his connection to the Honoré
women, became the shah's favorite and was assured protection
by no less than his royal highness. The *najes* Jew with a pollut-
ing handshake Muslims shunned was thrust into the unenvi-
able position of seniority over many of us. Then he decided to
resign, but his involvement with the import of diamonds was

such that he had to present a viable alternative before he dared submit his resignation."

Riveted to Mehrdad's beautiful eyes that seemed on the verge of tears, Simone asked, "What alternative did Cyrus suggest?"

"He offered to continue in his capacity as the royal jeweler while training someone to replace him."

"Who?" she asked, leaning closer.

"Me," he replied.

53

Mme Gabrielle rested her gloved hands on the wrought-iron balustrade, leaned forward, and glared down at the couple who ushered in the scent of lavender and civet. Reminded of the same sight with another Persian, the livid grandmother bunched up her skirts and sailed down the grand staircase. The man, she could tell, was nothing more than the shadow of Cyrus, yet Simone was intent on duplicating that tragic relationship. She wanted the mystery of Cyrus's murder solved, too, wanted that part of Simone's past put to rest. She wanted Simone to settle down into her intended lifestyle and to forget Persia, a country that had held appeal in the early days of her relationship with Alphonse but had fallen out of favor with its treatment of Simone. But she would not tolerate the same mistake twice.

Ignoring the puffs of disapproval from her grandmother's lips and the ballooning skirts swinging from her hips, Simone stepped closer to Mehrdad. Her grandmother deserved to be scared out of her self-serving skin.

Unaware of the brewing drama, Mehrdad found himself sinking into Simone's life-size image at the foot of the staircase. The photograph captured her pride and arrogance, softness and grit, fire and turbulence far better than the calling card ever had. Now that Cyrus was gone, and Simone was accessible, he had difficulty yanking himself away from her. He was dispatched to France for reasons far from romantic, he reminded himself, suddenly ambushed by lapis curls framing fierce cheeks, an ice-blue glare, and a satin-sheathed finger held up like a dagger.

Mme Gabrielle, having descended the grand staircase without the benefit of an audience, claimed attention with a flurry of hissing chiffon. "May I demand, Monsieur, whether you are calling upon me, my daughter, or my granddaughter?"

He seized her finger and brought it down to his lips. "*Bonjour,* Madame Gabrielle, Mehrdad at your service and, with your permission, I am calling upon all three Honoré ladies."

"Rather presumptuous of you, Monsieur M.," she spat out, gesturing toward the spacious foyer as if he had demanded her château in addition to all three women.

He fished into his coat pocket and presented the calling card. "This, I believe, will speak for me."

Mme Gabrielle furrowed her brows at the hand dealt her. The single act of giving that calling card to Cyrus in the president's palace had initiated an unforeseeable chain of disasters for which she, and no one else, was to blame. But she did not believe one had to suffer indefinitely for irreversible *erreurs*. Besides, tragedies occurred every day. One need not mourn forever. It was time Simone harnessed her grief. "Monsieur M.," Mme Gabrielle said, mouthing the *M* like a curse, "it is customary in France to hand such an invitation to a specific gentleman of one's choice, with the understanding it will not

be transferred to another. Moreover, in my country, a gentleman caller must notify proper ladies of his intentions via a
petit bleu or a messenger. Since you have followed none of our
etiquette, you leave me little choice, Monsieur, but to bid you
adieu."

"Madame, I apologize for any inconvenience I may have
caused. I bypassed formalities for the sake of secrecy and the
ladies' safety. I was sent to Paris to request Simone's help
in apprehending the perpetrators. Being the royal jeweler,
Cyrus was promised immunity by the shah. As such, his
murder is considered a personal affront to his Royal Highness. In the meantime, I must request that the Honoré ladies
remain in Paris until the matter is brought to a satisfactory
conclusion."

Simone let out a few coughs to clear her throat of what felt
like an expanding boulder. "I am not sure how I can help,
Mehrdad."

"You are our only witness. You could disclose what happened in the mountains that night, identify the murderer or
murderers. Reveal details Cyrus shared with you. All we know is
that he was shot, which tells us that the murder was premedi-
tated. Highly unusual in Persia, where impulsive honor killings
with knives are customary.

"His journal, which must be in your possession, might hold
other revelations." He swept his hand over his hair and stepped
back, as if to give his words more muscle.

Her suspicions resurfacing, she asked, "How do you know
Cyrus kept a journal?"

"I saw him take notes in it on more than one occasion."

Her heart thrashing, she said, "I don't have the journal, if
one exists. In addition, I will not allow you to imprison me in
my own home"

Mme Gabrielle tweaked the tips of her gloves, bared each
finger, her hands forming a pyramid. Although the gesture

meant little to Mehrdad, save the pleasure of witnessing the unusual performance of conniving hands, Simone recognized the unmistakable prologue to an unpleasant finale. "Monsieur M., *ceci ne semble pas raisonnable,* and we certainly do not have the leisure of chatting the night away. Alphonse! Alphonse! Show Monsieur M. out."

54

I settle under the shade of an expansive chestnut tree atop a Civet Cat hill, the panorama of Château Gabrielle and the lilac valley spread underfoot. The sun lounges on the horizon like a ripe melon. Geese wheel in the sky. The lake is a shimmering crystal sheet. A vendor is setting up shop on the opposite hill to sell roasted chestnuts to pilgrims. *Grand-mère* would not tolerate this invasion. She considers herself the proprietor not only of the château but also of the surrounding hills and their feline residents.

Laying Cyrus's Old Testament on my lace handkerchief, I rest my head against the tree trunk and wait for Mehrdad. I pluck a leaf from the spread of lavender and brush it against my cheek, the freckles Cyrus adored. You once told me I smell of nard at dusk. I asked what nard smells like. *A little lustful,* you said, *a lot of mystery, and very rare.* I don't know if I ever told you that you smelled of cardamom and tobacco. So does Mehrdad. Does he also chew on green cardamom to ward off the smell of corruption? These days, I question the accuracy of my olfactory senses, the reliability of my faculties. How can anyone resemble you in so many ways? Mehrdad is not you, after all. I don't know whether to believe that he is sent to Paris by an indignant shah to track down your murderer. Is he after your Bible, or did he truly fall in love with my image on the card? What did you mean by inscribing "just in case" on the back? You must have had a premonition that he might prove my only opportunity to mend. A welcome balm on the forming scabs. A necessity, not a betrayal. Another chance at that cherished sense of permanence and belonging you and I shared.

My gaze negotiates the hills, the château in the distance, and the winding road where his horse gallops toward the purple valley. He abandons the stallion at the foot of the hill, strides to the top and almost into my arms, as I rise to greet him. He takes my breath away with the clarity his presence injects into the surroundings. I lead him under the shade of the chestnut tree. Two civet cats scale the branches above. A horse's cough rises from the stables. He attempts to steal a glance from the book that lies facedown at my side.

Afraid to swallow my words, I meet his volatile eyes and ask, "Who is the murderer? How did I end up with a pouch of red diamonds?" Then I hear myself come straight out and admit, "I don't really know if I should trust you. I am not sure which side you are on."

He strikes a stone with his fist, grabs and tosses it across the hill, initiating a quake within the network of underground tunnels where civet cats scramble for shelter. He lifts his arms above his head as if my pistol points at him. "The truth, I hope, will put your mind at ease. Then, if you still want me to disappear, I will do so, although I will never be able to go back to Persia without you. That would mean execution," he says, lowering one hand.

I jump to my feet. Draw my revolver—an absurd reflexive reaction, I realize, even as I aim the barrel at him.

He presses the hand to his eye. "You have my word. You will never hear from me again, if that's your wish." He lifts both arms above his head again.

Cyrus, too, had touched his eye to promise he would never leave me alone again, just as he would never abandon the pupil of his eye. Conscious of Mehrdad's every move, I tuck the pistol back and lower his arms. "I don't know what I was thinking. You are a big man; you would have no trouble killing me."

"Dear Simone," he sighs, "I don't want to kill you. I want to marry you. I want to take you away from here."

"Marry me! Because you fell in love with my image?"

"No, Simone, I became obsessed with the girl on the calling card, but fell in love with the woman in Paris. Do not turn away from me like that and do not turn me down so quickly. In your religion, a man is charged with the responsibility of marrying his brother's widow. Cyrus was like a brother to me. I want to fulfill my responsibility."

"You carry none," I assure him, stunned by his unexpected proposal. "Tell me who killed him."

"Even if this will make it harder for you?"

"Make what harder?"

"Whom to blame."

"Even then," I reply.

∞

Pen in hand, the aging matriarch keeps court on the clover hill, preparing to bring her final introspections to a close. Her spirits lick her gossamer-gloved hands and frolic between her toes. Their buzz in her ears reminds her that she is a woman of a certain age, that it is time to extinguish her dormant guilt, or it will continue to multiply like her ghosts. They are an incessant reminder of her father's enduring anguish and of the rise of Jew hating. Not only around Europe but also inside everyone who is of a different faith.

She flings her arms up, scatters her ghosts with a frustrated shout. "Off with you! I've had enough. You are all over me. This is unacceptable!" She wipes perspiration off her cleavage and wonders what Simone is up to under the chestnut tree with that Persian. Nevertheless, she admits to herself that the couple creates a lovely portrait. She sighs, thinking that nothing is more essential to her than to be surrounded by wisdom, beauty, and the freedom to enjoy them. She tucks her pen between the vellum leaves of her journal. She had assumed that she was done inscribing the history of her life, done creating a road map for her granddaughter. But with the unfolding events, further elaboration is necessary.

Suddenly, Rousseau's ghost pops out from under the wing of a peacock. Levitating in front of her alarmed eyes, he announces that, despite having lived in a different era, he intends to join her repertoire of spirits and settle in the château.

"Impossible! Do not even think of it!" she shouts in her husky voice, her indignation echoing in the valley. "Even if you were my contemporary, I would have had no need for you, Monsieur, none at all. You are not welcome here! Must I remind you that I am a woman of literary merit? I have read your *Émile* and have not forgotten your ridiculous argument demanding separate spheres for men and women. In addition, Monsieur, allow me to quote your own preposterous words: 'Even if she possesses genuine talents, any pretension on her part would degrade them. Her dignity depends on remaining unknown; her glory lies in her husband's esteem . . .' Psht! Begone, Monsieur! Château Gabrielle has no use for men such as you!"

She chuckles with pleasure as Rousseau curls into a wisp of a ghost and squeezes himself back into a peahen's oily underwing.

She flips to the last pages of her journal.

My Living Will, Achievements and Failures

My beloved Simone, when I first addressed you on these pages, I had a vision of the Honoré women going down in history as Les Grandes Trois, the three most sought-after grandes dames of Europe. I had faith the three of us could keep alive the age of the grandes horizontales, *the virtuous women, as I see them, of the high society.*

But just as a wise lover reveals new pearls of wisdom with every visit, the process of reliving my life in these pages helped me discover and rediscover myself. I must confess now that although I might seem too ambitious to you, maybe even unrealistic in my expectations, I possess a rare and essential gift—the ability to disentangle myth from reality and look both squarely in the eye. And despite my dear Zola's insistence that I must not interfere, it is not in my character to allow fate to take its course or to lose without a good fight.

So, as difficult as it is for me to voice this, and as unbelievable as it might sound to you, I intend to hold myself responsible for the onus of certain choices I have made.

I will swallow my pride, chérie, *and agree that love granted you passion and maturity, absolutely. And the institution of marriage—despite your short-lived and tragic relationship—endowed you with admirable grit, perseverance, and complexity. But it also shifted the balance of power. I am afraid that, even in death, Cyrus continues to rule your life. I wholeheartedly reject any type of intimacy that demands conformity, even as I acknowledge the tragedy of your loss and share your pain,* ma chère. *And I applaud your heroic resolve to straighten your toppled world. I do not know what I would have done if I had lost Françoise, or you, Simone. I would certainly not have conducted myself with your grace and elegance.*

You have flowered into an intelligent woman who will find her footing, somewhere between Papa's Warsaw shtetl and the French Marais; somewhere between your Persian men and French heritage.

Exhuming my past and giving my memories a coherent shape also taught me the importance of compromise. And this, because of your still-

evolving maturity, you will need more time to appreciate for yourself.

Nevertheless, chérie, *you do not have my unequivocal blessing to wander far from your home.*

Let us discuss the path your future might take, a compromise between our shared desires. Let us confer as friends, give and take as equals. You have my promise never, ever to hand out your calling card to strangers again. In return, would you heed my advice and, for the sake of your mother and yourself, keep adding to the wealth I shall bequeath you? Women like us, despite our independence of spirit, remain financially dependent on our protectors. When they tire of us, they drop us faster than a slice of stale brioche. Our wealth saves us in such difficult times. And war is an ever-present danger. In fact, I smell the brewing stink on the horizon. If you have to flee another war, take your portable wealth, your jewelry, your mother, and Alphonse, of course.

In addition, I would be remiss not to beg of you to value your faith. I did what was right for me when I was your age. I abandoned the Marais and my Jewish heritage. But as much as I consider you an extension of myself, it gives me great satisfaction that a pious Honoré such as you will inherit my empire. When that day comes, ma chérie, *invite your great-grandfather to Château Gabrielle while the Valley of Civet Cats is still experiencing a semblance of peace.*

55

The sun sinks behind the long shadows of the fur-mottled hills. Gas lamps flicker to life around the château, and chandeliers scintillate in window frames. Geese return to the *parc* to sweep across the lake, trembling beneath a gale of flapping wings. A breeze furls chestnuts across the lavender and around our stretched-out legs. I shiver from the intimacy of Mehrdad's coat.

He worries a sprig of lavender between his fingers. "It all started after a confidential meeting took place between Cyrus and the shah. The meeting was a fatal mistake. Even before Cyrus left the palace, the minister was informed of the encounter.

"Eyes turned to daggers and hands closed into fists. The impure Jew became too brazen for his own good.

"When the first shipment of red diamonds sailed from South Africa to Persia, Cyrus was no longer an asset but a liability to the minister of court and Monsieur Jean Paul Dubois, for whom cruelty was a profession.

"In the meantime, the minister, aware of my growing friendship with Cyrus, appointed me as his spy.

"This is why, unbeknownst to Cyrus, I saw him conduct certain experiments on diamonds and take notes."

I place my hand on Cyrus's journal, the Bible he must have foreseen would become a source of strength in difficult times.

"Simone, I would never have done anything to harm Cyrus. Please believe that I fed the minister only nuggets of unimportant information—places the two of you frequented, mundane details regarding his mother in the Jewish Quarter."

In the process of spying, I became a force Mehrdad had to reckon with. I, who had fled Paris, my mother-in-law, and eventually Persia, settled in his heart. My image on the calling card, Yaghout's rejection of me, and my struggles to fit into the role of a Persian wife in the mountains became a reality more intense than an illness. The spying afforded Mehrdad an opportunity to step into my private life. No longer a detached spectator, if not a lover, he became a bit player in the unfolding events that would shape my future.

"In the hostile atmosphere of court," he continues, "a single word was enough to ignite the embers of hate. Fatwa, a legal statement issued by a religious leader, had long been used to eliminate Jews without the benefit of due process: *He who kills a Jew shall go free upon a small payment of blood money*." He holds his head in his hands; an artery beats at his temple. "Simone, I don't know who uttered the fatwa, who urged his followers to hunt and slay Cyrus, the supposed infidel. I can only guess that Monsieur Jean Paul Dubois and the minister of court, master plotters that they are, triggered the events that would prove more deadly than any.

"The night Cyrus was murdered, Muslim fundamentalists poured into the streets, setting fire to the Mahaleh and killing Jews without any reservation. At the same time, around the mountains, hordes of men lay in wait, expecting a triumphant cry from the man who had orders to murder you, Simone."

What the fanatics could not have foreseen was that nature would retort with its own turbulence that night.

The ensuing shouts that reverberated around the mountains were not of triumph but of terror. Cries of men fleeing Cyrus's ghost, which released red-green fire bolts across the Persian skies. Cries of men fleeing his French sorceress, whose tears had turned to shooting stars that rained fire upon their heads.

I squeeze Mehrdad's coat about my shoulders. A plump civet cat settles at my feet to crack chestnuts. The animal smells of burned nuts and of spilled blood. "I have not accepted his death. Not really. Not when I did not see his body."

"I am sorry to pain you further, but I promised to tell everything, and I will. I was told that his body was prepared according to the Shiite Muslim burial ritual—two pieces of willow wrapped in cotton placed under his armpits and some dirt along with a rosary on his chest, his body wrapped in an unsewn winding sheet. To further spite the Jew, instead of delivering his body to his family, as is customary, he was buried in a Muslim grave site."

"Then why wasn't I murdered that night?" I ask, one hand on the Bible, the other pulling hard at a curl, causing pain at the roots.

"Persians are a superstitious people. No one had ever witnessed the northern lights above the Elburz Mountains. It was a terrifying sight. The racket was translated as a widow's curses and the turbulent sky as Cyrus's revenge. And Beard, who came to your aid with his odd gait and ropelike beard, was further proof you consorted with djinns.

"This is why you came to be known as *Shaunce Banou* and why no one dared confront you, even later. Why the minister of court ordered me to deliver a pouch of red diamonds—doctored, I recently learned—with a note threatening you to leave

Persia. No one wanted your blood on his hands. Everyone hoped you would just pack up and disappear on your own.

"I shed tears of remorse when I learned what happened to Cyrus. I am mortified for doing nothing about the increasing hatred in court. A devout Muslim, I should have had the courage to challenge my brothers, voice my revulsion before I lost my friend. When the minister dispatched me—the only man willing to confront *Shaunce Banou*—to Paris to murder you, I welcomed the chance to redeem myself by doing exactly the opposite. By rescuing Cyrus's runaway wife.

"I warned you that the ultimate decision as to who murdered Cyrus would rest on you. No one can give you the names of the men who were in the mountains that night. But does it matter now? If you have to blame someone, blame the fundamentalist who is determined to silence anyone of a different faith.

"Simone, the bullet that pierced Cyrus's heart was laced with hatred of the Jew."

Winds gather force in the distance. Cats scramble out of underground tunnels to pepper the valley with their fragrant musk. Farther down, an ermine shawl flung sideways across one shoulder, layers of gossamer flapping about her, Françoise returns from her evening stroll. She lingers in front of the gates, bends down, and picks a rose, pressing her nose to its unbridled scent. She thinks of the roses of Persia, and of Alphonse's smile when he would receive the yellow blossom, the shade of his ice flowers. She sails through the gates and then veers back to pluck another rose, this one for her grandfather who was coming for dinner.

I pick up the Old Testament and press it to my chest as Cyrus had done when seeking solace in his synagogue. He had become infinitely more determined in his honesty, more certain of his principles, and less afraid of adversity.

In Persia, I realize, I was too young, too unharmed, too pure to understand the unraveling that took place around me. A woman now, I still do not comprehend the full significance of the newly revealed facts.

The air ablaze with my fragrance, I reach out for Mehrdad's palm, stroke his mound of Venus, slide across his heart line, and settle for eighteen counts of my heart on his contour of intuition. I do not know what I wish for, what it is I want. I think of turning on my heels and rushing down the hill, away from his scent, home to embrace my intended future as the Honoré matriarch. But is Château Gabrielle home? Essential to my identity—as it is to my mother and grandmother—as 13 Rue des Rosiers is to my great-grandfather?

Home is the anchor that would keep my heart from thrashing like an eel. Home is everywhere—Persia, Paris, Château Gabrielle, the Valley of Civet Cats—and home is nowhere.

I unbuckle my belt and lay my revolver down.

About the Author

DORA LEVY MOSSANEN was born in Israel and moved to Iran at the age of nine. At the onset of the Islamic revolution, she and her family fled to the United States. She earned a bachelor's degree in literature from UCLA, and a master's degree in professional writing from the University of Southern California. She is active in the Anti-Defamation League, the National Council of Jewish Women, and the Habib Levy Cultural Foundation at UCLA. She is the recipient of the San Diego State University Editor's Choice award and the author of *Harem,* a widely acclaimed novel translated into numerous languages. She lives in Beverly Hills, California. She can be reached at www.doralevymossanen.com.

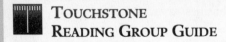

TOUCHSTONE
READING GROUP GUIDE

Courtesan

1. Describe the three women of Château Gabrielle, both individually and in the context of their mother-daughter relationships. What was your initial perception of Mme Gabrielle, Françoise, and Simone? Did your opinion change as the story progressed?

2. Given the limited options available to women in the late nineteenth century, do you understand the decision Mme Gabrielle—and later Françoise—made to become courtesans? Does their chosen profession make them superior to men, subservient to them, or of equal standing? What is their reputation, and how are they viewed by society?

3. Mme Gabrielle records the story of her life in a journal, with the hope that by revealing her past to Simone it will change her granddaughter's mind about continuing the family's role as courtesans. Do you believe Simone will change her mind after reading the journal? Why does Françoise feel betrayed when she discovers her mother's memoirs are addressed to Simone and not to her?

4. What does Mme Gabrielle gain from the process of revisiting her past? If she could live her life over again, do you think she would make the same choices? Mme Gabrielle describes herself as "Jew or Gentile, and proud of her accomplishments." Has delving into her past allowed her to reconnect with her Jewish heritage?

5. How would you describe Simone before she meets Cyrus? How about when she returns to Château Gabrielle after his death? From what you know about the time she spent in Persia, do you think she would have been happy living there, a place where she was met with hostility due to her Jewish heritage and her French nationality?

6. "One of a rare breed of women who were fortunate to boast a perfect balance of the preeminent male and female attributes, [Mme Gabrielle] utilized these assets to her advantage." What are these assets? Using Mme Gabrielle's encounter with the shah as an example, how do they work to her advantage as a courtesan and also as a businesswoman?

7. How do Simone's ideas about love and marriage differ from those of her mother? How have Françoise's experiences—not knowing the identity of her father, Simone's father leaving her for another woman—shaped her views of love and marriage? Does Simone's own experience of finding and losing love make her more understanding of her mother?

8. When Simone makes love with Cyrus at the lake, they are "unaware that Mme Gabrielle observed them from the clover hill, rejoicing that her granddaughter would belong to her, at last." Why does Mme Gabrielle believe this encounter with Cyrus will change Simone's mind about joining the family profession? What is your opinion of how she attempts to persuade Simone to become a courtesan? Why is it so important to Mme Gabrielle?

9. Discuss Alphonse and Mme Gabrielle's first encounter, which she recounts in her journal. What has made him stay with her for thirty years in such an unconventional relationship? Why do you think Mme Gabrielle has finally chosen to reveal the truth about Alphonse's identity?

10. How does Dora Levy Mossanen evoke the five senses—smell, touch, taste, sound, and sight—to enrich the story? Françoise tells Simone, "Memory and fragrance are intertwined in our emotional brain. Men will miss you when you leave your perfume behind." How does scent, in particular, play an essential role in the story?

11. Simone refuses to follow the profession of her mother and grandmother, and yet she uses the very same skills of seduction for a different purpose—revenge. Does the insight Simone gains alter her opinion about the life of a courtesan?

12. On her quest to uncover the circumstances of Cyrus's death, Simone seeks information from M. Rouge, M. Amir, and M. Jean Paul Dubois. What do you think of her methods for obtaining

the information she seeks? What drives her to continue the mission even at the risk of her own life?

13. *Courtesan* weaves together facets of different cultures and religions. What are the most distinct differences between Simone's life in France and in Persia? Why does Mehrdad tell Simone, "The bullet that pierced Cyrus's heart was laced with hatred of the Jew"? In what other instances do religious differences play out in the story?

14. When Mehrdad comes to Château Gabrielle, Simone at first believes it is Cyrus. What is the significance of Mehrdad's resembling Cyrus so closely in appearance and mannerisms? Why has he come to Château Gabrielle, and what does he want from Simone?

15. Discuss the novel's ending. What is your interpretation of Simone laying down her revolver? What do you think Simone decides to do—return to Persia with Mehrdad, remain at Château Gabrielle, or something else entirely? Do you see her fulfilling her grandmother's wishes and becoming a courtesan? Ultimately, do Mme Gabrielle, Françoise, and Simone each find what they are looking for?

**Discover more reading group guides
and download them for free at
www.simonsays.com.**